# THE OTHER PROFILE

Irene Graziosi

# THE OTHER PROFILE

*Translated from the Italian
by Lucy Rand*

Europa
*editions*

Europa Editions
8 Blackstock Mews
London N4 2BT
www.europaeditions.co.uk

Copyright © Irene Graziosi, 2022
First published by Edizioni e/o
Licence agreement made through Pietrosanti Agenzia Letteraria
First publication 2023 by Europa Editions

Translation by Lucy Rand
Original title: *Il profilo dell'altra*
Translation copyright © 2023 by Europa Editions

A catalogue record for this title is available from the British Library
ISBN 978-1-78770-467-1

Graziosi, Irene
The Other Profile

Art direction by Emanuele Ragnisco
instagram.com/emanueleragnisco

Cover design and illustration by Ginevra Rapisardi

Prepress by Grafica Punto Print – Rome

Printed and bound in Great Britain by Clays Ltd, Elcograf S.p.A

# C O N T E N T S

for Sofi

"I don't believe in your 'Good.' I believe in human kindness."
—VASILY GROSSMAN, *Life and Fate*
Translated by Robert Chandler

# PART ONE

B efore I meet Gloria, my life belongs to me. Well, at least it appears to be me.

Each morning, as soon as my partner Filippo closes the front door behind him, I wander out of the bathroom where I've been pretending to get ready and lie on the couch in front of the TV. If I look up from this position I can see, through the window, a triangle of sky framed by the buildings that loom over ours. Every so often, when it's not too hot or too cold, I venture to the supermarket and buy a bag of gummies in the shape of little crocodiles. The crocodiles are all different colors, but they each have a foamy stomach the shade of egg white.

On my way to the supermarket, I walk down a short stretch of road studded with billboards: they are inhabited by women frozen in time, crossing a street just like this one. Some are wrapped in tight-fitting dresses and others bubble over brightly colored frills, but they are all holding a sign that reads: *INCLUSION FOR ALL*. Each woman is a different color, like the gummy crocodiles. When I see them caged in those rectangles, exposed to everyone, I think of a story I read when I was young where witches trapped children inside bucolic oil paintings, forcing them to feed painted chickens for the rest of their lives. The campaign's tagline is *Be different—Be an activist*. After the billboards of the women forced to wear uncomfortable clothes and revolutionary smiles, I pass the neighborhood transformer box. This too is covered in posters advertising upcoming films and TV series on Amazon and Netflix: sometimes it looks like a monster is about to burst out of the locked door, like in those

Japanese movies pillaged by Americans with giant green lizards bursting from cracks in the ocean floor; other times it's Clark Kent unbuttoning his shirt to reveal himself as Superman.

The women at the supermarket look just like the ones on the billboards. They wander languidly up and down the Quality Produce aisle, poking at loquats as the AC ruffles their blush pink faux fur. They have lip filler and wear sunglasses with colored lenses, regardless of the season or time of day. I once heard two salesgirls whispering that a woman who had just left was the wife of a soccer player, then a third one interjected to say no she wasn't, she just looked like her.

I don't eat all my crocodiles: in the elevator, I open the bag and grab a handful, and when I get into the apartment I run to the kitchen, throw the rest in the trash, and pour detergent over them. I return to the couch with the surviving crocodiles held tight in my fist, put an episode of "Law & Order: Special Victims Unit" on, and eat them one at a time, starting with their foamy bellies.

I can't remember who told me that even though the gummies are different colors, which each correspond to a different fruit, they are actually all the same flavor. I don't believe it, because I like the green ones, for example, but not the yellow. So, while Olivia Benson resolves yet another case of sexual violence in Manhattan, I suck each sweet trying to reach a conclusion. I never manage. At first each one tastes different but, by the end, the taste in my mouth is always the same, and so I start again, crinkling my nose whenever I find a yellow one.

\* \* \*

My name is Maia, Maia Gatti. I'm twenty-six, I have stopped studying, and the only thing I do—reluctantly—to maintain contact with the outside world is work as a waitress at the local bar. I work there twice a week. I have a little black apron in which I keep my notepad, pen, and a corkscrew. Filippo tells me I look sexy and sometimes, when I'm on shift and he's on his way home from the university, he stops in for a beer and touches my ass stealthily, though everyone notices. He's the one who got me the job and I accepted it so that he couldn't say I'm not trying to better my situation. One evening he came home with a face full of manipulative joy and exclaimed that he had befriended one of the owners of the local bar. While they were talking it emerged that the guy needed someone to cover a couple of shifts. I say manipulative because it was the kind of expression someone has when they're asking you not to disappoint them, their eyebrows arched in entreaty. The subtext was clear: to reject this job would be to reject him.

Since then, I drag myself down to the Galeone twice a week. Despite being called the galleon, there's absolutely nothing nautical about it, but the four owners—losers in their mid-forties who at some point got it into their heads that a bar would be symbolic of their virile rebirth—decided to saddle it with that name to symbolize the marvelous adventure of being four random men. One of the waitresses who's been there the longest told me that when the bar first opened, they had the bow of a ship mounted on the wall behind the counter, which had a semi-nude figurehead that the owners affectionately called Clara. She was named after one of the first waitresses who had worked there—a real beauty, according to them. Nobody could have predicted that, during the jovial hustle and bustle of the first year after opening, a leak from upstairs would work its way down until, precisely fourteen months after opening night, the bow ruinously crashed onto the sticky floor, bringing down Clara with it. She lost a wooden nipple and a lock of hair in the incident.

The Galeone is frequented by an unchanging and anthropologically homogeneous clientele: middle-aged men who the other waitresses have renamed the "Fays," i.e., freelance professionals who reek of cologne and wear dark blue Fay jackets.

Each one has a ring on his finger, but after ten o'clock the rings come off and get spun on the table between thumb and forefinger like spinning tops. The Fay who keeps his spinning the longest wins. They drink a lot. They start with beer, then move on to gin and tonics and finish up with grappa. Every so often, one of the Fays will start a trend for a certain cocktail, and then for a few months we have to make Long Island iced teas or Moscow mules for them all, until they tire of it and go back to gin and tonics. When I started working at the Galeone the other girls warned me about the Fays. Without going into too much detail, I was made to understand that after a certain hour it was best to take another girl to the bathroom with you.

At first, I couldn't comprehend how on earth the Galeone attracted that kind of guy. On the surface, the four owners seem very different from the customers. Only one of them wears a wedding ring, for example, and they never wear branded clothes. One of the owners is fat, goes around in worn-out T-shirts, and starts rattling on about his ex-wife as soon as he's had one too many beers, how much he loves her and what he'd give to get her back. "You women need to be more tolerant," he once said to me with glistening eyes, as if I were the representative for womankind. Another is a cokehead who's had multiple heart attacks and spends a lot of time in South America doing some shady business. He talks about his divorce like it's the best thing that ever happened to him. He gets a new girlfriend every year, infallibly South American, each younger than the last. The third guy is the silent type who reads Bukowski and thinks that makes him sophisticated. He talks in a hushed voice, as if he's telling you a secret even when he's asking you to bring him a pastis—which I'm sure he doesn't actually like. Every so often he gets fixated on one of the waitresses and starts showing up every time she's on shift, bringing with him a pile of books and a ton of requests for the poor girl, whom he sits and stares at, surly, over the top of his book, thinking he's being discrete. His flames fizzle out quickly. The only one still married is the most attractive and, at first sight, the one you'd think was an exception. But as time goes on, I realize how much enjoyment he gets from being the most presentable: he never gets drunk, he raises his voice over the others and thumps his fist on the table to interrupt them, he enlists two of the others to humiliate the fourth one, and he takes the piss out of his friends in front of the waitresses as soon as alcohol leaves them vulnerable. This has made me dislike him, and has forced me, against my wishes, to re-evaluate the other three.

One time, the fat divorcee and the cokehead divorcee stayed on at the Galeone until closing time and, going by their table, I heard them making strange sounds.

"Screeez," one of them was saying.

"No, it doesn't sound right, it's too harsh. What about Yelaaas?" said the other.

When I asked them what they were talking about, the cokehead owner gestured for me to come closer, making room on his chair so I could sit down next to him. He put an arm around my shoulders and I could smell the alcohol and cigars on his breath. "Maia," he whispered as I repented having shown an interest, "we have a plan, but you must swear not to tell anyone."

"I swear," I said, trying not to breathe through my nose.

"We need to come up with a word that represents the bar. I mean we need to come up with a . . . Michele—" he barked over to the owner who was pretending to read Hemingway's *The Sun Also Rises* at a table in a dark corner, "what did you say a new word was called?" He closed the book letting out a long sigh, as if he'd been interrupted in the middle of doing surgery and, raising his eyebrows and revealing his pale gums, pronounced: "Neologism."

"Nice one Michele, neologism," Fabio continued. "Yes, we need to come up with a neologism and then start using it so that our friends start using it too," he explained, pointing at the last few Fays still standing, like bowling pins after an unimpressive bowl.

"Why?" I asked.

"To stir some *hype* up," Giovanni the fat one went on. "And then we'll get it printed on your T-shirts, it'll become famous, and we'll attract new customers."

As I was saying, for a long time I had wondered what the owners of the Galeone had in common with the Fays. I finally understood one day when the oldest of the Fays came to the Galeone, red around the eyes and chin trembling. He was getting divorced. In the months that followed the other girls and I witnessed his metamorphosis from hair gel, tidy beard, and glossy lacquered shoes to torn T-shirts and brightly colored sneakers. This Fay had become the prototype of the Galeone owner. What attracted the Fays to the Galeone was the invisible thread of predestination: they were identical organisms at different stages of evolution.

I don't like the Fays. I would like to say that this feeling is mutual, but the Fays don't seem to think about what or who they like and why. What they know about themselves is that they like going to the Galeone, flirting with the waitresses, and exchanging mystifying soccer memes. What they don't know is everything else. In the days preceding the shift that would inaugurate this job, I fantasized about being one of those waitresses you see in American movies: authoritative, brusque, sensual. My maternal aura would stir adoration slightly tinged with eroticism. Also in my head, the other girls and I would playfully tease the customers, united by an impalpable feminine wisdom. Sometimes I get lost in my fantasies and embellish them to the point where, when they don't come true, I develop an imaginary sorrow that's as painful as if it were real.

In reality, when the Fays are sober, they tell me to loosen up, and when they're drunk, they tell me to pull the stick out of my ass. Sometimes they run a hand through my frizzy hair and their rings get caught and they tug. As for the other waitresses, they wear long, pastel-varnished nails and, to my amazement, still manage to get all their tasks done. They don't want us to be a team, and, I must admit, neither do I.

The only Fay who's alright is the one who gets me weed, a short guy who wears jackets under his overcoat that look like they're made of cardboard. One evening this Fay gave me a joint. I had never smoked before, apart from at high school, but at high school weed made me paranoid. But this time it put me in a good mood, as if little fireworks were exploding along my cranium. Since then, he brings me some every week. In exchange, I send him photos of my tits. He texts me when he's in the office and asks if I can send him a photo. I then open my folder of pictures taken over the years and pick a different one each time to make him think I've taken it there and then, just for him. Men like to think they're special. I like my Fay because he never pesters. I've told him I'm with someone, and he's told me he's married. I let him think that if things were different, who knows what could happen between us, perhaps we'd be happy together. He bats his eyelids adoringly and says, "Yes, Maia, you are a fantastic, perfect girl. Who knows what would have happened if we'd met a few years ago."

The weed turns my brain into a pinwheel and for a few hours I have the feeling that the future holds all sorts of promise. When I smoke, I even manage to open a book and read a few pages. It's nothing compared to the concentration that belonged to the person I was a few years back, when I used to win scholarships, compose poems (that I'm now mortified by), and create diagramless crosswords to send into *Puzzles Weekly*.

Anyway, I think reading when you're stoned is no better than not reading at all. Once the THC wears off, I remember nothing of what I've read and am left with the familiar, melancholic sensation of having been sucked in by the pages.

Before Filippo and I moved from Paris to Milan, I liked reading. No, "liked" is an understatement: it was a reflex akin to breathing. My parents say as a child I would spend hours and hours flicking through books and magazines, and it was the only way of placating my compulsive and occasionally irascible temper.

I lost interest in everything when I quit university in France, the same time as my sister Eva died. I wrote to my supervisor, soberly explaining that I had just undergone a serious bereavement due to which I would need to move back to Italy and continue my studies there. It wasn't true, of course: I had absolutely no intention of continuing my studies. As I wrote the email, I knew full well that I wouldn't be transferring my credits, but I didn't want to let this professor down as I'd grown to like her over the months. I composed the email, removing all sentimentality because I thought minimalism expressed a more austere, and thus deeper, pain. I wanted to discourage her from writing to me in the months that followed; I didn't want to have to explain why I quit university. But perhaps I overestimated her interest in me, because she sent a quick reply and I never heard from her again.

Anyway, I felt absolutely no pain when Eva died, and I still don't.

Filippo says Milan is a dynamic city. He says people here are less pretentious and more welcoming than in Paris, but I suspect it's just because he gets treated with more reverence here than he did in France. In France he received continuous criticism: his weekly appearances in the papers weren't looked kindly upon in the academic world, nor was his use of social media, which had become spasmodic after the success of *The Secret Language of Fungi*. The book tapped into the Zeitgeist of a time when those who could afford the luxury of micropolitical activism were planting domestic forests of strelitzia, which are apparently very intelligent, like all plants, and now also like fungi. Neither plants nor fungi seem particularly smart to me, but I keep that to myself.

After the book's boom in sales, Filippo's social media profiles were fortified by people of note in the art and fashion worlds, even though he had studied botany first and then philosophy. Sometimes when I scroll through the photos he posts of himself with his arms around all these influential people, it seems to me as though he never wants to let go.

That book, where he wrote about pretty simple topics in a deliberately complex way, had crossed the line that separates academic essays from magazine features, managing to make those who read it feel clever and profound, and to convince them that their inability to understand certain paragraphs is symptomatic of the superior intelligence of the person who constructed them. Filippo rode the wave and wrote other essays that his colleagues mockingly called self-help manuals dressed up as contemporary philosophy. Those months were hard for him and gratifying for me. He would come home exhausted and bad-tempered, and it was my job to take care of him. I'd make him lay down on the couch while I cooked something, massaged his temples and whispered that all the critics were just envious of his success, and that you can't be liked by everyone. One evening he hugged me tight and announced, with a brightness in his eyes, that we would be leaving Paris like I'd always wanted, and moving to Milan to start over, just the two of us.

But it wasn't just the two of us. Everyone in Milan knew him, and they didn't know about the criticism he had received in other languages. So, mantled in the magic cloak of Abroad, Filippo swiftly reconstructed a life full of receptions, art exhibition previews, and flattery while I lost my role as loving support. Without that, and with no degree and no friends or acquaintances, I found myself with nothing to do but serve gin and tonic to the Fays.

I do not find Milan dynamic; I find it dreary. There's no sea and no mountains. There aren't even hills. When we were getting ready to leave, some Milanese friends of Filippo who had lived in Paris for years waxed lyrical about Milan's hidden treasures: the airy entrance halls, churches, alleyways. "Just begging to be walked!" they said. Now that we live here, I can't help suspecting they were victims of the warped nostalgia of expats. Most of the time, wherever I am, whether I'm walking to the supermarket or forced to travel farther to accompany Filippo to some social event, I feel like a figurine in an architectural model, and everyone around me is part of it too. A lady in a lilac mackintosh with her pedigree dog, slipping into a store surrounded by concrete that's meant to look like a designer boutique in a holiday resort; an athletic girl with ear-pods, walking in long strides and sipping take-away coffee, talking to herself; teenagers on skateboards in a gap between skyscrapers made especially for teenagers on skateboards; old people wandering between flower beds from which flowers the French call *rose trémière* stand like sentinels, nestled between the steel towers where the people who work in the steel towers next door park their cars; couples jogging together; Filippo in an elegant suit gifted to him by some eco-friendly stylist at whose art foundation he once held a workshop. And then there's me, and it isn't clear what I represent, but surely I was placed in that model intentionally. We have all been put here intentionally.

Asian, Black, and white faces roll along the sides of buses in ads promoting optimism and inclusivity; building facades are covered in cheesy murals with the logos of the banks that commissioned them; the girls dress like young women at their first job interview; and at events the guests study one another and try to work out which step of the social ladder they are on compared to the person in front of them in line for the open bar.

So I spend the majority of my time at home smoking weed and watching "Law & Order: Special Victims Unit." I've been watching it since I was little: it started in 1999 and is still being made. It's gotten worse over the years, but I try not to notice. If worst comes to worst I rewatch the early episodes when Olivia Benson is younger and the screenplay more sophisticated.

Olivia Benson in real life is called Mariska Hargitay, and when she started playing the role of Olivia, she got hundreds of thousands of letters from female viewers telling her they'd been raped. Moved by all the testimonies, she created a foundation that helps "special" victims, the same ones she helps in "Law & Order." I think about Olivia/Mariska often, because it seems to me she's found a purpose, and sometimes, especially since she's gotten older and her body has become more abundant, I lose myself in fantasies where she is my mother and I melt into her as she holds me in her arms, her face swollen with the botox she has recently started having a little too enthusiastically.

I think the summer in Milan is hotter than in Paris, but it might just be that I have more time to notice the weather. I keep the blinds closed, Filippo is against AC because it's bad for the environment, and from time to time I submerge my wrists in cold water because the weed lowers my blood pressure and I feel faint whenever I stand up. Sometimes Filippo goes away for days on end, like for a conference in the US that he couldn't bring me to because the host university couldn't add a plus-one. Filippo did confess that he'd feel a bit flustered were I to go with him: his sense of guilt for not being able to spend time with me would distract him from his work. If he is away for days on end and I don't have any shifts at the Galeone, I start to wonder, in the living room cut by a blade of light in which dust dances like ballerinas under a spotlight, if I really exist, or in general if we only exist when there's someone there to see us.

The truth, really, is that I should have more respect for the Galeone, because that's where this story begins, on the day Angela came in.

One evening, intent on cleaning the sticky glaze of alcohol off a wooden table, I hear a voice behind me squeal "Maia!" I turn around and see Angela. We did our bachelor's together. She was not a brilliant student: she harassed me for my notes and begged me to revise with her. I would try to wriggle out of her pleas for help but sometimes I would run out of excuses and find myself sitting in a café near campus, listening as she recited whole sentences lifted from textbooks. She had enormous breasts that sagged already at the age of twenty, and big blue eyes. I never understood her interest in me since I tried to speak to her as little as possible. She was boring, and her unceasing chatter in the face of my indifference made me suspect that she hardly noticed who was in front of her and really couldn't care less. This theory was confirmed when she talked about the men she liked, like Mario. Every summer, Angela went with her parents to a place on the Adriatic coast where she'd meet this hunky dimwit. Angela and Mario hung out in the same group and, roughly once a fortnight, when she was very drunk and he less-so, they'd take themselves off for a quick fuck that was unsatisfying for her and forgettable for him. The script was repeated unchanging for years: Angela's passion for Mario dwindled when October came—when he returned to Forlì and stopped responding to her messages—but took back up again every June, as if, at last, this summer might represent the completion of her romantic dream, silently embroidered over the winter. Anyway, Angela isn't a bad person. When she comes into the Galeone, she's wearing a blue blouse and a pleated skirt, and she drags me to her table where she's sitting with a friend.

"This place is near my office, but I hardly ever come in. What are you doing here? I imagined you in some prestigious university on the other side of the world." Then, turning to her friend, "Maia was the best student on our course, and she was accepted onto a super-selective master's in Paris. She helped me so much during our bachelor's; she basically taught me how to study."

I look at her suspiciously, but there isn't a trace of irony in her eyes.

"I'm here as a stop-gap, while I figure out what to do next, and this job pays the bills."

"You mean you're just working here? Not doing anything else?" Her eyes are even wider than usual, she looks like a frog.

"I met a guy who had to move here, and I came with him. He's a professor, a philosopher. Maybe you've heard of him, he's called Filippo Del Pero. I was bored of Paris; I needed a change of scenery."

Filippo's name doesn't seem to register with Angela. There's still this look of expectance on her face, as if she's waiting for me to finish the story. When she realizes that that's it, she looks away and runs her finger around the rim of her glass of watered-down beer.

"And what about you?" I force myself to ask in a natural-sounding voice.

"I work in publicity, I'm an AM. I moved here because it's the only place I could find work. We're both junior AMs," she says tilting her head toward the other girl, who looks up briefly from her phone to grant me a polite smile.

"Maia, enough with the public relations, come back to the bar!" another waitress shouts, to my relief.

"I have to go: Friday evenings aren't the best time to chat."

"Stay in touch though," Angela says with a sincere look in her eyes.

"Of course," I lie. I try not to make eye contact with her for the rest of the evening, and when I see her getting up to pay, I wander into the toilets and stay there for a few minutes, waiting for my past to disappear.

A few days later, Angela messages me on Facebook saying they're recruiting for an image consultant for someone called Gloria.

*She's a super famous influencer*, she writes. *But don't call her that. You have to say she's a creator.*

*Like Tyler?*

*?*

*Don't worry. Why can't we say influencer?*

*It just sounds crass. Like all they do for a job is take photos of themselves wearing brands' products, when actually they're creating content.*

*Got it. Thanks, but I don't think I'd be the right person for the job.* Mostly I'm just embarrassed that Angela is suggesting a career for me.

*The communications world accepts everyone, especially smart people. It's not like there's much to learn.* I wonder why on earth she was accepted, but keep that thought to myself. *Look, I'll give you the email of the HR person, and you can think on it.*

The call arrives a few weeks after I send them an email with my heavily embellished CV attached. It says I have a degree (lie); that I speak French and German as well as English (lie); that in France I worked in the scientific communications sector (lie); that I have experience working on set (half-lie: at school I used to put on these stupid plays where I'd force the whole class to recite *The Bacchae*); that thanks to my academic background in psychology I am particularly perceptive when it comes to knowing what people want to see. I ended with a couple of lines covering how enthusiastic this total fraud is about getting to know a world that is so different from her own.

It takes me a couple of seconds to realize who it is on the other end of the phone. I never thought they would actually call. But they're saying that my profile is different from the ones they've seen so far, and they want to meet me.

On the day of the interview, I turn up breathless outside a gray building in an industrial estate on the outskirts of Milan. It looks the same as all the other factories in the area that have been converted into open-plan offices, workshops, and co-working spaces: concrete boxes with windows that could only be made attractive by Milan's obsession with itself. The directions say this is where the interview will take place. Apart from the porter in the cloakroom at the entrance, who doesn't even bother looking up, the building seems deserted. I let out a little shout and listen to my voice echo, take my phone out of my pocket—the screen is cracked but I'm not fussed about replacing it, nor can I afford to—and re-read the instructions in the email. Second floor, right-hand elevator. The elevator is spacious, with a full-length mirror that shows me the image I've chosen to project today. I'm wearing a blazer from Zara. You can see a T-shirt underneath, also from Zara. I picked the blazer out of a line-up of very similar items, and I think it suits me, gives me a distinguished look. Ignoring the fact that both the jacket and the T-shirt are too big as I've lost weight over the last couple of years, I look decidedly more elegant than usual.

Unfortunately, the T-shirt has a hole over my left hip where I unceremoniously pulled off the security tag. But I think the blazer, which I actually bought, covers it up. I'm not particularly attractive: my nose is too pronounced and slumps slightly to the left, and my eyes are small. But the real problem is my hair. It's too curly and I hate it; it pings out all over the place despite having been fixed with bobby pins which now dangle despondently on my shoulders. When I was little, I was diagnosed with a compulsion that has a fun name: trichotillomania. To this day I am convinced that I never suffered from the ailment. I would challenge anyone not to pull out such horrendous hair, one strand at a time. Psychiatrists claimed they cured me, but the truth is I decided it was better to keep my hair and lose them. I take the pins out and stick them in my pocket. On my middle finger I wear one of my mother's gold rings—the only piece of jewelry I've ever owned. I like it because it has two forest-green rectangles that overlap and remind me, with a bit of imagination, of a Mondrian painting.

The elevator doors open onto a two-story loft with glass walls. For a moment I imagine the space filled with water. From the top of the metal stairs that lead to the upper floor I could dive in and swim down to touch the submerged desks, like shipwrecked relics. Instead, I sit down in front of a small table crammed with magazines. I pick one at random, open it to a page that's been dog-eared, and find myself looking at a photo of Gloria in a glamorous dress. She's holding the receiver of a rotary dial phone, from which a cord unravels across the page like a ringlet. In the other she is holding an antique gold-framed hand mirror. The title of the piece reads: *Mirror, mirror on the wall, who's the most photogenic of them all?*

In her eyes is the indecipherable expression I know so well and often see, even now, in girls on the street who aren't her.

I know what she looks like because I've already spent a lot of time scrolling through her profile. She has a clean grid: glossy photos taken with a real camera. They capture her as she wanders through a forest, fiddling with the high neck of her sweater. Or at the beach in a swishy skirt with the sunset behind her and her ever-absent gaze. She smiles in every photo, as if she has facial paralysis.

She isn't some great beauty. Not that she's ugly, but she has a common face, amorphous. She looks like one of those girls whose faces line stock image websites. An influencer should be breathtaking, celestial.

When they called me to confirm the interview they described her like a goddess, surprised that I didn't know who she was.

"What do you mean, it's Gloria Linares," her communications manager said (or was it her brand or content manager? I wasn't sure). "She has two million followers; she's been in two movies. She's an extremely important creator. Every year she is invited as a guest of the Italian president. She's written a book of poems that sold two hundred thousand copies; she brought poetry to the web generation."

(I would later discover that there are people who are able to say phrases like "web generation" without cringing.)

The more the woman spoke, the shriller her voice became. It felt as though her head might explode if I didn't calm her down by confirming that I did in fact know who Gloria was. "Oh of course, Gloria."

"I was sure you knew her!"

The first time we make eye contact is through the glass wall of the meeting room as I am going up the stairs I wish to dive from. She turns her head and looks at me as if her mind is still on whatever she was doing a second ago but her attention has just been caught by something more interesting.

She's only eighteen but looks like an adult. There's a certain benevolence about her and her head seems to tip imperceptibly, as if inviting me in. Her long, red, silky hair sways, creating glowing fragments of lava every time the sun shines on it.

When I think back to it now, I think I could already see in her melancholy eyes, the same ones that stare out of billboards across the country, everything that would happen. We recognized one another even before we spoke, as I stood on the stairs.

Three women are sitting next to Gloria. One looks about thirty-five. She has a delicate figure, wears cherry-red lipstick and a T-shirt that asks: WHO RUNS THE WORLD? I imagine, horrified, that the back says: GIRLS.

To Gloria's right is an older woman in a polo shirt and jeans.

They don't look alike, but when one of them does something—pours some water or checks her phone—the other moves too, as if their limbs were joined by invisible threads. The third is a woman in her forties who greets me with the same shrill voice that had exasperated me on the phone.

"Nice to meet you at last, I'm Loredana." Loredana is wearing a colorful skirt and electric blue boots. "This is Gloria, who needs no introduction. This is Anna Ricordi, Gloria's grandmother, and finally Valentina."

Her grandmother? What kind of teenager works with her grandmother? Valentina and Anna shake my hand. Valentina has sweaty palms and I have to stop myself from wiping mine on my jeans.

Loredana continues: "I'm Gloria's press officer. I don't only work for her; I appear and disappear as needed. I'm giving the girls a hand with these interviews because we're a bit short on staff. Valentina looks after brand relationships and organizes Gloria's commitments."

I pretend I know what she's talking about and nod.

"Would you like to tell us something about yourself? So we can get to know each other a bit better," Loredana asks me.

I start talking, relieved to not have to listen to her voice any longer. I tell them that first I studied philosophy, then psychobiology, and fail to mention my lack of a diploma. I fabricate a past job as social media manager for a sex toy brand, telling them how comfortable I am on set: how I love the magic of the unexpected and the chemistry with the crew (my high school classmates who hated me for putting them in a play they couldn't back out of without looking bad in front of the teachers). I talk about how we need much more philosophy in the nooks and crannies of the internet, and what a shame it is that the world of influencers has been devalued by a culture of elitism and snobbery—I lean quite heavily on this point as I see their eyes light up and their heads start to nod. I don't mention the Galeone.

Gloria interjects, addressing me for the first time: "Why do you want to work here if you studied psycho-whatever?"

"The world of research is too limiting for me, I need to be in contact with people, explore other environments." Christ!

"Have you had any more substantial experiences in the field of communications?" It's Valentina asking this question. When she opens her mouth, I notice that her incisors stick out at a forty-five-degree angle, almost like a beak. I respond no and see my first image consultant paycheck go up in smoke.

"We need someone with more experience," she says. Her lips are so sizable compared to the rest of her features that from then on I decide to think of her as a giant mouth.

"Valentina, it's me who knows what I need, thank you," Gloria cuts her off with a dulcet firmness. Valentina's face darkens and she shifts back in her seat as if hoping it might swallow her.

"I'll explain briefly how the job works," Gloria continues. "I travel a lot, and the person I choose will for sure have to follow my movements. In two months I have my final exams and I'll need someone who can help me in the public transition from being a high schooler to being . . . something else."

She's solemn, as if the lives of many human beings depended on this role. I keep nodding. I try to remember what I was like at eighteen. Wasted. Her grandmother doesn't open her mouth, but her gaze scours me. I don't have the courage to reciprocate because she has eyes of ice and, I imagine, the ability to see through a fraud, and I am a fraud. I start to sweat under my synthetic blazer. I take it off. I lay it over my knees and see Gloria's eyes lingering on my arms. I follow her gaze and remember I have hairy arms. Since I started losing weight, the hair on my body has multiplied in a desperate attempt to regulate my temperature. It's called lanugo. It's not like normal hair, but a fine coating of cotton wool-like fuzz. Fetuses have it too. I quickly pull down the three-quarter length sleeves of my T-shirt in the hope that at the very least nobody will notice the hole.

"You do know that you shouldn't buy fast fashion, don't you?" Gloria asks me.

I look at her interrogatively.

"She's right," Valentina butts in again. "You shouldn't buy clothes if you don't know the supply chain."

I wonder whether they're referring to my purchase or my theft.

Perked up by the fact that Gloria didn't stop her, Valentina re-emerges from her seat and goes on: "Didn't you see the news about the fire in Bangladesh? Loads of people died, workers exploited by high-street labels to produce clothes for nothing. Gloria stopped working with fast-fashion brands some months ago now."

They all shake their heads gravely, as if it were me who set fire to the factory in Bangladesh, after having invented capitalism. I look at my synthetic blazer shimmering under the light and feel a pang of shame in my stomach. Thank God the T-shirt looks like cotton.

"I'll pay more attention next time."

We remain silent for a few seconds.

"We'll let you know within a couple of weeks; we have to meet the other candidates first. Thank you very much for coming," Loredana says, with a touch of embarrassment.

As I'm about to leave I hear a raspy voice behind me, the only one I haven't heard yet. It's Gloria's grandmother.

"How old are you?"

"Twenty-six," I say, turning toward her. She has a cataract in her right eye that reflects the light as if the flash of a camera were permanently pointed on her.

"Are you in need of this job?"

I hear myself as a treacherous "yes" leaves my lips.

"You can go."

Before leaving, I stop in front of the coffee table where I left the magazine open on the photo of Gloria. My eyes fall on one of the interviewer's questions.

*What do you want to be when you grow up?*
*I don't know, but I'm sure about one thing: I'll be a mother.*
What an imbecile.

As I leave the building the fake voice whirrs around my head: "You do know that you shouldn't buy fast fashion, don't you?" I want to laugh but I can't. Parked on the sidewalk is a yellow CityCar. Inside, a pink plushie like the ones you win at a fun fair is hugging a little number plate that says "Vale." It must be Valentina's car. I scan the area to check if anyone's around and glance over toward the porter's booth. There's no one. So I take my keys out of my bag and discretely run a line along the side of the car. Walking to the metro station, I throw the blazer in the trash. I keep walking. I stop. I am struck by the impulse to go through the garbage and pull it out. I feel my nose tingle and keep going.

In the days after the interview, Gloria started following me on social media. It was strange, because after her many more followers came, girls who were evidently watching her every move. Reading two million, or 2M, on her profile made me anxious, maybe more for her than myself. I went back to my profile and tried to see it through a stranger's eyes. I've occasionally heard people say that you shouldn't judge others based on what they post online. Like my colleagues at the bar, who are not exactly geniuses and talk incessantly about things that are a world away from my life: threading, skin care, TV shows I've never heard of. They follow influencers and talk about them as if they were friends. One time, one of them, a girl from Sardinia called Giulia, was passing her phone around to show us a guy she was going on a date with the following day. On the dating app where she'd found him, he'd listed his passions as traveling, eating, Netflix & Chill.

"Original," I observed. They got all worked up and started telling me I was judgmental; that people are different in real life to how they look on the internet.

"Our brains are designed to judge. The idea that a person can look at someone without drawing any conclusions is absurd," I replied.

In the days that followed, Giulia tried to avoid making any judgements in order to prove her point. The result was comical: at the end of the shift, she came over in a frenzy and started telling me that another girl's new boyfriend was an idiot, but then remembered that she couldn't judge, so instead she told me that he spoke in a very loud voice and continuously interrupted his girlfriend.

"So he's an asshole," I said.

"No, I am just describing how he is." I smiled and Giulia looked offended. To be honest, Giulia is always offended. Except when she drinks. When she drinks she becomes verbose and, like all Sardinians, talks only about Sardinia. Sardinia this, Sardinia that. She never actually describes it though; to listen to her you'd think Sardinia was just a big lump of land rising out of the sea.

Anyway, the way I see it, social media gives us a better idea of who people truly are than real life does. I look at Filippo's Instagram, which is full of celebrities. On social media people reveal how they would like to be seen. What emerges is not what we are, but what we desire to be. There's nothing more intimate than our own desires, and yet I find them divulged everywhere I look.

In my photos there are many books, some cats, some brutalist buildings I find mesmerizing, and the odd soft toy abandoned in the street. I tried selfies, but I'm not much to look at. Then I tried those aesthetic filters that come with the app, but I felt shameful afterwards because I imagined everyone who saw them thinking I really looked like that. How pathetic that I imagined that, and that I assumed anyone actually looked at my profile.

I post a lot of photos of Filippo or with Filippo (he, however, never posts pictures of me), in which I try to cover my face with my hair or make it so only my eyes are in view. One of the last ones I uploaded is one of the few that I'm in. It's from a few weeks ago, when I accompanied him to Trapani for a conference and from there we visited Marettimo. I'm wearing a hoodie and jeans because it was late in the day and getting chilly.

> *I heard Marettimo was full of monk seals, but I haven't seen any. Every day, around sunset, I head toward the monk seal observatory, but you couldn't see a seal for love nor money. Then I head back, sometimes breaking off the stems of those plants I don't know the name of that look like giant spikes, and I remember when me and my sister were little and used to pretend they were poodles on leads. I drink a bottle of wine (two, actually), instantly fall asleep and imagine that the wine is resting on my internal organs, slowly melting them, because I wake up at four in the morning with my stomach on fire. So I get up, go into the courtyard of the guesthouse we're staying in and see that the trunk of the plant is still there, abandoned in a corner, only, in the morning it doesn't look like a poodle but a dead (or almost dead) plant.*
>
> *I'm still tired, I want to sleep.*

I'm back on Gloria's profile. Her at an event with some girls her age. They're dressed up, touching each other, and laughing. One hundred twenty thousand likes, 370 comments. The girls in the photo all have the little blue tick verifying them as VIPs. Gloria with her grandma, hugging on a couch. The caption reads: you are my life. Two hundred thousand likes, 780 comments. A selfie in which she looks prettier than in real life. One hundred eleven thousand likes, 870 comments. A photo of her holding a cat. Eighty thousand likes, 160 comments. Affection between humans gets the most likes. Then selfies, then animals. The hierarchy can be summarized as:

love, narcissism, cats. But then there's one post that has two hundred thirty thousand likes and two thousand comments. It's composed of three photos: one of Gloria with a small, ugly pedigree dog, one of her as a little girl with the same disgusting little creature, and one of her crying. The caption is too long and too uninteresting to read in its entirety, but the gist of it is that the dog is dead. Pain for dead animals does very well on social media, naturally. It's a pain we know is inevitable when we get a pet; it's a pain that all of society knows; it transcends class, gender, and sexuality, it is universal, and it doesn't make people uncomfortable when they see it on social media. Straight to the top: dead animals.

I'm rolling a joint when the notification appears. The phone lights up and when I read Gloria's name I feel momentarily dizzy. The message is a photo, one of the those that disappears once it's been viewed. I open it and it's her with a hydrating face mask on, taken from below. Underneath, it says: "Will you work with me?"

I don't know what to say and now she knows I've seen it. If I don't reply immediately I'll come off as rude and she'll no longer want to hire me. I type and delete for at least two minutes.

"Are you about to send me a novel? You've been typing for hours," she interjects.

"No. My phone's broken, I'm slow."

"Anyway, you can't say no."

"Why not?"

"Because the porter showed me the video of you keying Vale's car."

I turn the screen off and throw the phone to the other side of the couch. I stay curled up, my heart pounding. Meanwhile, the phone lights up with new messages. After a minute or so I get up and move toward it with caution.

"You shit yourself, didn't you?" "Don't worry I don't judge you." "Come into the office to sign the contract on Monday if it's cool with you—Loredana will call to let you know what time. For now, I've got your first task. I saw on your profile that you read a lot. Can you recommend me a book? Maybe with a female protagonist around my age, I want it to feel familiar."

I pick up the phone and write: "I've just read a book with a protagonist your age. It's called *The Idiot*." To tell the truth I didn't read it all—my weed ran out about halfway through—and I don't remember much of the first half anyway.

Sent. I re-read what I just wrote. Somebody please cut my hands off! As I watch the little cloud that shows Gloria is typing, I try to convince myself: this work does not interest me. Why on earth would I want to work for a famous dolt? Pull yourself together, have some dignity.

Gloria: "Are you trying to tell me something?" smiling emoji. I hold my breath. Then: "Kidding, I'll buy it right away. I assume it's the one by Batuman, not Dostoyevsky."

"Yep" smiling emoji. I've never used an emoji in my life.

"See you Monday then!"

I put the phone down and breathe. I feel like I no longer have a body, I'm weightless. I have a job. My first real job. I wallow in this information and the idea of writing to Angela to thank her passes through my mind. I let it through.

Gloria is never in a bad mood, and she writes to me every day to ask me out. It's like I've adopted a Labrador. I don't know what I expected from this job, but I certainly didn't imagine I'd be paid to interpret the role of friend. I read an article once about how in China you can hire a man to take to family lunches and dinners to show your relatives you're not single. I am shown to two million people. A few weeks after signing the contract, Gloria posted a photo of her reading the book I had recommended. She tagged me and I got two hundred new followers. What do these people see in her that's so exciting they want to follow me and my extremely boring life, purely because I know her? I see nothing extraordinary. Were she prettier, more intelligent, cunning, brash, zealous, maybe I'd get it. But she's none of those things. She's just a random girl.

She usually texts at around twelve, when she's about to get out of school, asking if I fancy going for lunch or a wander around some vintage market she's heard good things about. I'm not sure where the boundaries of my job are, so I always say yes. I don't have a car, or a moped, and Gloria is lazy. So she has forced me to download an app on my phone that allows her to hire the electric cars that are scattered around the city so I can go and pick her up outside the private high school she goes to. She put my info in because she claims she doesn't have a license and doesn't plan to get one. Then she put her credit card details in. Her credit card is silver and thick. Once she asked me to hold it for a few seconds and I felt the cold tile on my palms. It was heavy. I wondered if it was only rich people who had access to such exquisite credit cards. Mine is orange, peeling at the edges. It's not a credit card but one of those prepaid ones that also has an IBAN number, which I only use to transfer my share of the bills to Filippo.

"Why are you putting your card on there? What if I take advantage of it?" I ask her.

Gloria's lips stretch out into a smile.

"You think I don't have it in me?"

"Of course you have it in you, you vandalized Valentina's car." She bursts out laughing. I stiffen. Gloria gives me a pat on the back: "We are all potentially bad, but only if we're put into a situation that makes us do bad things. Anyway, it would be absurd if you robbed me after this conversation. Not that I would realize—seriously—I never check my account."

What game is she playing; what kind of master manipulator is this girl? She must be smart. As the days go by, I notice that Gloria often decides on my behalf what does or doesn't form part of my identity, based on a set of criteria I am oblivious to. "These are just so you," she writes, attaching a photo of a pair of boots covered in buckles that I wouldn't be seen dead in. "Always the same," or "Classic Maia," she responds when I ask her not to send me seventy-five selfies to choose the best of.

Despite myself, I come to learn various thing about her life. Her father died when she was very young. Gloria has lived with her grandmother since her mother, a beautiful woman with a past career as an actress in low-quality but lucrative TV series, decided to move to a villa in the countryside a few hundred miles from Milan with her new partner and their daughter.

Mrs. Anna Ricordi, née Aiello, was born poor. Gloria tells me this all the time, with a hint of pride, as if this detail, together with the Jewish blood, grants her the status of honorary poor girl. Her obsession with her grandmother's poverty, I'd discover later, has an interesting origin: the terror of being held up as privileged on social media, where a trend has started in recent years of carrying out complicated calculations to find out who, ontologically-speaking, is the least fortunate, and thus the most deserving of attention, followers, and money.

Gloria tells me that as a child Anna would walk home from elementary school with her friends and pretend to go into a beautiful salmon-pink building so that the others would think she lived there. As soon as her friends had turned the corner, she'd go and get on the train that took her out of the city to a run-down apartment block—the only place her family, who had emigrated from Calabria, could afford to live. There were no toilets in the apartments, so the residents had to piss and shit in chamber pots that were emptied at morning and night.

Today, Anna Ricordi is rich and nothing of Calabria remains, not even her surname. She started her career as a journalist at a local paper. Then she took a stab at being a photographer when a big paper needed someone who was willing to go abroad, even if she hardly knew how to use a camera. She lived in Europe and the United States when such a thing was still unthinkable for a single woman. Back in Italy, she became the director of a communications school and is now one of those professional figures who seem to be behind all sorts of projects. She's had three husbands, the last of whom died almost twenty years ago. Everyone knows her; everyone prides themselves on being her friend. She claims to be friends with no one.

Gloria goes to the Machiavelli School, a private institution for catching up on failed classes. She moved there from an academically demanding high school where she had flunked two years in a row. Her classmates had bullied her. "Being famous online was still a new thing," she explains while concentrating on her fruit gelato. One time, a group of older girls followed her into the restroom. They climbed up on the toilet of the next cubicle, leaned over the partition, filmed her peeing, then uploaded it online with the title *The pissing YouTuber*, making the cover image her face at the very moment she realized what they were doing. Gloria had written to Google, and they had removed the video, but it continued to circulate in group chats at her high school and other schools nearby. Gloria didn't stop filming herself. She changed usernames a few times, but it was useless: it started over again every time they found her. Etchings into the desks, whispers in the corridors, chanting on the stairs. She didn't tell her mother who was feeling guilty at the time for moving cities and leaving her with her mother-in-law. Nor did she tell her teachers, who disapproved of Gloria's choices. Though she hadn't said a word to anyone about what was going on, they all knew, and the teachers' silence was, for her classmates, as good as their permission to continue. One morning in December, the English teacher came into the classroom while the students were trying to get their hands on the last seats close to the radiators. She had brought in a crumpled tabloid, one of those you find in the metro. Among the pages was a short article that said Gloria wouldn't accept any job that paid less than twenty thousand euros. The teacher left the paper open to the incriminating page on an empty desk and announced: "Look who's washed up in the papers today. Linares, are you too famous to be quizzed? Must I give you at least twenty-thousand euros or will you condescend to coming up to my desk for free?"

Her classmates took it from there.

When she failed the first time, her grandma had blamed the stress of her mother's moving away. The second fail, however, she couldn't accept. She summoned Gloria: "Come with me, I'll show you pissed off." She dragged her into the staff room where the final exams grading meeting was taking place. She planted her feet so firmly on the floor they could have developed roots. She started shouting that everyone there was destitute, unjust, wretched. Her veins swelled under the flabby skin of her neck. The teachers remained silent until one of them, a charitable woman called Miss Palumbo, got up with a contrite expression on her face and, smiling, expressed regret for the situation. "Of course, adolescence can't be easy for a girl orphaned by her father and with an absent mother." She stretched her hand out toward Gloria's chin and held it a bit too hard, as if Gloria were a dog and she needed to inspect her teeth. "She's acting out over the internet. It's normal. But you have to understand that our job is to contain our students. We are sure that Gloria would do better in a less demanding environment. We're doing her a favor." All the teachers behind her nodded, grateful that someone had taken the reins. Mrs. Anna Ricordi continued to shake, her eyes burning with helpless rage: in that situation, for the first time in decades, she had no power, she'd become an Aiello again. Gloria searched for her hand, fumbling, and whispered: "Let's go," but her grandma shooed her away abruptly. She turned on her heel and walked out of the school in strides so long that Gloria had to jog to keep up. Once outside, they stood still in embarrassed silence. Gloria was tormenting herself. If only she'd studied more, or given up on those videos, she'd have never put her grandma in that situation. She was ready to swear to her that she'd stop, but at exactly that moment Anna stopped walking, took hold of Gloria's shoulders with her bony fingers, and said: "You must not bother with school. True as God, if what you want to do is be on the internet, that's what you'll do, and all those worthless, slimy little teachers will rue the day they lost you as their student." From that day on, Anna Ricordi used every tool she had to help her granddaughter carve her own path through the unchartered territory of the internet.

Everyone Gloria knows is rich. Her mother lives in a 1920s villa in the Piacentini hills. Gloria doesn't like her mother's new partner much but claims she understands why she is with him: "He looks after her, he cooks, he knows how to fix things when they break. My father could never do that, and my mother always said that for her next husband she'd choose a handyman. And that's what happened." What I would later come to learn is that this man, as well as being a handyman, also happens to be the heir to a large Tuscan family textile business.

Rebecca, the daughter her mother has with her new partner, says she's bisexual. She's twelve and hasn't yet had her first kiss: she says she wants to wait until her braces are off. One day Gloria tells me that on her mother's side, two out of three of her cousin's daughters are lesbians, and that one has started the transition to make her, I mean his, sex correspond with his gender. Nobody batted an eyelid, and they all use the right pronouns. Gloria's family call one another by their names, and when she tells me, I wonder whether this detail—linguistically eliminating the inherent power structures that exist in familial roles—along with the money, might hold the secret to their harmony. There are no visible conflicts in the Linares-Viale family. The villa her mother has chosen to withdraw to is surrounded by forest. The glass in the windows looks like a sheet of ice that will melt in spring. The windows are all different colors and when the light hits them it creates a lysergic kaleidoscope on the floor. A tower rises out of the villa's roof, stained glass windows on all sides.

"When I'm there, I swear, it feels impossible that magic isn't real," Gloria confides.

Friends and acquaintances pop up like fungi at least once a month for a party at the villa. Some order three thousand euros worth of sushi to reciprocate the hospitality and get it brought out in a little van from the best Japanese restaurant in Italy, which is at least a hundred miles away. In Gloria's family's eyes, even the people anyone else would call problematic become merely funny characters, stars serving as part of the social constellation in which they live. For example, one of Gloria's uncles is an alcoholic and she laughs as she describes this man wandering around with an expensive bottle of vodka under his jacket waiting for the right moment to swap it with the empty one he has just drained, so that no one discovers his vice. This man's daughter is the same age as Rebecca and they're friends. When I ask how this girl, Lorenza, is affected by her father's addiction, Gloria shrugs her shoulders and says she's used to worse: her father is also an opiate addict and there have been nights when Lorenza, making her way to the bathroom in the dark, has found him in a febrile half-awake state, sitting in a puddle of vomit. When I ask her what she thinks of all this, she tilts her head from left to right and says only: "He's a character, Uncle Giorgio." The way Gloria sees humans is completely free of judgment, I don't know if out of an absence of critical thought, or a limitless moral universe. "Characters," for her, are all the people who behave in unusual ways: a wide range of individuals that begins with her grandmother's hairdresser who, at the age of fifty after a straight-laced life, fell in love with this guy called Christian while walking the Camino de Santiago, and now enjoys telling everyone about the awakening of his libido; and includes her uncle who's high on opiates; and probably Pol Pot, if she knew who he was.

Indeed, another of Gloria's characteristics is ignorance. As far as she's concerned the Congo is a region of Venezuela. She doesn't know when the French Revolution was. She mainly reads self-help manuals or books with playful looking hard covers that contain exercises to make your life better. She tried to involve me in one of these: the title was *Find the extraordinary in the ordinary*. Instructions: take a photo of all the dogs you see in the park, match each one to one of your friends and then make a poster of them. Another was *Make other people's lives happier*. Instructions: flick through the phonebook, pick someone at random, phone them and ask how they are. My call was answered by a guy with a Southern accent who told me to fuck off, hers by an old lady who at first mistook her for her granddaughter and then, when Gloria told her about the game, kept her on the phone for an hour and a half. "What a character. A real sweetie; I must do this more often."

One day, while we were eating a sandwich on the steps of a bridge over the Darsena docks where up until a few weeks earlier, over the now smelly riverbed carpeted with garbage, ran a body of water, I wondered aloud whether they had closed a dam somewhere that usually supplied the water to the canal. The hypothesis Gloria candidly put forward was that the water might have evaporated in the spring sunshine. Thirteen feet of water, along the entire length of the canal.

I spend my time with Gloria searching for cracks in her varnished life. She doesn't hold a grudge against her mother for having moved away, maintaining that everyone is free to do as they like. "It's unhappiness that makes people bad, not distance."

The only remnant of misfortune I manage to find is the death of her father, when Gloria was three years old. But even this doesn't seem to represent a trauma for her. When I press her, she says: "It's hard to miss something you never really knew. But if you're so interested, I can show you a photo." I'm not interested, but it's too late now. Her father was a handsome man. Tall, with a square jaw and eyebrows thick like earthworms.

"You know, as a kid I thought he was talking to me through animals. Once a butterfly flew into the house and I was certain it was him. I still am."

"So your father was reincarnated as an insect?"

She laughs. She's never offended. Whatever I say just bounces off her privilege.

Apart from pretending to be her friend, I've still done nothing for Gloria that resembles the idea I have of work. I see her on social media, her face deformed by filters that swell her lips and lengthen her eyes, showing off an array of products: sets of natural shampoos that cost more than two-hundred euros; white, rough-cotton T-shirts that cost a fifth of my paycheck before tax (one thousand three hundred euros, never seen so much money in my life); sustainable energy providers; investment apps; flowers that cure cancer, and so on. She doesn't seem to need my help for those kind of things. She sits down in front of the phone and talks about the product for thirty seconds max. I have no idea how much she earns. Since I met her, I've started following other girls like her who I've seen tagged in her stories. They have the blue tick, and they too sponsor microplastic-free cosmetics and feminist calendars with illustrations by mediocre cartoonists who draw outlines of women and call it art.

On social media everyone is good, especially the ones who belong to a non-privileged minority. If you're unfortunate, you can't be bad.

Apart from the heterosexual men, who are free to be anything they choose, everyone seems obliged to be sensitive about every cause. They declare themselves to be empathetic and, in the name of this empathy, indignant against anything that violates their moral standards. In a single day it's possible to see a person post four or five different images that contain commitments to as many different causes. Against beekeeping that exploits bees, against plastic, against transphobia, against fatphobia, against fast fashion.

On the Day for the Elimination of Violence against Women, Gloria, her friends, and all their emulators post infographics, videos, and newspaper articles about the issue. On World AIDS Day, red ribbons pop up all over the screen. On the anniversary of the G8 summit in Genoa all these girls who had only just been born when Carlo Giuliani died, commemorate 2001 in touching tones as if it meant something to them, only to begin instructing their followers to follow the lifestyle vilified by their bible *No Logo* on the very next day, in a bizarre moral short-circuit. Gloria carries out all of these actions mechanically, but the cause that is closest to her heart is her extremely personal battle against plastic packaging.

Gloria shudders every time she sees me buy something wrapped in plastic, as do all her certified-VIP friends. The thing that arouses the most terror is packaged prosciutto. When she asked me to drive her to the supermarket, I saw her giving the side-eye to all the wretched people buying packaged prosciutto. She stared at them indignantly and nudged me with her elbow as if I give a shit. I once took a photo of some strawberries in a plastic container and received a tidal wave of fury in my inbox from the gaggle of Gloria's followers who have started following me for my connection to her. I tell Gloria, hoping for sympathy.

"They did the right thing. That's how we change the world," Gloria tells me, completely sincere. "If all of us stop buying plastic, they'll stop producing it. If you get called out for something you've done, you stop doing it. It's bottom-up power: we're educating others and the brands. It's all thanks to call-outs that I've stopped buying packaged prosciutto. One day I posted a photo of a dinner with my friend Sara and on the table there was a plastic prosciutto packet. I got some really harsh criticism and since then I always buy it unpackaged. Like you with the strawberries."

"Oh, I just stopped taking photos of them."

She looks at me suspiciously. I continue: "You really think

everything people say they do is what they really do? If that were true, we would have solved all of humanity's problems ages ago. Does your life mirror everything you show on social media?"

"I try to make it that way: it's important to behave well."

As a consequence, the thing that she and all her friends hate most are the girls—other influencers—who have loads of followers, but, unlike them, don't put out positive messages. She believes they are irresponsible and that they should disappear from the face of the earth; that their indolence could poison fragile young minds and inculcate the idea that smoking, being selfish, having issues, and glamorizing your suffering is the right way to live.

"Hold on, are you saying that people start having issues only when they see other people having issues? Is it not more likely that if you're suffering or you're a dick then you feel better represented by someone who suffers or is a dick? How is that any different to a person who follows someone to make themself feel good?"

Gloria shrugs her shoulders, looks at me with baffled eyes full of compassion and asks if I want to play one of the games from her colorful book.

Another strange thing about Gloria is that when I ask her a question, she responds as if she's talking to an audience. One afternoon, sitting in the car outside her house, I asked her what she wants to be when she's older, and she answered with a big smile: "I don't know yet, but I know that I want to be a mother."

"You said that in an interview too. What kind of answer is that?"

"Do you not want to be a mother?"

"That's not the point. The point is that being a mother isn't exactly a life plan. You can have kids but also do something else; you don't live in the 1950s."

Gloria squinted her eyes, still smiling. Her smile annoys me, it's as if her face is made of porcelain and if I gave it a reasonably solid flick it would crumble.

"Why are you always smiling?"

"The more you smile the happier you become. When you see someone else smiling it makes you smile, and so you create a chain of smiles and positive energy. Why shouldn't I?"

"Because if you smile too much, you'll get wrinkles. Imagine the irony, given all the money you spend on your beauty regime."

"Alright, from now on I won't smile when I'm around you. Is that better? I want to see how you find it." I think she wanted her voice to sound angry, but it came out velvety as usual.

I didn't manage to hold in a laugh.

"Now why are you laughing?"

"Because you're funny."

At that point Gloria got out of the car, slammed the door, and went into her grandmother's building. I continued to laugh for a few seconds, then went home.

Despite the forced company I have to give Gloria, I'm happy to spend some time out of the house: I hope it will prevent me from sabotaging my relationship with Filippo. Before I met Gloria, I would go and rummage around in Filippo's computer whenever he went out. One time I was almost caught. I had already logged in when I heard the key in the lock. To avoid being caught red-handed, I pulled out the plug of the computer and pretended to mess around with the multi-socket. He said he'd forgotten his wallet and, on seeing me crouching under the desk, asked with a hint of worry what I was doing down there.

That episode prompted me to refine my technique. Nothing special, I simply waited a few minutes to be sure he wasn't coming back. Filippo has two laptops: a lighter one he uses for work and another one he leaves at home. One day he called me from an unknown number and asked me to go into his computer and read out the code of a train ticket, because his phone had died. The password was: Belalugosi197!

Never forgotten. Every morning I tell myself it's the last time I sneak into his business like a thief, but I never manage to keep my word. As soon as I hear the lock snap shut, my guts awaken. It's one of the few things that relieves my apathy. My stomach is in knots even before I've pulled my intentions into focus. I try to restrain myself. I open the fridge, close the fridge. I make a coffee. I go to the toilet. I flick through a book, feigning interest. I try to deceive myself. But the more minutes that pass, the less I'm able to ignore the whisper in my head luring me into violating someone else's privacy. I put the book down, get up, start to wander around the study as if looking for something. I need a slow approach. It helps me convince myself that it happened by chance, that I just found myself in the area. When the whisper becomes a shout, I sit down in front of the laptop, open it, and type in the password. The passwords to his social media profiles are saved in the browser's memory. I check the last people he befriended. I read his latest message threads.

Filippo is an extremely intelligent and busy man. Apart from being a philosopher, for a while he has also been curating contemporary art installations: a few reasonably well-known artists have been fascinated by his books and call him when they need to fill room upon room with plant life or put on a symphonic concert for spruces.

I put my name into the search bar and read what he says about me to others. My ego gurgles when I violate his conversations, because being considered "smart" by him is an honor. And his friends agree when he describes me as a brilliant girl. I like scrolling down through his intimacy to the early days of our relationship, when he first told them about me. He wrote to his friends that he didn't know what to do, because I was too young but he liked me. He had fallen in love, even. He told them how mature I was; said that if they met me, they'd never guess my age.

The recent messages are harder to decipher. Since Eva died and we moved to Milan I have not been a good girlfriend. I have stopped cooking and I very rarely tidy the house. Also, with him no longer in low spirits, it's difficult for me to offer him much support. Yet, when I scroll up to the present, I see that he tells his colleagues (all his friends are his colleagues) that I am well and soon to graduate in psychobiology; that it's energizing to be with a young, lively girl. They're all lies, and I feel confused. Only once—to his ex-wife in the middle of the night—did he write a long, long message in which he said he was desperate because I was crazy; that I wasn't doing anything except waitressing. She never responded.

I don't know which way to turn. There are days when things feel a bit better and I try to repeat the actions that punctuated our routine years ago. I knot his tie before he goes out (I learned on YouTube as soon as I met him, because it seemed like something a grown-up woman should know how to do). I force myself to cook something. I try to keep the house tidy. I try not to smoke weed. No chance! I only manage to sustain this personality for a maximum of six hours every two weeks. Then I deflate like a beach ball in the sun and go back to watching "Law & Order: Special Victims Unit."

To be fair, it's not like he only bad mouths me behind my back, quite the opposite: he's very direct. He's confessed multiple times that he can't go on like this. I can't keep sulking and I have to start eating again. Once, exasperated, he blurted out that my pussy was skinny. I would have done anything to rid him of his disappointment. It's just that I really don't feel like eating, apart from the gummy crocodiles. I told him he can cheat if he wants. "Don't pull that crap, Maia. I love you; you're just trying to make me crazy," he responded in his melodramatic way. He added that I was awful for saying such a thing.

"I'm serious, I know I'm a sad person to be around. Don't tell me if you do, just know that you can."

He remained silent.

A part of me has always hoped Filippo would cheat. I first

realized this just after I moved in with him, after a long period of insisting that we take that step. There were weeks of negotiations before he gave in. I was so happy, happier than I'd been in years. Being with him without living in his house felt like a threat to our love. He wouldn't respond to my messages for days and when, trying to stay calm, I brought it up, he'd call me controlling. Living in his house gave me official girlfriend status. He still didn't respond to my messages, but this recognition was sufficient. Filippo was an adult, so I had to grow up. My lack of possessions worked in my favor. I wouldn't be taking up space; every inch of that apartment belonged to him. I was a parasite, like one of those birds that lives on a hippopotamus's wrinkly skin, or one of those fish that cling to the sides of whales.

When I was forced to admit to myself that I wanted Filippo to be unfaithful, it was late in the evening and I had already gone to bed. He had invited the university Chancellor back to the apartment after a conference: a man in his sixties on whose meaty nose sat a pair of gold-framed glasses. They were sitting in Filippo's study. They were both tipsy. I was woken by their footsteps, the click of the light switch, and their excited voices, each attempting to restrain the other. I lay in the dark for a few minutes, then slid out of bed like a shadow and tip-toed down the hallway and into the bathroom. One of the walls was thin, and if you pushed your ear against it, you could make out the voices in the study. They were talking about the conference; gossiping about this or that colleague. They commented on the appearance of their least attractive colleagues and gave them unflattering epithets. Then they moved onto the young assistants. One in particular: Lucrezia. I knew who she was because I had seen her name among the senders in Filippo's mailbox. She was a bit older than me. She had milky skin and few photos on her profile. She had studied in London: her first posts, around the time that I was starting university in Paris, portrayed her drunk at house parties full of international students. Then she was in Italy and her photos memorialized her in short, tight-fitting dresses. She wore round glasses, her wavy black hair was tied at the nape of her neck with a few strands falling over her forehead. She had thick thighs. In contrast to mine, which had already begun to shrivel up, I imagined hers soft, plump, and sticky with sweat. At the time, I imagined Filippo delicately lifting the skirt of that cheap flowery dress.

"If I were twenty years younger I wouldn't think twice about getting her along to all the conferences abroad and accidentally booking only one room," the chancellor commented.

Filippo's laughter. "What, can you no longer get it up?"

"You're still young. Let me tell you about old age: I have a tumor on my prostate," —coughing— "it's benign, nothing serious. Although if I don't take the drugs, it grows, and if it grows it presses on my bladder and I spend the whole night pissing." Pause, clinking and refilling glasses. "But this drug dries my mouth out. It's like sand under the sun; I'm incessantly waking up to drink. This is old age, you see? Deciding whether to lose sleep due to thirst or incontinence. I couldn't screw her, Lucrezia. But you could."

Filippo laughed again. He was embarrassed. The age gap between them meant they were working with two different sets of morals and prevented him from agreeing with his companion.

"She'd fuck you without question, you can tell. And were I twenty years younger, she'd fuck me too, both of us. We'd have a ball." He paused again. "I have to piss. I didn't take the drugs."

I wouldn't be quick enough to leave the bathroom without being seen, so I switched on the light and ran the faucet, making it seem like I'd just gone in. The moment I put my hand on the handle to pull the door, I felt an equal force push it toward me. I found myself standing in front of that man, to his evident surprise. I was wearing only a T-shirt that came midway down my thighs. Under his beard you could see wrinkles that suggested the existence of many necks. His eyes were small, and age was graying them. I acted sleepy, then shocked.

"Who are you?"

"Maia."

Meanwhile, Filippo had appeared behind him, looking annoyed. "Go back to sleep." Then, turning to the chancellor: "This is my girlfriend, we woke her up." He sounded hesitant and looked down, ashamed. Of me?

"I had to go to the toilet, I couldn't go in bed."

"Filippo, don't be rude to your little lady." The man smiled. He pressed himself up against the wall to let me pass, and the outline of his stomach in profile looked like the moon. A shirt button had popped open over his belly and a few hairs peeked out through the gap. The chancellor made a bow, his arms twirling elegantly as if rolling out an invisible carpet for me.

I disappeared down the dark hallway. Their voices started to whirr in the air again, indistinct. Once I was in bed, I took my T-shirt off and ran my hands across my hips.

Then my fingers moved down toward my clitoris, making their way through the hair, and I started to touch myself. I was Lucrezia in the cheap polka-dot dress, the elasticized spots stretching over my big breasts. The chancellor and Filippo were consuming me, biting me, leaving scratches and bruises, slipping inside me like butter until I melted. Nothing was left of me, of Lucrezia, by the end, just flesh cloaked in rags. Once I was finished, I lay awake in the humid warmth of the sheets, breathing in my salty odor, watching the darkness until I could no longer tell if my eyes were open or closed.

Filippo doesn't cheat on me, even now. He responds courteously to students who try to flirt and coldly to approaches from women his own age. I want him to. I want to find proof of his wrongdoings in his messages. I want to have a reason to hate him, to explode, to lay on him the blame for all my failings, for my being such a mediocre girlfriend. I squander my time away lying on the couch that makes me sweat in summer. When I look out the window, I see the taxi drivers in the stand and they look like seagulls. I want to close my eyes and take flight, and it would be a dream if it was all because of him.

My role as image consultant becomes clear about two months after signing the contract: I have to help Gloria decide how to present herself publicly on occasions that require more sophistication than product promotion. At first, I don't understand why she needs me: she seemed perfectly able to make her own decisions. I finally get it when I'm asked to participate in my first meeting with a brand. In the world of publicity, people pepper their sentences with random fashionable expressions: "The deal is," "we have to be on our game," "get real." None of these people have ever actually lived in English-speaking countries, so adopting this mongrel tongue with the flimsy excuse of being confused by their multilingualism is really not justified. Before the meeting starts, I get called into the office with Valentina the woman-mouth and Gloria. Gloria has already explained more or less what it's about, and she has shown me the profiles of the other girls participating in the project. But it's up to Valentina to explain the inner workings of the job.

"It's very simple," the mouth explains, punctuating every word. "Advertising is how Gloria earns money. Brands call her and ask her if they can affiliate themselves with her face and her social media profiles. The first level is what you've already seen: Gloria talks about a product for a few seconds on her social channels. Then there is a classic, more structured situation where Gloria is the face of a brand's campaign, so all that she has to physically bring is her appearance. Like an actress. Finally, and this is where you come in, there's the option that a brand asks her to talk about a certain topic in her own words but within a frame provided by the brand. For example, she'd talk about feminism or ethical consumption on a set provided by a brand trying to tell their story. In this case what matters most is her work as a content creator, her tone of voice, her personality."

What personality, I wonder. Instead, I ask: "Why should she talk about feminism if she has never called herself a feminist?".

"All intelligent women are feminists; there's really not much to know. One's own experience as a woman is sufficient. We are all oppressed by unrealistic beauty standards. We all call other women sluts, and so on. Anyway, that's where you come in. Your job is to write the script for Gloria's content, so listen to everything that's said in the call."

I glance at Gloria. She's not as chatty as usual. She seems to have disconnected from herself, like in the photo in the magazine. It's the first time I've seen her like this.

"Today we're talking with Glow. It doesn't seem like you take much care of your skin, but I imagine you must know them. They're a cosmetics brand. They've won a whole host of prizes for the originality of their ad campaigns." Pause. "They're revolutionary. It's extremely difficult to get into their creative team," Valentina adds with a sigh. "Today's call is a check-in. That means we can join over video from the office, since we've already met the team and we're just catching up on the progress of the campaign." Valentina takes visible pleasure in explaining it to me. Then she taps at the keys with her purple-painted fingernails, making them click, perhaps on purpose, and the monitor illuminates her porous, foundation-covered face.

The meeting is full of women. For the first seven minutes they flit around from nicety to nicety: Darling, you look great; I saw on your Insta that you've started going to the gym; I haven't drunk for two months; There's so many of us; It's great to see you again; How's our Gloria; The holidays are coming; Your daughter's already three?; Fabulous hair.

The other four faces of the campaign are a feminist influencer (four hundred eighty thousand followers), a mom influencer (three hundred nineteen thousand followers), a fat influencer (one hundred four thousand followers), and a Black influencer (sixty-three thousand followers). The latter has been pinched from a competitor who accidentally sent her a shampoo for non-afro hair. The Black influencer filmed herself in a blond wig with the product smeared all over it and, crying, denounced the brand's racism, looking into the lens and asking whether her hair looked better now it was more Western.

A woman in her forties starts speaking. The virtual background behind her shows a tropical beach with the Glow logo hanging from a palm tree. "We are delighted with the work we're driving forward thanks to our ambassadors: Gloria, Serena, Donatella, Eugenia, and Mary. The #realbeauty campaign is going fabulously. Let's recap what we've done so far." She shows slides full of data and graphics that list the campaign's total number of views. Then more slides appear with women of various kinds. In contrast to the brand ambassadors in the meeting, the women in the slides are all ugly. Every so often, the lady who's speaking glides her cursor over their faces and enunciates the words *diversity* and *inclusivity*. "Glow has always made it its goal to represent all kinds of beauty. As we Italians say, *the world is beautiful because it's diverse*, and we are committed to representing all of this diversity. We want to boost the self-esteem of the women who feel crushed by the weight of our culture's beauty standards. We want to overturn society, to topple the stereotypes that link beauty to a single form. Even today girls are too often valued by their aesthetic appearance. But *girl power*, thanks to *body positivity*, has shown us that all women are beautiful and deserve to be represented. And this is where you girls come in, with your diverse and unique forms of beauty."

Valentina nods, won over by the speech. Her lips often move without emitting a sound, finishing off the sentences that come out of the computer's speaker. When it's her turn to speak she says she is proud to devote her time to such a socially committed brand. Then she grabs Gloria and pulls her into the frame. "And Gloria is also proud to be able to be your ambassador on such a crucial message."

Gloria gives the crooked outline of a smile. Now it's the

mother-woman's turn: "As you know, I'm a mother. And as a mother I am happy that my daughters will grow up in a world that I have helped to make safer for them. And if one of them becomes a hairy exhibitionist I'll know who to thank—myself and Glow—for giving her too much confidence!" Laughter.

Now it's the Black influencer's go: "I would like to express my emotions." Everyone's face turns grave. Mary is beautiful, and when she speaks, she brings her hands to her chest, making a shield over her heart. She talks about how important it is for her to be represented, echoes of the shampoo affair rebounding in her long silences. She complains of all the times she has been racialized, called a Black Pearl. Everyone applauds when she finishes speaking. "You are so brave; we are so moved."

The fat influencer brings her experience too. "When I admitted to myself that I was fat, I felt this wave of courage come over me." Before the meeting, Gloria had told me that the fat influencer had contacted the brand personally to be part of the campaign. Whereas Mary, the Black girl, is in fact the daughter of an American diplomat and runs courses on personal branding for her followers. "You have no idea what an honor it is for me to be here," the fat influencer is saying, "I've always had enormous admiration for Glow. Even if I haven't yet met you in person, I can feel good vibes coming off all of you." Donatella's eyes are wet. She explains that she lives in London and when she describes the microaggressions that she receives online every day because of her weight, tears roll down her cheeks cutting glistening paths through her face powder. Everyone shakes their heads. Everyone brings a hand to their heart. It's really not O.K. that the world is like this.

The feminist influencer takes the floor, brushing a golden lock away from her lips which have been enlarged by injections, and says that feminism is the only weapon we have to "tackle the standards to which women are continuously held. I myself, aware of my white privilege, make an effort every day to pass my megaphone to less fortunate women."

When it's Gloria's turn, I struggle to hear what she's saying, even though she's sitting right next to me. "Thank you all, I'm also happy." She speaks fast, as if the things she said wouldn't exist if she got them out within a certain amount of time. The others wait for her to say something else, but essentially Gloria is thin, rich, and white, so all she can do is atone for her guilt in silence. They go on for a few more minutes praising one another for having the courage to be themselves. "You are all warriors. In fact, let's give ourselves another round of applause, all together this time, please." The sound of the hands of all the participants crackles out of the speaker. "We'll check in soon to decide on the content for July," concludes the woman who spoke first. "Ciao sweeties."

Kisses smacking, hands waving. One by one the smiling faces disappear from the screen. Valentina, satisfied, closes the computer. "We're doing an amazing job!" Gloria keeps her head down. She takes her phone out of her pocket and sinks her chin into her aqua green hoodie, sucking on the drawstrings. After a few moments she changes tune: "I need some air. I'll wait for you outside."

As soon as Valentina is sure that Gloria is far enough away, she turns to me:

"Hmm, how does Gloria seem to you?"

"She doesn't seem anything to me. I still barely understand what my job is. That meeting told me nothing, and I don't know if Gloria is aware of the boundaries of our relationship, which is a professional one. Or at least it should be. It seems to me like my job is to be her friend."

Valentina gets up and closes the glass door.

"First of all, your job is to get her to work. She's no longer the only princess on the internet, now TikTok and all the other social networks are full of girls just like her. Plus, she's a *white girl*, and the brands want more than that." She lowers her voice and looks around the room as if someone might emerge out of the walls. " . . . .Gloria is a spoiled brat. If she's gotten so far, it's entirely down to her grandmother, who is an extremely stubborn woman. She got her in everywhere. You know, she once refused thirty-five thousand euros to do an ad for a brand of chips. A teacher earns that figure in a year." Valentina puts on a sorrowful expression, eyes turned to the sky as if there was a clutch of poor teachers dangling above her head. "She turns down those kinds of figures. So, your first priority is to convince her to work. You've just seen how little enthusiasm she puts into it. Any number of girls would love to be her, and she acts up like a princess. But sooner or later the good times will come to an end."

"And if it all comes to an end, what will you do?"

"I'll click my fingers and change job. In fact, I'm already starting to look. I hate to tell you this because you've just started, but this is a sinking ship." Suddenly Gloria seems like someone I could hang out with. Valentina continues, taking my silence as permission to offload: "You have to give her a personality. It's simple. That's how she works; she's an empty vessel. We managed to fill her up for a bit, make her not say stupid things in interviews, and now she knows how to respond to journalists. But when she meets someone new who she likes she clings on like a limpet, and now it's your turn. Also because it was she who chose you. You've never worked in this world, why else do you think you're here? Last year she was going out with Giulio, another guy from the circuit, and he claimed that he loved meditating. Moral of the story: she spent three months meditating in some monastery God knows where." My eyes turn to the door through which Gloria just left. I bring my thumb to my mouth and focus on a little bit of skin, trying to pull it off with my teeth. "Gloria has no form, except that of whoever is beside her in any given moment. So right now, she has yours." The worse the stuff she says, the more golden Gloria becomes in my eyes. "I hope you are wise and make the most of the opportunity you've been given. This is a springboard, but you have to be careful to get out in time." She puts on her coat like it's a cloak and shoots me a complicit glance from the doorway. "Just give her a personality." She winks and prances down the metal staircase.

Gloria is waiting downstairs. She's sitting on a step looking at her toes and when she sees me coming, she smiles weakly. "Did I do well in my inaugural call?" I ask her, sounding chirpier than I feel. Am I trying to cheer her up?

She nods.

"Are those meetings always like that?"

"Sometimes they're shorter."

I sit down next to her. "Isn't it you who's always saying this is how we change the world? You're subverting the beauty standards that imprison us. When they see you looking so gross all the other girls will finally see that they too, despite being gross, could star in an ad one day."

Gloria smirks. "Stop it."

"Is it true that you refused thirty-five thousand euros for a TV commercial?"

"Did Valentina tell you that? She's never forgiven me. But yes."

"Why?"

"Because I was sixteen, and they wanted to put me and some extras pretending to be my friends in a pool, all of us half-naked and wet. And they wanted me to say that the chips, because they were spicy and had a weird shape, were a *fun twist that makes me happy and spices up my friends*. If you're going to tell me that I'm spoiled, there's no need, I know that already."

"Better to be spoiled than a moron."

Gloria looks up at me, trying to gauge if I'm being ironic. I'm not. I get up and hold out my hand. She takes it and we walk along the blisteringly hot sidewalk. I drop her home in one of those stupid electric cars.

It's the beginning of June; the sky is a blue so intense I feel nauseous. Gloria and I spend most days together. We don't have many commitments. We sit in silence in a park, wander around the scorching city. I'm amazed at how easy it is to exist in the same space as her without being required to do anything. She scrolls through her phone, every so often laughing and sending me a TikTok video that she finds sidesplittingly funny and that I don't get. I've started flicking through books again and so I bring one along with me or get lost down a train of thought I've never followed before, which has been happening more and more since I met Gloria, as if her presence alone is capable of opening up new air vents in some recess of my mind. I have to admit that Gloria isn't so bad. She doesn't talk much; she isn't annoying. Sometimes I catch her staring at me, spaced out, so I ask her what's up, what she's looking at—maybe there's a stain on my clothes or something stuck between my teeth. She always answers: "Nothing, nothing."

I can't stop thinking about what Valentina told me about Gloria. She had to film herself for Glow talking about how, in her life, society has made her perceive herself as female, and therefore inferior. When writing the script, I came up with a teacher who made a young Gloria feel insecure in science class, and a principal who asked her to stop wearing miniskirts. Although it was all made up, hearing her recall memories that weren't her own in a language that also wasn't hers was unsettling.

"Valentina said you were an empty container," I tell her one afternoon while we're drinking Coca-Cola in the shade of a tree in the park.

Gloria stiffens for a moment, then her usual vacuous smile. In that moment, looking at it more closely, I see that it's a sad smile from an ancient sadness, washed away by time. We don't talk about it again.

One day she turns up at the Galeone, face beaded with sweat, with something very important to tell me. Despite the job with

Gloria, I'm still doing my shifts at the bar. I was going to quit, but when I picked up the phone to call the fat owner and tell him, my throat closed up and I started to hyperventilate. I wondered why my body was rejecting the idea of not spending six hours on my feet serving beers and wiping greasy tables, and realized that the Galeone is the only place that belongs to me. Even if it was Filippo who got me the job and it's the place he has our packages dropped when the porter for our building is away, it's more mine than his. The sickly odor that impregnates the walls is familiar, just like Giulia's accent and her blabbering on about her homeland. I've worked there for almost a year; when a new girl starts it's me who warns her about the Fays and shows her how to make a Bloody Mary. Sometimes Angela comes in to see me and tells me about her work at the agency, or gossips about this or that influencer, or how slimy her bosses are. I don't really listen, and she doesn't really care. I've grown used to her chatter. Having her there, showering me with rumors, makes me feel safe, as if time were a straight road with no bumps in it. The Galeone is my territory, mine and theirs, the other girls with whom, sighing, we talk about what we'll be like when we're grown up and this place has the blurred outlines of youthful memories.

Gloria has never been to the Galeone before: I have always been careful that she didn't find out about my kingdom. I didn't want her to think I was so desperate for work that I had to be a waitress. And I didn't want her to see me in an apron. She already treats me like the help as it is: I chauffeur her around the city; I call the toll-free number of online stores when she needs to return something because she's embarrassed to; I accompany her to renew her passport. I imagine she behaves like this with everyone. It's just what happens when you're told, for years on end, how important you are: other people become mere enablers of your comfort.

Since we weren't supposed to meet that day, I had said I'd cover another girl on the afternoon shift. Afternoons at the

Galeone are rarefied, I have time to do sudoku or read a book without being continually interrupted by the Fays' requests. But straight after lunch Gloria called me. I told her I had plans.

"What are you doing?"

"A favor for a friend."

"You don't have friends."

"Yes, I do."

"I'll join."

I tried saying no in all the ways I could think of, but it wasn't happening. She insisted with such strange urgency over the phone that in the end I gave in. I thought of calling in sick, but there was no one to cover me and I'd never missed a shift before. My commitment to the Galeone had become almost sacrosanct. I felt that were I to violate it something would change that I didn't want to.

Gloria comes in, out of breath, her hair woven into a complex structure of ribbons and hairpins. She looks around, trepidation clearing the way for curiosity, as if it is just dawning on her that the bar is an actual bar. Her features soften when she sees me.

"What is this place?"

"It's where I work."

"No way. You're a waitress?"

"Among other things."

"Amazing," she comments with her mouth wide open and her eyes bouncing off the walls and over my dark uniform.

"Are you kidding me?"

"Not at all, you're like someone from a TV show. You're so normal." She bites her tongue. "I didn't mean to offend you, it's a compliment."

"Sure, who wouldn't want to work for seven euros an hour."

Her face darkens. "I mean it, I'm sorry."

"Fine, what's up?"

"Can we sit down for a minute?"

I roll my eyes back to highlight my annoyance and let myself be dragged over to the same table where Angela had been sitting a while back.

"Something has happened, and I don't know who else to talk to."

Sara is one of Gloria's classmates. She's the daughter of a sad-looking couple who own a tobacconist. Gloria has known her since elementary school. They started making YouTube videos together, then Sara stopped because it was "for dorks." When Gloria started to become popular, Sara's responses to her messages thinned out until they disappeared altogether. So Gloria witnessed her friend's changes through adolescence via social media. Sometimes she would find herself scrolling through her photos, hypnotized by this girl who was constantly evolving but, in some ways, seemed to stay exactly the same. In the photos she shows me she has bleached hair and tongue and nipple piercings. She used to work as a dancer in an afternoon disco for teenagers, the management of which has since been reported for some sinister-sounding behavior. She skipped almost a whole year of school pretending to have glandular fever, until the teachers called her parents and she was caught. There were rumors about her promiscuity based on an alleged clitoris piercing that she'd had since the age of fourteen. There were guys who boasted of having taken her home on their mopeds and received a hand-job under their windbreakers en-route. The better-off ones who had a car talked of blowjobs. The service increased in line with the luxury.

Just after the start of the school year, Sara wrote off-handedly to Gloria saying she was going to be in her class and couldn't wait for them to be classmates. And, indeed, she arrived, sat down next to her, and never left again.

Sara liked older men—Gloria lowers her voice as if someone might hear—and every week she had a new story to tell. Gloria would listen, captivated, though she tried not to let Sara notice.

She wasn't sure if all the stories were true, but it didn't matter. A while ago, Sara's parents added a bar onto their tobacconist. It was nothing fancy, but it soon became an important feature of the suburban area of middle class homes that back onto soccer pitches. After school, Sara would help her parents. She'd pull on a pair of push-up jeans that hugged her ass and wear white cotton T-shirts without a bra. When her parents weren't there, the customers flirted with her. Sara enjoyed the flattery, which often came with gifts: silver chains, hand-made leather bags, new sneakers. One time she asked for a gold ring, identical to one Gloria had been gifted by a brand, and came into school showing it off to Gloria, proud but slightly contemptuous.

The man of the moment would come and pick her up and take her out for drinks in a bar far away from Sara's parents'. Then they'd retire to a car park where Sara would straddle him and he would pull aside her panties and penetrate her. One time she told Gloria that she had accidentally leaned on the horn with her pelvis in the middle of sex and like lightning the guy had pushed her off, his eyes wide with terror. Sara found that exciting.

Another time, she ended up in a loft that overlooked a 3-lane elevated highway. The cars looked like toys. The apartment was small and bare, but it had a huge terrace. Apart from the guy who had brought her back, there was also a friend of his, who had a lot of cocaine. They ordered three pizzas that nobody ate because they'd started snorting straight after calling the restaurant. When they offered Sara some coke she accepted flippantly, even though it was her first time and her heart was pounding. After three hours with a bank note stuffed up their noses, the two of them tried to fuck her. They grabbed at her ass and sucked on her tits, but neither of them could get it up. At the end of the evening Sara called a cab—paid for with their money—and went home. When she came into class after all these stories, the fabric of her jeans hugging her thighs, Gloria felt like she could smell her sweaty groin, repellent like the sickly sweet scent of tropical flowers.

Gloria told Sara little about herself. After all, it was hard to find someone to talk to about her life: the private concerts she was invited to with international superstars, the brand events overflowing with food and alcohol, the tours to promote a new product, film, or book of poetry.

"If I tell people about these things, it'll seem like I'm trying to make them jealous, don't you think?" Gloria told me as we were on our way home one day from a trashy film that, unsurprisingly, given her terrible taste in everything, she liked. Yet at the Galeone, as she was talking about Sara, I caught a glimpse of something else. The stories of her classmates' lives were about conflicts, embarrassing discoveries, and seismic events that forged their paths toward adulthood. Nothing about Gloria's stories, no matter how astounding, seemed to have brought about any kind of change in her. She watched from above, untouched, as the others wrestled down in the dirt.

But this is not the reason she has come to the Galeone. During the year, she has been losing bits of money at school. Twenty euros one day, fifty the next. Eventually she calculated she'd lost almost a thousand euros. After a few months she confided in Sara, who immediately launched the idea of an investigation. They'd pretend to fall asleep on their desk, waiting for someone to make a move. Or they'd get up, as if going to the restroom, and spy on the classroom through the crack in the door. They would leave Gloria's wallet in plain sight, taking note of the faces of the people in the room, then check if anything had gone.

That morning Gloria had turned on the video on her phone and left it on in her bag. At the end of the school day, she watched two hours of film, skipping forward to the moment in which a hand appeared, rummaging, with a golden ring.

"What did she say?"

"That it wasn't her."

"Even when faced with the overwhelming evidence?"

"Yep. She started crying and told me it wasn't her."

"Are you angry?"

"No. Does it make sense to be angry with someone who's so sick? If she'd admitted it, I'd have been furious, but what's the point? I love her, I'm not going to keep going on about it."

Gloria's display of moral superiority swoops down on me all of a sudden. I feel humiliated, that I belong to a different species, a more mediocre one than hers, the same species as Sara. Maybe this is what happens when you reach success: the main privilege of those who don't have to struggle is the absence of anger. Gloria is magnanimous. She floats a couple of inches above the ground, watching the common mortals as we tussle to pick up the scraps of her fortune.

"You're Gloria, aren't you?" Giulia's here. The evening shift is about to start, and I didn't see her come in.

"Can I get a photo?"

I turn around and see the other girls confabulating in a corner. I've never mentioned that I work for Gloria. They look at us, dumbstruck, and start whispering again. Then, one at a time, they come up to the table and mimic Giulia. "I'm older than you but I've followed you, like, forever—since you were a little girl"; "We actually met before, in the Gherlinda mall in Perugia, but I'm sure you don't remember me." Hopeful giggles.

In that moment I witness one of Gloria's metamorphoses. When she was telling me about Sara, a throbbing energy emanated from her body, her eyes shiny, her hands drawing unusual figures in the air—in that moment she became beautiful. Now behind her eyes there's a black screen. She is a puppet doll, animated by an invisible hand. She smiles kindly at Giulia and responds: "Sure," and the photo is taken.

I watch her as she hugs my colleagues, and for a minute she looks like the loneliest girl in the world.

Unlike me and Eva, Gloria and her sister Rebecca get on

well. More than well: they are like the main characters in an advert to persuade couples to have more children. They are the sole holders of the keys to an enchanted world, that has taken years to build.

On the day of Gloria's high school final exam her sister comes to watch the interview part. Once it's over I tag along when they go shopping in the city center to celebrate. Gloria rubs sun cream into Rebecca's freckly skin, gluing the front of her sunset-colored hair into a greasy tangle. At first glance they don't look like sisters: aside from their red hair, their skin tone and eye color are different, like two distinct, not-yet-invented seasons. But their facial expressions are clearly molded from the same family clay. They both gesticulate, creating invisible architectures in the air; they both zone out with the same deflated gaze. When there is something unpleasant in front of them, they both arch their eyebrows and curl up their mouths, creating what they call the Queen Elizabeth. If one of them does the Queen Elizabeth it means an item of clothing is not going to be purchased. They both move through the world as if everything already belongs to them and nothing is dangerous. They both know how to talk to anyone, no matter what class, transmitting the sensation of being as "human" as the next person, while preserving an air of inaccessibility that makes you feel that if you reached out to touch them, you'd grasp only air. They glide around on invisible skates, suspended just above the ground. Even the insignificant blunders that sometimes slip out when each of them is alone—a flash of anxiety in their eyes, an awkward gesture that knocks a glass over—disappear when they're together, as they furnish one another with whatever the other is missing. I wait for them in the corners of boutiques and the store clerks eye me with suspicion while the two of them lose themselves in spontaneous choreographies, lifting their heads like meerkats whenever one loses sight of the other for too long. As soon as they have verified each other's presence, they squeeze their eyes like secret agents and return to the hunt.

At the cash register, Gloria pays for everything. Every so often she asks if I want to get something for myself. I always say no.

Once they've finished, we come out into the suffocating midday heat and head toward Gloria's grandma's house.

"Maia, are you coming up with us?"

I've never been there before. Rebecca throws a sharp glance at her sister that only I perceive. She doesn't want me to join.

I smile at the twelve-year-old, "Sure."

Anna Ricordi's apartment is gigantic. Gloria explains that it was once owned by a wealthy marble family whose descendent was kidnapped in the seventies. Even though the bribe was paid, they killed him. Twenty years later, Anna Ricordi befriended the elderly mother. The woman was torn between her love for that house and the desire to let go of the memories that haunted it. She sold it to Anna at a lower price than the market value under the condition that, were she to change her mind, Anna would give it back ten years later. The woman died six months after leaving the apartment.

Every room is clad in a different marble. The reception room is a dark red shot through with white veins, like live flesh. One bathroom is blue, another black with white steps leading up to a bathtub that shines like the inside of a shell. The kitchen is gray, one of the living rooms forest green. The hallway floor is herringbone parquet.

Gloria's bedroom is at the end of the hallway. It isn't big but it has an en-suite bathroom. The walls are lined with big colorful posters covered in photos. "My fans have given them to me over the years." She points at the ceiling where there are more, crumpled and half unstuck, the putty stuck like chewing gum to the flaking plaster. Plushies holding hearts and faded polaroids, a vague smell of stale sweat, piles of clothes in various places around the floor, words written in lipstick on the mirror on the bathroom door—*Rebecca and Gloria, You're craaaazy, I love you*. And then hearts, some dates, an eye with thick lashes, a heap of boxes wrapped in ribbons and colored paper. I move closer: they're all the gifts she's received from brands. The little cards, hand-written by unknown employees, are signed with hearts and cutesy scrawls.

I didn't expect Gloria's room to be like this. I thought I'd find myself in an elegant chamber with immaculate walls and objects that hinted at the private Gloria, far from the eyes of the world: the bedroom of the grown-up from the social media photos, who describes her work with managerial expertise, and authoritatively silences her collaborators. But no, Gloria lives in the bedroom of a child. I look at the hoodies, the compact and brightly colored cosmetics that call to me from the bottom of translucent make-up pouches. There's a small, long, mysterious box that, on opening, reveals a silver pen. I pick it up and am astounded by the coldness of the metal, the weight of the designer object. As I close the box an unpleasant taste rises in my throat.

Gloria and her sister are absorbed in their respective phones, sending each other videos that make them cry with laughter. I pretend to be interested in the rest of the room, but that's all there is. I regret coming up here. I don't belong in this place. Every time Gloria turns her attention to me Rebecca draws it back.

"Maia, come and look at this video." She makes space between them on the bed. I smell the sugary scent of Rebecca's chewing gum. As I get closer, she chews with increasing fervor. On the screen there's a girl Gloria's age filming herself while buying a lock and chain which she ties around the handles of her wardrobe. "Now let's see if my little bitch of a sister steals anything else." Gloria and Rebecca laugh uproariously. Rebecca's face has gone the same color as her hair, and she has to drag herself to the bathroom so she doesn't wet herself.

"Isn't it insane? What kind of psycho would do something like that?"

"Mental," I mumble. I kept my wardrobe under lock and

key throughout high school to stop my sister from stealing my clothes. And still today I feel that if someone wore my clothes, they'd be breaking open my identity to plunder the contents of it. As if deep down I'm nothing more than what I wear, a man-nequin who, stripped of clothes, would quickly evanesce.

Gloria, on the other hand, is unflappable. Perhaps because her job is to be copied by as many people as possible; or per-haps, a hypothesis that doesn't rule out the former, because she was born when the sun was already beginning to set on sub-cultures. She herself was an unbridled fan of various boy bands and fought furiously with the other fans for the object of their love. Perhaps Gloria is just a conformist. In any case, she doesn't mind her sister taking her clothes, not even when she packs them in her suitcase to take to the villa which is miles away.

My parents had always asked me to be kind to my sister, as if even before she was born, they were sure that I would not have been gentle with the newcomer. Sometimes I wonder whether things went the way they did because of their nervous words, illuminating the true nature of their preoccupations: the suspicion that, ever since childhood, I was nasty. I don't know whether this suspicion was justified. What I do know is that, nasty or nice, I never liked Eva.

She was born with see-through skin, her first blond hairs already adorned her head like golden threads and her body was fragile and sickly. She soon began to suffer from all the maladies newborns can get: sleep apnea, reflux, loss of appetite, diffi-culty gaining weight, uninterrupted crying, gastrointestinal is-sues, insomnia. In the three years that followed, my mother lost weight and energy, and my sister's tantrums left her without a single moment to herself. Eva had a sulky temperament that didn't change over time. Unlike me, she was beautiful: a severe, imposing kind of beauty. She was sensitive to all stimuli: too-bright lights, too-loud noises, mysterious smells that only her perfect nose could possibly detect. My parents never learned to say no to her. Whatever she desired, it was an order that, if not fulfilled, made way for a silence that could last for days. My sister never forgot an injustice.

As she grew up, realizing that the way she looked was setting her further and further apart from her peers, Eva also started to make herself up, deepening the differences, and would spend hours and hours in front of the mirror. When, not infrequently, she forced her chubbiest and most awkward friends to try on her dresses, which on them looked like circus costumes, a shadow of a smug smile would appear on her face, which remained there while she consoled whichever poor girl it was this time, trying to convince her that she looked great, that a tight, pink microskirt did not in fact draw attention to her waist.

Eva was also indolent. Despite her great potential for a range of talents, she didn't cultivate any of them because she had no patience, nor did it serve her to know how to do anything: she was always surrounded by people who worshipped her. My father, following her every whim, convinced that she would soon become a multi-faceted genius, bought her flower arranging manuals, canvases to paint, upright pianos.

It was my father who would soon make us poor. The fault of our ruin is all his: his obsession with the travel agency, which for reasons that remain shrouded in mystery he considered the most lucrative business to throw himself into. I like to use the term "ruin" because it suggests that we were once wealthy, which isn't true. But even if we had never been rich, I fondly remember our ground-floor apartment with no direct sunlight, tinted by an apple-green light reflecting off the buildings opposite. My father didn't believe in the internet. It's funny now, but between the end of the nineties and the start of the new Millennium many people thought the internet was just a phase. Even when the more sophisticated people started buying their own plane tickets and organizing their own holidays from the comfort of their living rooms, my father said it was just a passing craze that would soon disappear like the others. My father was offered a tidy sum to sell his agency around that time, but he refused it, maintaining that the offer in itself was proof things would soon start moving in the right direction. Then the low-cost airlines arrived and he started getting into debt. My mother left her job as a kindergarten assistant to help him, given that he could no longer pay his employees, and someone had to accompany the groups of elderly people, the only clients left, on their jaded vacations in coaches and half-board hotels.

Eventually the bank came and took our ground-floor house in the neighborhood with the flower beds and twisted wrought iron fences, Eva began to get sick, my mother's eyes became empty, and we migrated to a place on the outskirts, on the edge of an enormous highway torn up day and night by the roar of noisy cars.

When I get home Filippo still isn't back. I lie down on the couch, which has loyally preserved the shape of my body. I light a joint. It numbs me but not enough to quiet the sense of anguish that has been creeping in throughout the day.

I stand up, hoping to shake the feeling off. It doesn't work. I take a plastic container out from under the bed where I keep documents and other paperwork that I probably won't ever need but am afraid to throw out. I pull out an old album with photos of Eva. It has a dark blue spine. I took it from my father's house without telling him the day after her funeral. Eva is cupping a swallowtail butterfly in her hands. She was five years younger than me. She looks out from the photo at me, full of wonder, her blue eyes stained with dark blue streaks, her face sullied with curls of hair like the ones little girls always have in adverts for those shoes with light-up soles that we longed for as kids. As she was learning the rudiments of the violin before abandoning it in a corner of the room, I was pulling out my eyebrows, hair by hair, then moving onto my head. She was fussy and needy: she'd only eat food made with the best quality ingredients, while I only wanted to eat animal-shaped pre-cooked breaded chicken (I'd still eat them now if I didn't have to put up with Filippo's judgment, which is why I make do with the gummy crocodiles). At her parties her classmates competed to get her the best present. I was usually only invited to other people's parties because my mother asked if I could go, and then she'd bring a really embarrassing present, usually a book. No one wanted a book.

Eva's smile reveals a missing milk tooth. Her skin is browned by the first sun of the summer. On the same page there's a picture of her with her hand in a plaster cast. She'd broken her fingers in a rock-punching competition with me: I was only pretending to hit the stone; she, stupid, hit it for real.

Psychiatrists call the under-the-threshold symptoms of mental illness prodromes; the ones that start to show in a person's development before the illness is properly unleashed. When I start digging for Eva's prodromes I only manage to find the flaws that I hated, but I find them much more evident in myself. It's as if I was the one afflicted by the prodromes of her illness and at some point our destinies were accidentally swapped. It was me who set light to ants' nests with a magnifying glass; me who wet the bed until I was eight; me who, when I was put on the soccer team in third grade of elementary school, head-butted a boy who tried to tackle me and broke his nose. Eva looked after the butterflies that I caught to harvest the dusty substance from their wings, having read in a book that if you spread it on the shoulder bones of a newborn baby, it would take flight.

In all her mushy sentimentalism, Eva was perfect.

I turn the page. A five-year-old Eva, bundled up in a midnight-blue down jacket that had once belonged to me. Behind her is the Genoa aquarium.

During that period, my impatience with my sister gave form to two new made-up personalities to add to my repertoire: Iris the monstruous demon, and Azzurra the good fairy. The two of them continuously swapped places within me. Iris's job was to slaughter all of Eva's toys, leaving them for her to find, disemboweled, under her pillow. Certain children's objects are transitional: they help the child to introject unspoken notions, like the emotional presence of a parent who is physically absent; or give them confidence in new situations; or simply act as imaginary friends to play with when they don't have any real ones. Eva's stuffed animals, which she'd started talking to more than usual when she was around four, were Iris's favorite target. Every morning Eva would wake up in tears, blindly believing that it wasn't me who'd done this to them, but Iris. She would beg for Azzurra to get here, who would console her but only for a minute, substituted swiftly by the silent eyes and gnashing teeth of Iris, who ordered her to say nothing to our parents.

Like dogs or mice, humans who undergo any level of pain that they can't control develop a sense of stress that hollows them out, just like I hollowed out Eva's toys. It's called learned helplessness.

Eva never actually saw the aquarium in the photo. Iris didn't let her. If Eva had so much as glanced at a manta ray, Iris would have slit the throat of the last of her companion animals, a cloth iguana. Eva didn't dare and spent the whole day with her back to the tanks. When our parents or random couples wearing fanny packs asked her why, she opened those pathetic blue eyes wide and responded in a honey-sweet voice that she liked it better this way. The next day Iris cut the iguana in two regardless, and when Eva started to cry, my maleficent alter-ego tied a red cord around her throat, leaving a mark that still hadn't disappeared by the time we were on the bus home.

In fact, the thing that annoyed me most about Eva was her willing subjugation. She could be a devil around others, but with me she was a little lamb, submissive and adoring. I've always been sure, deep down, that this was a strategy to make the job of punishing her more painful.

I turn the page: me hugging Eva from behind, both of us wrapped in a wet towel. It's the only photo where we look affectionate. We're at a summer camp, a mediocre parenthesis before a vacation somewhere random with the agency. Eva is six; I'm almost twelve. The photo must have been taken by one of the camp staff. We were staying with fifty other kids in a hotel the shape of a parallelepiped with neon lights and three bunks in each room. Each morning we were taken to Aquapark, an expanse of concrete covered by patches of synthetic turf and scattered with sky blue water slides. Being a group of excitable children, we were immediately ostracized, our towels strewn like used tissues across a strip of fake grass at the very edge of the park. The most important thing was not to bother the paying weekend customers.

I hated the other kids at that summer camp. In contrast, I hated Eva less. Those were the only days I remember ever loving her. Or rather, loving her and showing that I loved her. I also loved her when Iris tied the lace around her neck in Genoa, I just didn't like her. Or rather, I loved the Eva that lived inside me, the image of a sister who by virtue of the family bond that joined us I had to love, in an abstract way. Whenever she was far away, whenever I couldn't see her, I felt a wave of love washing over me; the thought of that frail body rushed into me like a torrent. Her tantrums became a symptom of her suffering, her vanity a symbol of insecurity and fragility. Yet every time she was in front of me, I was gripped by an uncontrollable urge to hurt her. Or maybe it was controllable, because after all it wasn't me, it was Iris.

Anyway, the first days of the summer camp had been happy. We avoided the other kids like lepers, we didn't even enjoy the slides that much. Our attention was entirely devoted to the adults: in the mornings, as soon as we had laid down our towels, we would choose an adult to shadow like spies until evening. It was always a man because we found them ridiculous even then. We would observe them as they stared at the young girls' butts, as the ash from their cigarettes fell to the floor and melted into puddles of water. We were disgusted by the ones who did jump rope and then threw themselves into the pool covered in sweat, their mouths full of saliva. We crouched down by the walls and pretended to be talking to each other if someone looked suspicious. The riskier the mission, the more adrenaline pumped through our veins, and we melted in laughter and excited squeals. One day we followed a man who was around fifty and had rolls of fat around his stomach like a pile of tablecloths. We were on him until he got to the toilets, where we watched him bypass the blue cubicles toward an area hidden from the other customers. Initially we thought he wanted to pee without having to wait, exasperated by the line that unfurled all the way to the bar. Fair enough. We watched as he pulled his willy out. Only, instead of the golden jet that we were anticipating, we saw him turn it over between his hands, floppy like a mollusk. He examined it as an entomologist would a rare insect. Little by little the penis grew—not much—and he started to wiggle it slowly to start with, then faster and faster. From the tree we were hiding behind we couldn't contain ourselves. The image I remember from that moment is the porky little face of the man, shocked and humiliated by our laughter, and us running out into the sun. We ran like crazy, convulsing with laughter, holding our stomachs as if we might collapse and, tears in our eyes, made our break on our most adventurous mission yet; him panting, trunks loose around his hips.

We were punished. We were no longer allowed to go on the slides, so going on the slides became the only thing we wanted to do. Eva looked at me as if I was the most wonderful person she'd ever seen. I remember her looking completely enchanted, as if I'd done some kind of witchcraft. I stirred her from her adoration with a pat on the head and we wrapped ourselves in our heat-stiffened towels and sneaked to the steps, climbing up to the slide with our towels like cloaks. The aim of the game was to go down the slide without getting our towels wet, not even when we shot out at the bottom into the blue water of the pool. We had to hold them up above our heads like trophies. It took them four hours to find us again. They put us in separate rooms. I ended up with some other twelve-year-olds who read articles that promised to reveal all the secrets of heavy petting in magazines for retards. Eva was put in a room with two sisters who were seven and eight and had brought a whole box of plastic dolls with them. She started playing with them, first just in the evenings but then in the daytimes too. When I went to get her, her eyes begged me to let her stay with her new friends. High treason. My blood boiled violently in my veins as I told her: "Sure, what do I care. I was doing you a favor letting you hang out with me, I'm much better off without your stupidity."

The following days I faked a sudden illness and stayed in the hotel all day watching a regional channel where horny women rubbed themselves against couch cushions, giving glimpses of their butt holes to get viewers to call the number on the screen to talk to other women who were probably fully clothed. One evening I went down to dinner just as the others were coming back from their day at the water park. Eva hadn't yet entered the hotel's filthy dining hall. I waited, and at a certain point she walked in. Her face was pale, and she was walking as if her legs were made of lead. What happened? It only took a few seconds to find out, because as soon as she was spotted a chorus of "shit pants!" filled the room.

That morning Eva had actually had a stomach bug and shit herself. If I close my eyes, I can still see it as if I was there: her face white as a sheet, the shame pouring out in tears, her eyes searching for me, my own stomach contracting. I want to hug her, save her from the humiliation, protect her. I want to tell her that nothing bad will ever happen to her again, that I'm always going to be there. I see her as she runs toward me to hide under my clothes; I see myself dodge her, as if I've never seen her before in my life. I let the chorus of voices drown her with a victorious smile that breaks my heart.

PART TWO

T he party was in a post-industrial pavilion with a tiny door supervised by a bouncer. We got a taxi because I had asked Gloria for a night off driving.

"What are you wearing? Have you ever been to a party?" she asked as she came out of her house. She was wearing a high-necked body-con dress that came down to just below the knee, and black moccasins with a brass strap. Apart from her make-up (her eyes were encrusted with glitter in an aesthetic effort that made her look sweet), she was dressed like a lady.

"I don't need to cloak my insecurities in a blanket of glitter."

Gloria sulked for the rest of the journey, right until the taxi dropped us off at the entrance to the club. I watched the outline of her profile, clear against the glow of the traffic lights.

I'd spent more than two hours trying on various outfits in the mirror at home. I don't buy many clothes, although ever since they pulled me up on my shopping habits, I try to buy a cheap accessory every time I walk past a fast-fashion chain, just for kicks. Or I steal stuff: nobody ever notices anyway. I always have a little pair of curved scissors in my bag so I can remove the electronic tags. My T-shirts are riddled with holes. I've only been caught once: my pockets were full of cheap earrings when two big men took me into the back room of one of those many stores selling trash at inflated prices. They told me I was banned for life from all the stores in the chain.

"Even the ones in Indonesia?"

"Yes, all of them."

"Even in Mexico?"

"Don't try and be smart with us, we said all of them."

They tried to make me believe that from then on I would be recognized by the facial recognition devices that guard every store. Sure. For a moment I felt it would be a relief if it were true. Maybe one day I'd be lost in Jakarta with no memory of myself or my past life, no passport, no nothing, and I'd just have to wander into a clothing store to be immediately recognized by a camera. The camera, at least, would remember who I was.

Two months after the business in the back room, I went into that very same store and stole almost three hundred euros worth of clothes, which I threw out the next day. Stealing reveals things for what they really are: rags.

Gloria pays the taxi driver. I go to open the door but she stops my hand. She closes her eyes and breathes in deeply, facing the headrest of the seat in front. She opens her eyes, lifts her chin, her hand rises, as does the child lock. She puts her leg out onto the tarmac, as if trying to toss it away, grabs my wrist tight and heads into the crowd, which is shouting her name. She drags me through the bodies and with a nod of her head signals for the bouncer to pull to one side the velvet rope that marks the border between what is within anyone's reach and what is exclusive.

Music pounds from inside. We go into a semi-circular room; the bass vibrates around the walls, blanketing the details of every sentence uttered. I read Gloria's lips silently articulating "Bar." We struggle to find it because it's half-concealed by a partition wall of red blocks, but at least behind it the music is slightly softened.

The party is hosted by a Korean phone company in partnership with a low-end vodka brand. At the far end of the room there's a photobooth with a platform in it. When you stand onto the platform it starts to spin and the four phones in its corners take a sequence of photos that are immediately uploaded to Instagram with all the right hashtags. There's already a line.

"Why don't they let the people waiting outside in?"

"Because that was never going to happen. They post about the event on social media in order to draw a crowd, but the guestlist is already full."

"But aren't they taking a risk that nobody will come next time?"

"Are you kidding? Even more will come. They let about fifty people in randomly and let them take a few photos, so that all the others think they have a chance. It's like the lottery."

It's true: in the middle of the floor stands a clump of frightened teenagers who don't seem to have a clue why they're there. Every so often one of them points at one of the two balconies that loom over the dance floor.

The girls up there are beautiful. Phosphorescent eyeliner marks their faces like war paint; fake eyelashes; white tops that gleam under the strobes. They're stick-thin, much cooler than my influencer-nun.

Gloria passes me a horribly sweet cocktail that already tastes like a hangover. Her eyes jump around the room with ill-concealed frenzy.

"Who are you looking for?"

"No one."

I let her lie. What does it matter to me who she's looking for. What I don't understand is why I've been dragged here. Couldn't she have called one of her pick-pocketer pals? In any other situation I'd have said no, but I felt guilty because a few days earlier I walked out of an Amazon Home event. She'd tried, out of nowhere, to pull me into the frame to have our picture taken together for the brand photos. Press officers and other professionals with undefined roles milled around us. They were smiling, but it looked to me more like they were gnashing their teeth. A moment before the shot was taken, I slipped out of Gloria's grasp, ran outside, and went home. She stood there smiling moronically in front of a canary-yellow fridge.

We remain propped up at the bar. The room starts to fill

up; on the balconies people are piled on top of one another. Two girls approach us. They look about my age, but like all the people who circulate in this parallel universe where the entrance ticket is your face, they look about ten years older than they are. I have two theories for this phenomenon. The first is that only after thirty-five is it statistically likely that a person has the kind of salary that can afford them expensive treatments, thus these impeccable faces automatically look like the faces of grown-ups. The other is that when you get successful and become a "personality," your features no longer recount the bewilderment of youth and the search for an identity.

I've seen these two girls before. They're called Michela and Vanessa and they're non-indentical twins. I remember them from one of Gloria's photos taken at a gala dinner for a magazine. Under the post there were hundreds of comments from followers thrilled by the entanglement of famous people. Followers love it when influencers meet and have their photo taken together, staging a friendship that doesn't exist. While studying the twins I discovered that they are both psychologists. They post photos of them standing on an elegant staircase, light pouring through the glass windows, always in different outfits. Under every post there's a caption that tells the reader how to live: what to eat, if and when to meditate, how to give yourself a hug (shudder). Every so often they change it up with a promotional post for a bubble bath that can help you avoid emotional breakdowns; one post about the stress of social media and another on the performativity of social media; a post on eating disorders, which are really just a cry for love, and so on. Recently they've even launched a line of health drinks with a low environmental impact in an attempt to exorcize everything that makes humans human: glass bottles full of cucumber-flavored water which, according to the packaging, promise all their followers the erasure of guilt.

The twins smile as they hug Gloria, revealing a number of

teeth that to me looks higher than the norm. Their lips and gums are thin. Like Gloria, they're dressed more soberly than the other girls, wearing the same dress in different colors.

"I heard you're part of the Glow campaign. Have you met Donatella Pernice?" Conspiratorial giggle. "You know she nominated herself as an ambassador?"

Donatella Pernice is the fat influencer from the meeting a few weeks ago, the one who cried about insults.

"What a character," says Gloria. They both stop laughing.

One of the twins sighs: "What I'd give to have even a quarter of her self-esteem," (since brands began to pummel consumers with the concept of self-esteem rather than beauty, the two terms have become interchangeable, apart from the fact that that one of them—self-esteem—is socially acceptable and the other isn't.) "Anyway, she's adorable. She takes it all so seriously," the other smiles inanely. She pushes her lips out, her thick, perfectly plucked eyebrows arranging themselves into an expression of tenderness as if she were talking about a three-legged dog. "She once wrote to us asking us to ask Glow to let her do testimonial promotions. It's amazing how far she's managed to get on her own."

Neither of the two twins has acknowledged my presence. "We didn't think we'd see you here, Gloria, this isn't your kind of party, is it?"

"I know, but it's summer and I've just graduated, so I wanted to make the most of it."

"So, Giulio has nothing to do with it?" one of them says with a hint of malice.

I interrupt: "Who's Giulio?"

The twins are startled.

"Sorry, I haven't introduced you. This is Maia, my . . . a friend of mine," says Gloria.

"And how does she not know who Giulio is?"

Gloria glares at me.

I say, "Oh, *that* Giulio. I was thinking of another."

"Are they your friends?" I ask Gloria after they've gone.

"Yes, why?"

"Because they seem like bitches."

"Look who's talking. They're very cool; they post information, and they make other girls feel good. They amplify positive messages," she barks. Then she continues sucking alcohol through her straw and staring at the liquid as the purple reflections of the lights wriggle like eels.

Giulio, she tells me later, is her ex-boyfriend. He became famous doing live-streams on Twitch, a place on the internet that's owned by Amazon where the community pays their favorite content creators. It's mostly inhabited by gamers, violently virile men who play up their political incorrectness, some slutty women, and then lots of maladjusted guys who throw money at the first three. Nobody has described Twitch to me in these exact terms, but it's what I've intuited from the roundabout ways Gloria and the others talk about it. On Twitch the word "virgin" is outlawed, banned from the platform: they're almost all virgins.

She shows me a photo of Giulio. He's one of the guys who play up their virility, with tattoos up to his neck. In a recent post, he is holding the head of an inflatable doll against the fly of his jeans with one hand, while holding a bottle of beer, tilted to the side with a thin stream of urine-like liquid trickling out, in the other.

They had a tempestuous relationship, Gloria explains. He cheated on her and left her multiple times. He always teased her for the saintly image she projected, making herself eligible for any kind of publicity work that came her way. He has never stooped to brands' blackmail, never presented himself as respectable just to earn money through his virtual imago. He feels pure, invested with the admiration of those who pay him to exist on the internet. It so happens that recently some photos have come out of him and a girl, another influencer, fucking. Lavinia someone. I ask Gloria if I can see them, but she yells at me, horrified, saying that looking at other people's intimate photos is an act of violence. I shrug: if you ask me, she's just jealous of her rival.

"Anyway," she adds, "Lavinia isn't alone with Giulio in those photos, some of his friends are there too."

"Like an orgy?"

"Yeah, kind of."

In any case, since the Lavinia scandal, he and Gloria haven't spoken. Clearly, she thought he would be at the party, but there's no trace of him. She tells me about how much solidarity she received from other important people on the internet. "Even some feminist influencers," she confides with great solemnity, "who have publicly said that it's not O.K. to spread other people's Instagram photos, wrote to me privately agreeing with me: Lavinia is on an eternal quest for the male gaze. That's just how she is. And she's not a good role model on her social media. She's always high, dressed like a . . . dressed in a way that leaves little to the imagination. But the worst thing is that glorifying her own pain makes it desirable for the girls that follow her. It doesn't send a positive message."

I have a knot in my stomach and I'm drinking too much. Or maybe it's all this bullshit, who knows. I've never loved parties, but this one is particularly depressing. It feels like nothing unexpected could happen in this place. We drink the brand's alcohol and listen to the watered-down music of some DJ who has more than ten thousand followers on Instagram. It's as if each person is following a script written for them by the writer of a TV commercial. Everybody knows everybody but likes nobody. Gloria elbows me every so often to point someone out and give me a few lines of their biography. Over there is a tattooed trap rapper with his new girlfriend. He gets a new one every six months, and each of them, for her allotted time, gets in photos with him and sees her follower count go up. The peak is reached when he lets the girl of the moment wear his gold and diamond brass knuckle ring, a gesture that usually symbolizes the beginning of the end. As soon as he leaves them, the girls collect all the photos in a single post and put it where it's most visible on their profiles, like a new job on their CV.

At the other end of the bar there's a girl who Gloria tells me is the same age as her but looks ten years older. Gloria explains that when you could still do this, when nobody really understood how the social media world worked, this girl had posted her own photos with the randomest selection of products, pretending that the brands were paying her. She started buying herself followers, and under her photos comments appeared from Indian bots that were all identical. In her case, fake it till you make it worked: she went from impostor to influencer, and brands now actually ask her to promote their products.

"Her like count," Gloria explains, "is tiny compared to what she should get with those numbers. But the brands are only just starting to clock on, and they don't actually care. Often, they get to November and still have a ton of marketing budget left and they have to spend it before the end of the year, otherwise the team will get less money next year. And so just before Christmas they throw money at anyone, just to spend it all."

She stops and pinches me on the arm. Following her gaze, my eyes land on a girl who has paused at the entrance; she must have just come in. She's beautiful: a brutal, vulgar beauty. Her lips are turgid with botox, and her cheeks also look more swollen than what's normal, as if she's chewing something. This puffiness spreads out toward her eyes, which have ended up a bit squashed and thus supplicant. She looks around, intimidated. She's wearing a sparkly top that comes down to her ribs and reveals the gentle curve of her breast, extremely short shorts, and shocking pink fishnet tights. She touches her elbow and moves her weight from one foot to the other. She's very tall, and when she moves it looks like her body is a mask, or a dress that's too big, concealing underneath it a little girl who's desperate to disappear. She takes a few uncertain steps on her high heels. Everyone's eyes are glued to her. She looks like a victim, and that makes her sensual.

"Who is she?"

"Lavinia. The girl I was telling you about before, the one Giulio cheated on me with. I can't believe she has the nerve to show her face here."

I'm completely drunk. I don't usually drink at the Galeone. Alcohol bloats you, wasted calories. The last time I drank this much was at a book launch. I went with Filippo. I like accompanying him to events. He wears a white shirt that makes him glow. I tie his tie and wear a black skirt that used to be my mother's with a slit up one side and a skin-tight bodysuit that makes me uncomfortable all evening. I have one elegant bag: a red purse adorned with little coral pearls that I move my fingertips through when I'm nervous. Just before going in, I squeeze Filippo's hand, knowing that we won't exchange any affection until the end of the night. He will flit from guest to guest, the men slapping his back, the women applying a gentle pressure on his fingers, like a light shake, laughing at his jokes without listening to them.

I will stand alone, next to the buffet table. The servers will approach me sympathetically, but I don't want their pity. Filippo's friends won't talk to me; they'll just send a few kind smiles my way, as you would a child.

The first and only time I got wasted at one of those parties I snuck off with a young, blue-eyed server. We were making eye contact all evening until finally he came to personally refill my glass. For the first time in years, between the coats in the cloakroom, I had sex with a man my own age whose stomach was still smooth and white like an opal. When we finished, I felt ferociously happy: I felt like I'd torn off a piece of life all for myself, a shred of experience that was mine and no one else's. He left me his number on a piece of paper. I still keep it folded up in my wallet, worn out at the corners, and every so often I take it out and look at it. *Mattia 340986543*. I've never felt guilty; not in the days after, not now.

Gloria is blinded by the blue and pink lights that alternate across her face.

"Are you envious of Lavinia?"

"No. I could never be envious of such a . . . a . . ."

"Whore?"

"You can't say that. I didn't say that."

"We're all whores to someone." My head is spinning faster now. I continue, "Anyway, if it makes you feel better, from the outside you both look tragic and insecure."

Gloria is scandalized, but then a flash of what looks like curiosity lights up her face, as if I possessed some truth about her that she wanted to hear more of. It lasts milliseconds. "To me she only looks beautiful." She observes me, disconsolate, as she says it.

"Never said she wasn't."

Then she adds something else, but the racket coming out of the speakers obscures her voice; the room begins to twirl around itself, I lean on the bar, my legs tremble, an acid wave rushes up from my belly button to my throat. I collapse, and the music roars through my chest.

I'm kneeling next to the toilet bowl, the icy porcelain cool on my cheek. Gloria has wiped the bowl with a napkin and is sitting next to me. She's holding my hair at my back while I retch from a now empty stomach. Her fingers brushing my neck remind me of my mother, when I was a teenager, stroking my head until my tears ran out; I feel like I can almost smell her almond oil scent. I try to speak but nothing comes out. We stay there for what feels like a lifetime, until someone knocks on the door and I wake up. Gloria turns back into Gloria. I wash my face at the sink where the exquisite girls from the balconies look at themselves in the mirrors, sniffing to show that they've just done coke.

We leave the club and sit down on the empty steps, where the people not worthy of entering thronged a few hours earlier. We light a cigarette.

"Don't you find all this gross?" I ask Gloria.

"All this what?"

"This . . . being famous for the sake of being famous, brands, publicity, your bitch pretend friends, this horrendous place, the shit music . . . I could go on until the sun comes up."

She looks straight ahead. "It's not always like this."

It has stopped raining, but the air is still humid. I sense that Gloria, like me, doesn't want to go back inside. If we went back in, we'd be swallowed again by that senseless diorama.

We light another cigarette and are contemplating the silence when we hear a thud of metal and a scream coming from the bit of road hidden behind the wall that surrounds the club.

"Shall we go and see what's happening?" Gloria asks, alarmed.

I don't want to get up, but when she does, I resign myself to meekly following her. About fifty yards away, under the light of a streetlamp, we see a figure pressed against the side of a car with three silhouettes bending around her. Every so often one of them throws their head back and bursts into metallic-sounding laughter.

Gloria lengthens her stride. I stumble and have to grab onto a lamppost.

There's a series of flashes and in the bluish light I recognize some of the girls I'd seen in the club. Curiously, as Gloria walks toward the group she appears to get bigger and bigger while the distance makes her smaller. I hear her shout: "What are you doing!"

The flashes pause. An indistinct bustle, shadows fidgeting under the streetlight.

I hear Gloria's name repeated. "We're doing this for you Gloria," "You'll thank us later Gloria." More laughter.

Gloria stands still; the girls bounce away. They come toward me, then past me, resounding like little bells.

I breathe out, stand up straight and feel my way over to Gloria. When I get to her, I notice her stomach rising and falling fast under her clothes. The other girl is also panting, folded in on herself like a napkin.

I reach out toward the stranger and lightly touch her on the shoulder. Slowly her body unfurls; she moves her arm away from her stomach, rests her hands on her knees, breathes in and lifts her chin, showing me a face framed by bleach blond hair. The reflections of her sparkly top dance over her long neck. It's Lavinia. I look for Gloria's eyes. She knew who it was before I did.

I ask Lavinia if she's O.K.; she nods imperceptibly, keeping her eyes down and fiddling with her fingers. Meanwhile Gloria pulls herself together and, without a word, dials the number of the taxi company. Then she turns toward the club. There's people stumbling out, and some are walking in our direction.

"Let's avoid making any more of a spectacle," Gloria says, yanking us out of the strip of light. When the taxi arrives, she orders Lavinia to get in.

And Lavinia, for the first time, looks her in the eye. Her swollen lips and the makeup running down her face make her look somewhat grotesque.

"It's not how you think it is with Giulio," she says in one breath.

"Get in."

The car's headlights disappear into the night. Gloria tries in vain to call another taxi.

"Fuck it," she says after a few minutes waiting. "Follow me."

"Glo, I'm too drunk to drive."

"Shut up."

I run after her as she walks quickly toward a point marked on her phone screen. She stops in front of a moped parked on the sidewalk. She touches the display and I hear the click of the top box opening. She takes out two helmets, passes me one, puts her one on and then, seeing my confused face, takes the one she's just given me out of my hands and puts it onto my head. As I stand there incredulous, she gets on the scooter and indicates for me to do the same. I climb on and she presses the ignition.

"You told me you didn't have a license," I mumble, confused.

"If you want to have a competition for who's been the most truthful, go ahead, but know that I'll win."

The vehicle hiccups as we drop off the sidewalk. I hold onto her waist and feel the wind lash my face. It feels great.

"You saved your worst enemy from those girls," I say. "Pardon?"

I don't repeat myself and she doesn't ask me to.

"You're sleeping at mine tonight," she shouts.

I hold her waist tighter. When my fingers brush her stomach, I feel her stiffen. I pretend I haven't noticed and rest my head against her back, while the tips of my fingers draw little circles around her belly button.

When we arrive outside her house, I let my arms fall and wrap around her stomach for a moment before getting off the bike. We put our helmets back in the box and go into the building, trying not to make any noise. On the landing, Gloria lifts one of the oil paintings off the wall to reveal a recess that contains the keys.

Once we're in, I'm assigned a T-shirt for the night. She pulls a brand-new toothbrush out of a box in the bathroom and passes it to me.

She removes her make-up and gets changed in front of me. Only in that moment do I realize how long it's been since I've seen a woman's body that isn't my own. Gloria's body is still immature, with the messed-up proportions of youth. When her face is eventually bare, her skin is snowy white, and she has the fluctuating features of someone to whom life has not yet given a definitive form. I quietly observe her as, in the darkness of the room, she runs cotton wool pads over her slightly oily skin.

"I shouldn't really use cotton wool pads, but I've tried the eco ones and they just don't work."

"Just as I was starting to like you."

"Idiot."

I get undressed too. I feel Gloria's gaze move over me timidly. I try to cover my stomach by curving my shoulders.

She asks me: "Are you ashamed of your body?"

I don't respond.

We lay down on the bed, Gloria turns the light out. I can hear her breath. The pillow is fresh, and the sheets are rolled up at the end of the bed. I have the urge to reach out and feel the warmth of her hand, like on the moped. I don't.

Instead, I whisper: "Why are you still hiring me?"

She stays quiet for long enough that I assume she's fallen asleep. Then her voice floats through the darkness like a dream: "Because you tell me the truth."

Filippo is lying on the couch next to a stack of books. He's trying to read one of them, but his eyes keep wandering elsewhere. Eventually, he takes off his glasses—the lenses are so thick they look like they're made of frosted glass—and places them on his stomach. His shirt is unbuttoned, sleeves rolled up to his elbows. I struggle to recognize him. It's not a sensation that goes away with time: without glasses Filippo's face is watery. The tortoise-shell frames that trace his eyebrows lend his face an artificial structure that makes him familiar. He has a white toothpaste stain on his beard. I would like to get up, lick my thumb and rub it away, but it's too hot and I'm sitting on the floor. At least the parquet is cool, as is the wall I'm leaning against. There's one fan in the house, which I ordered off Amazon. It isn't put together properly and makes a metallic noise that neither of us notices anymore.

We brush our teeth with the same toothbrush. It's a ritual we started when we first got together, when he still wouldn't admit to himself that we were getting serious—not that we were telling anyone—and refused to buy a spare. And I never brought one with me out of superstition. I'd noticed that every time I thought I was going to stay the night at his and prepared for it, it wouldn't happen. When he saw me cleaning my teeth with toothpaste on my finger one morning, he said, "use mine." Those two words symbolized the granting of access to a slightly gross, and thus elective, intermingling.

I like being in the same room as Filippo when he's reading or studying. What happens when I'm with Gloria doesn't happen with him. With her I get lost in my thoughts and memories, but with Filippo my attention is all on him. I surveil him discreetly, drifting away from myself. I get caught on his beard, following it as it spirals across his cheek. I check his fingernails to see if he's been chewing them, a sign that he's more tense than usual. Filippo barely talks about himself or what's happened during his day, and these are the only moments that I am able to intuit something from the network of signals spread across his body. I feel honored, like I'm seeing a hidden part of him, inaccessible even to himself. I like him most when he's sleeping because he looks so vulnerable and I get to watch over him. We are all children when we sleep.

"Edoardo has invited us to spend August at his and Francesca's place in Alonissos," he says, not looking at me.

"That wasn't the plan. We said we'd do a road trip across the Balkans, just the two of us. If you want, we can do it in Greece, but I don't want to not do it at all." I try to maintain a calm voice.

Filippo picks up his glasses and starts fiddling with them: "If we do a road trip I'll have to pay for the whole thing."

"No, I've saved some money from the bar and working for Gloria."

"I don't want you to throw away your savings for no reason. We'd be guests at Edoardo's, no cost."

"The cost is spending the whole time with Edoardo and Francesca."

"Stop being a baby, please. Don't make my life difficult. And anyway, you said you liked them. That you wanted to be like them, remember?"

It's true. The first time I met them was at a party on someone's terrace when I hadn't been with Filippo long. Edoardo and Francesca looked like a celebrity couple; they seemed taller than everyone else. Unlike the other women who pulled their lips into an embarrassed smile when I made eye contact, Francesca was kind. When I asked her how she and Edoardo met she called her husband over and repeated my question. They gave one another a knowing look and then launched into the story of when they first met, performing, in turns, a narration that they had clearly constructed together and rehearsed so many times that I was sure neither of them could remember how it really happened.

Edoardo was the assistant of an old professor of philology at Rome's Sapienza University. She wasn't even taking that course, but when she had been with a friend and seen Edoardo teaching she pretended to be a student.

"The problem was, I didn't know how to get his attention, you know?" she continued, miming with an amused look the same bewilderment she felt then.

Edoardo's turn: "Of course I had noticed her. It was impossible not to: she was marvelous. She still is, to me she hasn't changed a bit. But I didn't have the courage to make a move, because it would've been inappropriate in those circumstances."

"So I turn up to the oral exam regardless, even though I'm not enrolled. When Edoardo calls some student with the surname Cosimato, and I realize she isn't there, I go into the room instead and sit down in front of him."

"I almost fainted; I was dazzled."

"I tell him that I'm only there for him, I'm not even enrolled in the course, but I'm sure that I can't live another day without him. He doesn't respond, so I get up and leave, purple with embarrassment."

"While I was just left bewildered by this courage that I didn't have, still don't. And when I come to my senses, I realize I have no idea what she's called. I search Monica Cosimato and call her in to see me, but it turns out she's a horrible-looking thing." They both laughed.

"Poor Monica, don't be unkind."

He kissed her. "In the end, after weeks of searching . . ."

"Weeks that I spent hoping for the ground to open up and swallow me, certain I'd made a big mistake . . ."

" . . . after weeks of searching in vain I print fifty leaflets that say: 'If you know who you are, and I know who I am, let's meet on Friday at midnight in the piazza whose name you stole.' I stuck them up all around the faculty, in the hope she'd see one."

"I'm hardly leaving my apartment by this point because I'm just so embarrassed, but eventually a friend of mine brings it round with her lecture notes. When I see the leaflet I can't believe my eyes. I'm sure it's him, but I don't want my desire to be so explicit. So I go to Piazza San Cosimato, pretty much in my pajamas, no jewelry or make-up, just so that if I'm wrong, I won't be reminded of my error when I get home and look in the mirror."

"But there I was . . ." They kissed again, this time slower. For the me standing on that terrace, drunk on the early days of falling in love with Filippo, the story of their happiness achieved the goal for which it had been architected: to cause envy and reinvigorate the hope that that kind of love was, with a bit of luck, within everyone's reach, even mine.

"And you told me that they were so affectionate because they're privileged middle-class hypocrites," I respond, remembering Filippo's comment. My praise of them had annoyed him. He had started saying that they were cheap petit bourgeois, thrusting their pretend marriage in everyone's face when really Edoardo was doing nothing but taking his students to bed. I hadn't believed him: to me his spite looked like a proxy for envy. Around that time, Edoardo was made associate professor, was awarded a prestigious European grant for his research project, and he and Francesca had moved into a sumptuous loft apartment that had been in his family for generations.

"Privileged but nice to be around," he responds with a twitch of intolerance.

We stay silent for a few seconds, then I decide to stick to my guns.

"I would prefer us to go on a trip alone. We've never been on vacation on our own."

"But I've already bought the tickets. Edoardo told me we had to decide quickly, otherwise they'd invite someone else. We'll do a road trip somewhere next year." That final sentence sounds like a branch splitting.

"You have toothpaste in your beard."

Filippo scrubs it away, then puts his glasses back on and picks up the open book on the top of the pile.

I don't feel like arguing; there are other things bothering me. One in particular. The morning after the party when I woke up in Gloria's room she wasn't there. I went to look at myself in the bathroom cabinet; its mirrored doors reflected both my profiles, and I didn't recognize either. Then I tip-toed out, following the echo of the voices coming from the kitchen. I heard Anna Ricordi tell Gloria that she didn't like me.

"Since you've been hanging around with her you've stopped eating and you're much more agitated. She left you alone at the Amazon event, and it's not acceptable for a person who works for you to come and sleep at our house after getting drunk at a party. She is responsible for what happens to you."

Gloria's response was concealed by the sound of footsteps moving toward the kitchen door, so I ran into the bedroom, got dressed in a fury and left without saying goodbye. Later on, I wrote to her saying I'd woken up late for an important meeting. Gloria replied that there was no problem, but she would've liked to say goodbye to me before the holidays. I didn't want to see her. I wasn't going to give her the chance to fire me before the summer break.

That moment marked the start of a sense of anxiety that I just can't shake. My dreams are full of scraps of scenes that are always the same: me opening a message from her and learning I'll never see her again; her and her sister all dressed up at a party and neither of them acknowledging me.

I peel myself off the floor and go and tidy the kitchen with the sensation that I'm playing a part, the part of a grown-up woman who can keep a house together while enduring her husband's oppression. I rinse the pot and the frying pan under the faucet before putting them in the dishwasher, despite having bought detergent capsules that were advertised for their cleaning power, and so shouldn't require that intermediate step. I feel impeccable.

Filippo cooked, like he always does when he's at home. When I realized he was a man who could cook and build bookshelves from planks of raw wood, I was astonished. You'd never guess from looking at him; his appearance suggests fragility and impracticality. Just like it's easy to be astonished when he opens his mouth: you expect an insecure, timid voice, but what emerges is an assertive, even cold, tone.

When I go back into the living room Filippo has fallen asleep and is sweating. I go back to sitting in my cool corner, unlock my phone and tap lazily on the Instagram icon. Photos of people already on vacation. Girls lying at the water's edge. Plants, cups of coffee, books. People smiling, long captions, short captions, warning signs, ads for things I need, sponsored profiles, newspaper articles, faces moving frenetically.

Nestled in the inbox for people I don't follow are the message requests from Gloria's fans. They implore me to ask their beloved icon to film a video for their little sisters' birthdays, their best friends' birthdays, and so on. At the beginning I found it touching and their wishes seemed easy to grant. But when I asked Gloria to do those things, she would say she didn't feel like it. I thought it was selfish of her to not do something for the people who made her what she is. It only took a month of receiving these messages, each one identical to the last, for me to come round. Now Gloria's fans incite the same indifference in me that beggars incite in tourists visiting India. When the pain belongs to many, it may as well belong to none. Those scrappy supplications remain unread and, after an undefined number of days, disappear.

When a photo of Gloria appears in my feed, I immediately close the app, as if she might see me through the screen and ask me to reply to her. Instead, I open the dating app that I downloaded a few days ago and swipe through dozens of faces of men I don't fancy.

I match with some of those men but never write to them, nor do I respond when they write to me. After a few minutes I can no longer distinguish between them. All of their masculine faces look identical, symbols of themselves, prototypes of man. This thought reconciles me to Filippo for a while, who is at least just one, and is mine.

When I walk past him on my way to the bedroom, I brush his hair with the back of my hand and turn out the living room light. Whenever Filippo sleeps, he returns to being the man I fell madly in love with years ago, when just his presence emitted a glow, and his familiar warmth made me feel protected.

In the bedroom I take a Xanax out of the blister pack, silently thanking the rosy-faced pharmacist who never asks for a prescription, and fall asleep in a matter of minutes. Only in the middle of the night, numb from the substance, do I feel the mattress sink on Filippo's side; his embrace, his voice saying sorry, that next year we'll go wherever I want. I fall back into a heavy sleep. In the morning I don't know whether it really happened.

In August Filippo and I land in Alonissos, an island in the Sporades. Edoardo and Francesca are there waiting for us, in their villa that sprouts up along a white path that winds over the hills and down to the sea. We are staying in the black stone outhouse. The windows frame a slope studded with strawberry trees and kermes oak.

Unlike Edoardo, who was born in a high-ceilinged apartment in the center of Rome, Filippo came into the world above a small town grocery store in central Italy. His mother was a nurse who had got knocked up, in the biggest cliché, by the head general surgeon, some guy called Salvatore. Filippo's father had never formally recognized him, but he took him hiking in the mountains every so often.

"We would spend hours hiking on trails through the forest, which would suddenly open up in an expanse of blinding snow. My father was silent, with his cap and his pipe. He was an incredible man; I'll never forget those days."

I can't imagine anything more boring that spending an entire day trudging along behind a taciturn man who has never recognized you as his son.

When Salvatore died, he left Filippo a rotten wood cabin that he'd built himself. His villa, his car and his savings all went to his real family. Nonetheless, Filippo saw a cryptic message in this gesture, a treasure map that would lead him to paternal affection. He spent years after Salvatore's death trying to get the moldy hovel back into shape. One morning in early summer, a few months after our arrival in Milan, he got up and, under a rusty sky, trudged to the cabin laden with tins of varnish. As he was getting close to his destination, he noticed a column of smoke rising through the trees, and arrived to witness, in shock, his inheritance turned to ash. He didn't speak for four days.

Filippo is in therapy with a Jungian psychoanalyst, thanks to whom he's discovered that his origin familial archetypes remain a spoke in the wheels of the present, directing his attraction toward severe and distant women like his mother. I asked him if I am part of this pattern too, and he told me that I'm still too young to say.

Filippo's ex wife is, in his words, a horrible woman: the spoiled daughter of super-rich French insurance brokers. In the five years they were together they hated each other silently, first in Berlin, then in London and finally in Paris. She unhappy, he a martyr in the name of the familial harmony he'd been denied as a child. Six months after their return to France, Filippo, coming home one evening in January, found her looking more sullen than usual. At dinner she confessed that she'd fallen in love with a Canadian actor touring in Paris. She moved to Canada soon afterward. Filippo and I would meet a year later.

When I found the message Filippo had sent her complaining about me, I became suspicious of his version of events and started to wonder whether that woman's role, while they were together, was the same as the one assigned to me: vestal, holder of the access codes to the limited knowledge he had of his own feelings. I immediately stopped the thought.

Filippo's mother has developed a form of dementia over the last few years, and he got her into a long-stay clinic. He never visits but he pays the maintenance fee every month. I've never met her. From the photos, she looks austere.

When I ask him if he misses his mother, he responds that familial affection is a societal superstructure and cites a quote from Napoleon: *Ma supériorité vient de que je pense plus vite que les autres hommes . . . et je pense plus vite parce que je n'invente pas.*

During our daytrips out on the boat with Edoardo and Francesca, when Filippo's body is removed from the intimate frame within which I'm used to seeing it, I realize how much he has aged. When we met, he was still pretty toned. Now, his swimming trunks reveal a flabby stomach. His hair is almost completely white, and his posture is slightly hunched over. He drags his feet along like bags of rice when he walks, and when he forgets his glasses his mood darkens and he gets a headache. But the strangest thing is his breath. I had never noticed it before, but now, when he penetrates me from behind in the morning, I try to bury my face in the pillow to avoid the trajectory of his breath, which smells of rotten fruit.

He likes my body less and less too. We go for a walk one day along the white trails that climb up the hills scattered with low brambles. Edoardo and Francesca walk fast, chatting and stopping every so often to let us catch up, handing us their water bottles with indulgent smiles. As we trudge along behind them, Filippo lists the names of the plants to himself. Once or twice, Francesca turns around and teases her husband for not knowing the name of a plant, then walks back to link arms with Filippo, feigning interest for a few minutes in the names of the flowers, as he laughs, embarrassed. Edoardo and I could come up with a similar little display, but we have nothing in common. His presence makes me uncomfortable. He asks me what I do for work, and when I tell him that I curate the image of an influencer he seems to light up for a moment. He tries to find out what goes on behind the scenes, but I am not capable of making my life sound exciting and after a few minutes of me talking about meetings with publicists I see his gaze zigzagging more and more insistently in search of his wife. They pair back up like magnets and move into the lead again.

When we get to a clearing, we find them already lying on the sunburnt grass. I'm walking toward them when Filippo grabs me by the belt loops of my jeans and lifts me a few centimeters off the ground. "You're too thin: your crotch is down at your knees." I feel the rough fabric cutting into my groin. Then he sits down next to the couple. I join them and lie down with my head on his stomach. I try to remember the last time someone did what Filippo just did to me. My mother, perhaps; when I was five and she'd lift me up by the waistband of my tights so that my tiny body would sink down into the elasticated fabric.

One evening we go out for dinner. Edoardo drives the Fiat Panda which, for the rest of the year, he keeps in the garage of one of the island's residents, who looks after it for a bit of cash. The holiday car suggests an even more boundless luxury than the holiday home. Sure, the villa is beautiful, with the purple heather blowing in the wind and the view of the sea, but it wouldn't be the same without the car. You know you're doing well when you have a car you keep at your holiday home.

Francesca gives Filippo the front seat and gets in next to me, her Junoesque body covered by a transparent sundress under which she's wearing an elegant one-piece swimsuit with a bone ring over the sternum. I've noticed how Filippo observes her when he thinks I'm not looking. His eyes comb every inch of that body that's so different from mine: her sagging breasts streaked with stretch marks, and tufts of hair that sometimes pop out of her swimsuit. Whenever their gazes cross, Francesca, smiling suggestively, pulls at the synthetic fabric to cover what's escaped. Then, to restore cosmic order, she goes and puts her arms around her husband, who may or may not have noticed.

The car hurtles through expanses of green from which square stones poke out every so often. It takes me a while to realize they're gravestones. The Panda struggles up the hill that leads to the island's Chora. We sit down at a table in a restaurant that claims it's Italian. I order fettuccine paglia e fieno, which is drowning in cream. It was the fattiest option on the menu, but I've worked out that if I only order a salad—which I would actually eat—my dinner companions ask me why I'm not eating, while if I order something heavy and then leave it, I get away with it.

Edoardo is talking about his father, who bought the villa in the sixties. He was a linguist before becoming a university big shot, and also the host on a radio program called *The ABC*, among whose participants ranked a Nobel prize winner, a detail Edoardo takes every opportunity to remind us of.

Edoardo is good-looking. The beginnings of a receding hair-line are outweighed by the still dark curls that bounce onto his forehead whenever he gets animated. In those moments Francesca, with a mechanical gesture that she's perfected over the years, tucks the lock of hair behind his ear.

Francesca is devoted to her husband. Even though they have a housekeeper who takes care of everything, including the cooking, she spends her days making Filippo's environment as nice as possible for him. She weaves little gray cotton bags, fills them with lavender flowers that grow on the terrace of their loft apartment, and slips them into their underwear drawers. Every day she buys bunches of tulips and gerberas tied up with daisy chains. She goes personally to do the shopping for her Solidarity Purchase Group, adjudicating the most tempting tenderloin or the freshest vegetables. She embroiders her husband's initials onto his shirts. Every time Francesca does something—every time she alters the space around her—her little piece of the Earth is made better than it was before.

I would later understand that this was the true, purest meaning of privilege: not the flowers in themselves, nor the little bags, or the expensive food, but the luxury of occupying oneself with the least useful thing in the world: beauty.

Francesca notices that I'm not eating. Women pay a lot of attention to what other women are eating. She reaches out to touch my shoulder: "Why aren't you eating? Men like women with a bit of flesh on their bones, otherwise you'll always look like a child. You look younger than you are, but remember that's only a good thing once you're over thirty-five."

"I'm always telling her she's a skinny little girl," Filippo interjects.

"I get it," says Edoardo. "Eating is boring for some people; it distracts us from more important thoughts. Maia is just deep in thought, right?"

I fake a smile.

Edoardo goes on: "I didn't eat when I was young, I just wanted to read."

"It's true," Francesca agrees. "He was so thin; I've seen the photos." She turns toward him, her boobs getting squashed against the table. Filippo notices and Francesca catches his eye. A sly smile flashes across her face, communicating that he can look as much as he wants because that's all he's getting.

"What were you like when you were young, Fili?" Edoardo asks.

Filippo freezes. It happens every time someone asks him about his adolescence. My suspicion is that people humiliated him in the way young men do to anyone who's desperately different. One time, at another dinner, he argued with one of his friends who was waxing lyrical about the male changing room as a democratic space in which to gain intimate experience of other men. Trembling with rage, Filippo slammed his fist down on the table while his friend was talking, and everyone fell silent.

"Maybe that's how it was for you, but don't you dare put your *democratic* experience, as you say, onto everyone else. Changing rooms are violent places for anyone who doesn't take part in a certain type of macho performance, and they are the reason feminism is still having such a hard time in this country."

On that occasion I loved him for having the courage to hold a position that was so different from all the other men around the table. But on the way home from the dinner he was silent, and didn't speak again until the following afternoon, despite my jittery attempts at flattery to reward his nonconformism. I felt tender toward him, sensing a fragility that brought him closer to me.

At the table with Francesca and Edoardo, however, I do not experience the same sensation. I pull my phone out of my jeans pocket. "I have a photo of Filippo as a teenager, I'll show you."

It's a photo of a photo. I took it on one of those days I spent raiding Filippo's past, rummaging through red cardboard boxes, and finding pictures of him when he was younger.

THE OTHER PROFILE · 109

The boy version of Filippo was skinny and disgusting. On the grainy celluloid his face is confusing, as if the packaging contains no substance. There's a flash of fear in his eyes, mottled with aggression. Over time, Filippo's face has lost that vagueness. His features are harder now, even if there's still a tinge of mystery, as if the deepest kernel of his character remains unfathomable to anyone, even himself.

I hand the phone over to Edoardo and Francesca. Filippo has turned ashen.

"Well, it's a good job you had brains!" Edoardo laughs.

"I am certain that brain broke many hearts, like our Maia's." Francesca squeezes my shoulder with her ring-encrusted hand.

When we get back to the villa, Filippo is anxious to say goodnight. He walks silently along the mule track that leads to our outhouse. As soon as we're inside, he closes the door behind us.

"Where the fuck did you find that photo?" He's calm, his voice is flat.

"I found it in one of your boxes," I respond. My heart beats faster.

"I have never given you permission to root through my things like a rat. Nor to share them with my friends." His tone is almost robotic now.

"But they're your friends, it was just a bit of fun." I might even have had a point, but as I was showing them that photo I was well aware that I was breaking a clause of our unwritten contract.

"Am I laughing?"

I don't answer him. My temples are pulsating.

"Do I look like I'm laughing? Answer me." He steps closer. "You knew perfectly well that was a thing I would not have wanted you to do. I know how your manipulative brain works."

I always want to cry when we argue. I read an article that said women cry when they're angry because culturally we don't know how to express anger, so it morphs into frustration. I also know that Filippo gets even more irritated when I cry because my tears, he once explained, are emotional blackmail.

"Why are you still with me then?" I ask him.

"Because unfortunately I love you, despite the fact that you're a nasty person."

"I'm sorry," I mumble. "I did it because I'm jealous of how you look at Francesca." Filippo inflates like a frog's neck.

"You're mental. You're mental just like your sister; you see things that aren't there. Francesca is my friend and the wife of my best friend. How can you even think of saying such a thing?" He breathes heavily, holding his arms rigid at his sides. Then, quietly, "Get out of this room."

"Where should I sleep?"

"Sleep outside, on the deckchair. Take a sweatshirt, do whatever the hell you want, but tonight I do not want to sleep next to you."

In the darkness of the room, I pull a light jacket and a Xanax pill out of the suitcase and leave.

The nylon of the deckchair stiffens under my weight. The night gets gradually cooler; the white streak of the galaxy is brushed across the sky; crickets chirp in my ears, merging with the sound of the waves. I close my eyes and I see Gloria, and with minimal effort I can feel her body breathing softly next to mine.

In the days after our fight, Filippo and I ignore each other. In front of Edoardo and Francesca we exchange the minimum words necessary. We rub sun cream onto each other's backs, but our actions are merely functional, stripped of any affection.

I open my dating app and for the first time start writing to some men.

Every evening I take a Xanax pill, then one and a half, then two. Some evenings it's Filippo who passes me a little blue pill when he sees me sitting on the deckchair, reluctant to lie down. I swallow it and follow him meekly. I lie on the bed and wait while he squeezes lube onto his hands and then puts it on my pussy. As he penetrates me, my mind focuses on the edges of my body: hips, knees, jaws. I will my sharpness to perforate him. When he's finished, he falls asleep next to me and after a while I too slip into a viscous sleep from which I wake at dawn, dazed by the benzodiazepine. I go to pee and get back into bed. He is turned away from me, wearing a worn-out white cotton T-shirt, and I wrap my arms around him delicately. His warm back rests against my stomach. I bury my nose in his smell and I want to tell him how sorry I am, how horrible I've been, and how much I love him.

I go out less and less during the day. I make up debilitating headaches and spend entire days in bed. Only when I know that Edoardo, Francesca, and Filippo are out on the boat do I set off down the mule track that leads to the black sand beach, my footsteps causing the lizards to scamper.

On those blinding days, under the amphibious shrubs that bury their roots at the edge of the sand, I check what Gloria's up to. After looking at the last few days' posts—her freckled face smiling, a cocktail in hand, sitting on a towel in some bay somewhere—I scroll back through time. I study how her face has changed over the years. I don't recognize her at fifteen with her blond highlights, and at sixteen she's a different person again, her eyes made up with heavy lines of kohl that sink them even deeper into her face. For the first time I also go and watch the videos of her as a young girl. She talks about arguments with her friends, teenage love affairs, parents, incidents at school that I'm sure I also experienced but have no memory of. Under the videos there are hundreds, sometimes thousands, of comments from girls her age who idolize her. Her more recent content has fewer interactions. She has lost two hundred thousand followers since I met her, and she has stopped posting as much as before. Sometimes a comment from a hater appears under an image, calling her a worthless nobody. Between shoots at the Amazon event, before I abandoned her, Gloria explained to me in a very professional tone that someone calling her a slut on social media and someone asking her for a selfie in the street is all the same: "Every interaction, even the most odious, earns me money. In fact, it's usually the negative content, the stuff that sparks a bit of controversy, that generates more clicks, more interactions, more everything. Because the algorithm rewards indignation. But I don't want to spread hate, so I don't encourage those things," she hurried to add.

Whenever Gloria told me about her work she spoke with nonchalance and a hint of pride, as if the rules of the game were easy, you just needed to know how to use them to build your audience. But in Greece, my feet anesthetized by the heat of the sand, it occurs to me that I can count Gloria's bad moods on one hand, and each one has coincided with forced exposure to an audience of strangers.

After I've finished my research on Gloria, I get started on Lavinia. In contrast with the former, who shows the camera a version of herself who talks lots but says nothing, the latter eviscerates her own adolescent intimacy to an audience of millions. The result is grotesque. She doesn't recount the little crossroads in her everyday life. Instead, she talks about her brother's Down syndrome and the hostile divorce her parents are going through—crying at night under a sheet, the light of a torch painting unsettling shadows across her tear-streaked face. In some videos she looks drunk or high: her eyes roll around in their sockets as she stumbles over incomprehensible phrases. The comments under her posts are more violent than the ones Gloria gets. The masses lock onto her brutal fragility and refuse to let go.

As other internet personalities talk so obsessively about themselves that the recital becomes their identity, Lavinia puts an agonizing fragmentation on show which perhaps reflects that of her viewers and stirs up a visceral disgust. Gloria is, without a doubt, the shrewder of the two. And yet, lining them up side by side, my sense is that, in service to the image she has built for her community, Gloria has renounced a deeper part of herself, blindly following the direction of silent feedback, driving herself to an erratic and perennially smiling state in which she is never truly there.

That's the game, after all: being famous not for something you do, but for the insistence with which you force your own identity, edges sanded off, onto other people's screens. The brands pay the people who give most of themselves. They pay fat people to film themselves saying how proud they are to be fat in an ad for underwear that holds in their fat; they pay the people who understand that ideals, like identities, can be sold to the highest bidder. Feminism, anti-racism, environmentalism: the more fervently you support certain isms, the more the brands will pay for your two-dimensional pantomime to promote the new 50% recyclable Coca-Cola bottle, or their Women's Day special on cosmetics that donates 5% of profits to some organization that supports women. The brands are friends and allies of the flattened faces that inhabit that world. They greedily drink up the self-centered ambition of people who want to be seen; gorge themselves on money and empty sentiments encrusted with the performativity that cloaks the denizens of social media, while a flock of accounts cheer on whoever seems the most morally intact.

On our last evening, Francesca asks me to go out to pick some sage with her. I follow her into the garden. As I break off some stems, I feel the humid earth and have an impulse to sink my hands into it.

"Filippo told me that your sister died and you never talk about it," she says suddenly. I almost laugh at the absurdity of the sentence, but it passes when I turn my face toward her. A smile pulls at her lips and her eyebrows rise in the middle into an expression that I imagine intends to communicate empathy.

Fucking Filippo: he definitely put her up to this, revenge in the guise of benevolence.

"You can talk to me, even if we don't know each other that well. Filippo told me you don't have many friends." I perceive, in this proposal, a desire less to be a friend to me and more to be able to tell herself she was.

"Don't worry, I have Gloria."

"But she's so young, and she's your boss. That can't be a healthy relationship. In any case, Filippo told me you think she's vacuous and stupid."

"I've never said anything of the sort. Gloria is amazing; she's aware and profound."

Never said anything of the sort. In reality, I've said nothing but bad things about Gloria since I met her, especially to Filippo, who goes wild for stories of how privileged and frivolous she is. "You're kind, but honestly, I have people I can talk to."

"O.K., but if you change your mind, you know where I am. I've also lost two important people in my life." Then, lowering her voice, "Two babies. Edoardo and I can't have them. They get to the fifth month and then . . ."

She stiffens, taken by surprise by the unplanned confidence. Then she stands up, straightens her skirt, and walks gracefully back to the house. I follow her, clutching the sage leaves.

Actually, Francesca is right, I don't talk about Eva to anyone. I've tried with Filippo, but each time I do he throws some variation of "You have to make peace with death" back at me, or, if he's in a kinder mood, offers to take me out for an ice cream. After Eva's death, scrolling through Filippo's messages one day, I was surprised to see he had ascribed the word "mental" to my sister when talking about her to a friend. I didn't recognize my sister in that word, not coming from him.

It's strange not talking about Eva, because it feels like she's taking on a secret life, and the quieter it is the bulkier it becomes. I keep a folder of images on my phone called "Eva," where I've saved the photos she took for Instagram. After the incident, she'd film herself wearing skimpy dresses and using filters that filled out her lips and blurred the skin on her face. As if the moment her mental health abandoned her, the vainest elements of her character sprung to the surface. She made herself up with heavy eyeliner and bold lipstick. Sometimes she posted images of dreamlike fashion shoots. Up until a little while before, Eva had been just like those beautiful models.

I couldn't stand her when she was well, let alone when she was sick. I used to envy the way she looked, but since she'd gone insane, I was embarrassed by her every detail, as if her illness was contagious. She swelled up. Her hair, once shiny and thick, had become opaque and thin to the point that it looked glued to her temples, and her eyes lost their brightness. I can't be certain, but I think she might have lost some eyelashes too, for her gaze became less intense. Her face, yellowish, was assailed by pimples and little wounds.

I was struck by the distance between the Eva standing in front of me and the one who inhabited my memory. The shape of her nose, her slightly slanting eyes, her asymmetrical upper lip: in the new Eva, all of these elements seemed imperceptibly but inexorably modified, until she was a whole different person. I remember seeing a documentary about an American sociopath in the seventies who went around planting bombs. Her mugshots revealed an extraordinary transformation that ran in parallel to her crimes: a beautiful young woman unrecognizable at fifty, as if her face had melted as a result of her wrongdoings; her features now bobbed around aimlessly on the surface of her face.

However I looked at her, in person or in one of her self portraits, I couldn't catch sight of the Eva I remembered, the one with the pigeon chest, the gap between her teeth, and tissue paper skin. Part of me was sure she was doing it on purpose. Her sudden madness would occasionally seem like her ultimate tantrum, her life's work, an explosive demand for attention, bringing with it the blackmail of pity, which I was determined not to feel.

Her friends abandoned her like the courts abandon a deposed queen. Surrounded only by people who desired to live under her radiant, persecutory wing, once the original characteristics had disappeared, so did all those who, in envy and fear, had once admired her.

The fact that she had no friends on social media meant that each of her posts echoed in a relational void. A few months before she disappeared, she bought herself a tripod for her phone to take selfies. But when she uploaded the photos online she would write in the captions that she was happy to have someone so special in her life, someone who made her look so good in photos. In her worst moments, when her lucidity was crumbling away, she would curse God. She would become seriously paranoid, like when she insulted her doctors, convinced they were spying on her via Instagram. She had clocked that whenever she talked about something, it would appear in her adverts, in the invasive banners, as suggestions for online purchases. But rather than taking it out on surveillance capitalism, she took it out on the doctors.

Eva's solitude made my toes curl, so after a while I made a rule not to look at her social media, only to give in and save all those photos, in an attempt to conserve some tangible proof of what was happening to her. Far from home and from Eva, I couldn't believe her transformation. I saved the image of her in the courtyard of the psychiatric ward where she was admitted after her last crisis: she's wearing sneakers without laces, pulled on like slippers, and a white hoodie that had perhaps once belonged to me, also missing the cord around the neck. She's sitting on an exercise bike which, for reasons that remain a mystery, was parked in the sad cement rectangle bordered by the walls of the hospital, where the sun shone just once a day around lunchtime. In my memory, her face is covered in glitter that I brought her with the nurses' permission.

Eva was more bearable in that place than she had ever been when she was healthy. In the psychiatric ward for suicide attempts she returned to her infantile core, spoilt but also humble, because she was aware, deep down, of her own defeat.

A few obese women wandered around the ward growling and mumbling to themselves. We called one of them Madame Ogress. She fidgeted under the neon lights with her hand constantly stuffed in a packet of chips that she scattered on the floor as she walked. If you got close, she might attack. Just like we'd done at Aquapark more than a decade before, Eva and I would spy on her, squatting down behind white doors and pillars covered in chipped paint, setting off, if we were lucky, her wild rage. In those corridors, I have to admit, I loved her again, for the second time in my life.

On that Greek night I fall asleep listening, for the last time, to the sound of the tide. I see Gloria immobile on the exercise bike wearing a white hoodie. I brush her cheek. She tells me with an absent look that everything's fine. In my dream, I believe her.

The return journey is on a small plane that takes us home from Skiathos in the prickling heat of a disappearing August. My tan is already fading when I see Gloria again. She calls me midway through September. I was sure she wouldn't, or that she would contact me to put an end to our working relationship. I see the phone light up with her name and feel, like the first time, my heart drop down to my ankles and ricochet back up. She doesn't want to fire me. She tells me to meet her at the station, explaining that we have to go and pick up a prize she's won in Naples for her best-selling book of poems. It's called *Here I am*. The things inside that she calls poems sound more like publicity copy or verses from horrible pop songs. I open the book at random and read:

*You are like Christmas*
*I wait for you all year*
*Like a child*
*Then when you arrive*
*I don't like you anymore*
*And I realize*
*That I'm grown up now.*

Gloria sends me an email with the information about the ceremony. I'll be responsible for getting us there.

Over the course of the summer, I've bitten all my nails down to the quick and rediscovered my childhood passion: pulling out my hair. It's not trichotillomania, it's just that with the salt and the sun my hair becomes weak and pretty much falls out by itself. Might as well give it a hand. When I look in the mirror, I see a shadow of myself, and I like it. For my body to reflect my spirit, that's all I can ask of it. Gloria has also lost weight. Now her legs look like toothpicks even in photos with other famous girls. Pictures of books and brutalist buildings have started to appear on her Instagram grid, with captions that sound a lot like mine. When I read her words appropriating my tone, I push down the sting of indignation and tell myself that, at the end of the day, social media is not my world. I fantasize about what it will be like when I see her again.

At the station, my stomach in turmoil, I search for her head among the thousands hovering under the departure boards. I spot her. She's reading one of her books for eight-year-olds, leaning against the wall of one of those monobrand stores that sprout up like mushrooms in the middle of stations and stay there for a couple of months before being replaced by something new. The current pop-up is selling sunglasses made of colored plastic. When she sees me from afar, Gloria smiles. As if the summer hadn't happened and we were still the same as the night of the party. I want to hug her but remind myself that our intimacy lives only in my mind. I've spent so many days talking to that imaginary Gloria that I'm no longer sure if she and the one in front of me have anything in common. She skips over like she's playing hopscotch. When she reaches me I notice how thin she is, thinner than me now. Gloria takes a breath; she's about to say something but I get in first.

"This prize is ridiculous. Have you actually read how it works? They may have told you that you've already won, but two other people have won too. And seeing as the world you live in is a world full of retards, we are going all the way to Naples so they can choose the Super Winner."

Whatever Gloria had wanted to tell me softens into an expression that is first bewildered (maybe it's because I said "retards"), then disappointed. Eventually she comes out with a delicate smile: "At least we're traveling first class."

Inside the carriage I try not to reveal my enthusiasm for the unexpected luxury. Leather seats and a compartment all to ourselves. A woman in uniform knocks every hour to ask if we would like anything. I would like everything: three packets of mini salamis with crackers, two packets of parmesan shavings, two Cokes, three waters, a packet of shortbread, and a cereal bar. I slip it all into my suitcase under Gloria's curious gaze. "You never know," I say. Putting food away is another of my tics. I don't eat it, but having emergency rations calms me and I think it also extinguishes any hunger pangs: a bit like knowing I have Xanax in my bag curbs my anxiety, even if I don't take it. The problem with food is that it goes off. I forget where I've hidden it, and months can pass before I rediscover a packet of withered chips at the back of the wardrobe, or a wrinkly apple in a gym bag under the bed.

Now that I can look at her properly, Gloria really does seem different from how I remember her. In some ways she's more beautiful. She's lost weight, her face is more sculpted, her hair is styled, and she's also changed her look: she's wearing a blush pink top that comes down to her ribs like the one Lavinia was wearing at the party, no bra, and black cargo pants covered in buckles, identical to the ones I've seen American models wearing in fashion ads.

I feel betrayed by her transformation: she's turned her back on the relationship I've been building in her absence. She puts her earphones in and rests her forehead on the window. I can almost feel the cold of the glass on my own skin. Her eyes look beyond the infinitely unravelling scroll of the landscape.

"You've lost a ton of followers," I say after a while.

Gloria takes her earphones out. "What did you say?"

"I said you've lost a ton of followers."

"I hadn't noticed." Of course she had noticed.

"Of course you noticed. Why do you think you've lost them? Did you fail to preach one of your moral precepts?"

Her eyes become two slits, she's about to whisper something but then she puts that magical mechanism of hers into motion and instead of flames comes a void.

"They've probably done a clean-up of fake accounts." She puts her earphones back in, closes her eyes, and pretends to sleep.


A driver comes to pick us up from the station. He explains that the hotel is in Fuorigrotta, a little way out of the city center. "But it's a beautiful place, built during fascism. The Mostra d'Oltremare is a huge exhibition center, full of gardens, aquariums, restaurants. There are fountains, lawns, swimming pools, entire floors of maiolica, and it's all white."

The car speeds under overpasses wrapped in emerald-green vines that are reflected in Gloria's opaque eyes as she refuses to talk to me. The Naples bypass unwinds through the window: apartment complexes covered in cracks, sheets flapping in the wind like flags of surrender, a yellowish end-of-the-world light. The driver takes us farther and farther from the city center and comes to a stop in a circular piazza paved in red. It's deserted, apart from some runners so far away they look like they're moving in slow motion around the circumference. A bright white marble building that looks like it could have come down from space towers up in the middle.

I turn to the driver, perplexed: "Are you sure this is the right place?"

"Yes, we're out of season now and there are no exhibitions on, but if you look over there, follow my finger, miss, do you see the gate? That's the entrance to the exhibition hall. And the stadium that you see over there is the Armando Maradona stadium, the *mano de dios*—do you know it?"

Gloria starts walking toward the entrance to the hotel. The floor of the lobby is a chessboard of black and white marble. Transparent glass doors open onto the internal courtyard, which is adorned with a rectangular stone pool, full of water that looks like it's been stagnant for a long time. There's nobody at the reception desk. Gloria rings the little gold bell impatiently until a boy in an un-ironed, untucked shirt rushes in apologizing and checks us into our rooms.

"It's not how I imagined," I murmur. "Where are the lawns and mosaics? Where's the swimming pool?"

"Who cares. I just want to lay down."

In my room I fall into an agitated, fragmented sleep of disturbing dreams.

At 7:30 I go down for dinner. It's organized by a blonde woman in her seventies who reminds me of Donatella Versace. We've already had some brief phone conversations about the event—brief because I don't understand a word she says. She introduces herself as Laura, but she might have said Lara, on the phone I'd heard Ilaria. When Gloria joins us, La(u)ra asks us to follow her as the other guests are waiting for us in the restaurant, where they're having aperitivo. Gloria is still enveloped in her mutism. I hadn't expected such an enduring glower. I could ask her to stop, but I don't want to give her the satisfaction. We walk toward the red piazza. Gloria is in front of me, head bowed and walking quickly, when suddenly she is attacked by a shower of mahogany hair with two thin arms that lock around her neck. Instinctively, I lunge forward to detach her from the grip of this newcomer, as La(u)ra, with unexpected speed, makes to hit her with her quilted gray purse.

"Stop it, I know her," says Gloria's voice, suffocated by the girl's body. She gets her breath back: "Amanda! What are you doing here?"

"I came to see you. I took the train from Ancona; it took ages but I read that you'd be here." Amanda's face is bony with little round marks on her forehead, perhaps scars from childhood chickenpox.

"Look, I can't stay. Here, this is the key to the room. Hold it against the little flashing black box outside the door and go in. Tell the concierge I gave it to you. I have to go now, I have a work dinner; I'll see you when I get back."

The girl looks at her adoringly, throws her arms around her neck again and kisses her cheeks, leaving a wet mark.

"Thank you thank you thank you," she says looking malevolently toward La(u)ra and me.

"Why on earth would you just give your keys to that nutcase? Who is she?" I ask Gloria once the girl has left.

"She's an old fan of mine. And don't call her a nutcase. She's had a tough time."

"How so?"

"I'll tell you later. I don't feel like it right now."

Of course I now desperately need to know.

La(u)ra, who seems to exist in a completely different space-time dimension, asks Gloria, despite the exchange that just happened right in front of her eyes, if the girl is one of her little friends.

"Why is she talking to you like you're six years old?" I whisper to Gloria, and finally she smiles.

The restaurant is in a cube, also white, on the third floor. We go up a flight of stairs that look like teeth and into a room that's illuminated, even in the daytime, by blinding spotlights. There's a tacky bar on the right-hand side which isn't open and has a depressing bowl of chewing gum and lollipops next to the cash register. Around a single, large round table in the middle of the room sit the four people who make up the jury and who, when the time comes, will present the prize to the Super Winner.

"The other candidates aren't here yet," La(u)ra explains, "they arrive tomorrow morning. Their train journey is shorter as they live nearer to here."

The faces of the guests suggest a desire to be anywhere other than that table. I can empathize.

Gloria and I sit down next to a man in a gray suit with small, distant eyes. He looks like a tax collector. His name is Ugo, and he introduces himself as the nephew of a famous writer who died a few decades ago. He's a high school principal and loves literature, thanks to his aunt. Opposite us sits a woman in her forties. I recognize her; her name is Frida. Before she was famous, she worked in a toy store. One day she wrote an ungrammatical post online denouncing the way toys are targeted according to gender: the pink ones that reflect domestic life for girls, the scientific ones in more austere colors for boys. The bombast of her opinion stirred up support on social media, but her real success happened a while later when, on Women's Day, an American influencer with millions and millions of followers tagged her in a list of feminist influencers across the Western world.

Frida immediately gained three hundred thousand followers and became, overnight, the touchstone for online feminism. She then gained a further following when someone pointed out that the books she'd hastily published following her boom looked like they'd been written by someone illiterate, and she created an uproar against Italy's classism. The brands now wheel her out for any campaign to promote feminism, usually ideated by middle-aged men who grope the interns. I know that because

Angela told me as much one afternoon at the Galeone. Angela was an account manager for one of these agencies before she discovered that the bosses wished to "choke her to death with my bell-end." Verbatim. She found out when her computer died and she temporarily borrowed a male colleague's. She was confronted by thousands of Telegram messages in which her superiors exchanged photos of half-naked girls, often underage, and commented on the physical appearance of female colleagues.

"So, what did you do?" I asked her as I cleared a table.

"Nothing. After three months I mentioned the messages to my supervisor, who told the CEO of the agency, who in turn ordered the deletion of the message thread and we never spoke of it again."

Angela didn't blackmail the company like I would have done, nor did she sue them. She said the episode had traumatized her too much, and she trembled like a leaf as she talked about it. From then on, she has been posting words of hatred toward men on the internet, confirming my idea that social media, when the illusion is wiped away, is the death of the revolution: it makes its users believe they are fighting to heal the world's injustices, when in reality it is just a broken vent for the frustrations that consume us in real life.

In any case, from one outburst to another, Frida the feminist influencer has become a juror for a literary prize.

Next to Frida sits an editor who looks after the Ultrapop! imprint of a large publishing group. Ultrapop! publishes only low-quality books that rise up the sales charts for two weeks, then vanish into oblivion only to pop up again years later in a second-hand book exchange. He's called Giacomo Rosa, he's about sixty, and I've seen him at one or two of Filippo's book events. He's a cultured person, and deep inside him there must be a little voice that shames him for all the crap he publishes. And indeed, to soften this inner conflict, he markets every Ultrapop! book as the literary debut of the century, giving interviews left, right, and center in which he explains that there's no such thing as high culture or low culture and that he, unlike others, is definitely not a snob.

The woman sitting next to Giacomo Rosa, Gloria whispers in my ear, "is called Serena. She used to write for a local newspaper. Then she started only interviewing people who had large numbers of followers on Instagram or who worked in TV and moved onto a bigger paper. She interviewed me once and was super flattering and then I overheard her out in my courtyard talking on the phone too loud calling me an imbecile."

Serena is laughing noisily and squeezing Giacomo's forearm. Frida is about to publish her second book with him and is sitting, composed, not eating. The writer's nephew is telling anecdotes about his aunt that are clearly lifted from her published biographies.

"He was obviously her least favorite nephew; I bet he never even met her," I whisper to Gloria, who chokes on her water.

The conversation of our dinner companions shifts to Frida's new book. Giacomo Rosa says he's astounded by how well it has sold: "I don't agree with anything that my star author has written," he says as he puts an arm around her shoulders. "But it evidently speaks to many women."

"You are the most sexist man I have ever met," she laughs. "It would be nice if my book spoke to you."

"But I believe Frida's book speaks only to Frida's community, or am I wrong? If you didn't have so many followers, you wouldn't have sold anywhere near the number of copies you have," says the journalist. "They're buying you, not the book."

Giacomo Rosa smiles and sinks back in his seat, ready to enjoy the show. Before Frida can formulate a response, Ugo intervenes: "Well that isn't exactly surprising, that's just how publishing works. When my aunt was alive things were different: people really knew how to write. They had Montale, Spaziani, Ortese . . . If we still followed the same publication criteria as back then, nothing would get published, and it would be a blessing."

Giacomo Rosa's smile transforms into an aggressive sneer: "And yet you self-published on Amazon, didn't you?" The journalist looks relieved that the attention is no longer on her. Frida pulls her phone out of her bag and turns to Gloria.

"The most deserving of us here is Gloria, who has written a book of poetry that's been read by hundreds of thousands of her peers." She turns her phone ninety degrees, opens the camera, and takes a selfie with Gloria, immortalizing her as she takes a sip of water and a rivulet of liquid runs down her chin.

We are no longer invisible. The journalist takes the opportunity to ask Gloria some blunt questions about her book: did you write it yourself, how long did it take, why is it so short, why do you think it has sold so well. Gloria utters monosyllabic answers as she pushes mashed up gnocchi around her plate.

"That isn't very elegant," Ugo reproaches. Gloria stops, picks up her phone and starts moving her thumb over it distractedly.

"Weren't you taught not to use your phone at the dinner table?" he interrupts again after a few minutes. "How were you brought up? At dinner time, we talk." Gloria puts her phone down and stares at a point beyond Giacomo and Frida's heads. I search for her hand under the table.

"Perhaps you'd like to tell us something about your book—that way you'll have a chance to talk about yourself. Isn't that what you young people want? It seems to me that all my students want is to talk about themselves," Ugo presses her.

"I don't really feel like it," she responds tonelessly. Her hand is cold and damp in mine, different to how it felt the evening of the party when she touched my cheeks. She picks up her phone again, as if hoping the screen will open a wormhole that will suck her out of this room. In an abrupt movement, he knocks the phone out of her hand and it falls on the floor with a clatter. Gloria looks at him, stunned. She looks as if she's about to say something, but whatever it was evaporates.

Ugo continues: "What on earth could a girl so young have

to say, I wonder. What did you say to convince all your peers to buy this book of poems?"

"Whatever it was, if you want to repeat it in prose I'll publish it immediately," Giacomo interrupts, laughing, while the journalist can hardly conceal her annoyance.

Gloria stares at the plastic flowers in the glass vase. I stare at them too. I imagine how they'd feel to touch. They'd have a light fur covering them. They'd feel like carnations.

"Oh, satisfy our curiosity will you: tell us what a little girl could possibly have to say that is so urgent she needs to write a book."

I stand up and my chair scrapes across the floor. Gloria's hand, torn away from my leg, hangs in mid-air. Everyone is looking at me. My breathing is irregular. I hear my voice as if I were not the source of the sound.

"Seeing as you're judging this prize you should probably know what's written in her book." I turn to Ugo with a tone that's almost a growl: "What can a young woman possibly have to say? I guess you'd pose the same question to your aunt, would you? And she'd tell you that you're an imbecile, but unfortunately she's dead, and I'm sure you barely knew her anyway since all your little stories are pilfered from her biographies."

I yank Gloria by the arm, pick her phone up off the floor, and pull her to the door which spits us out into the windy night. I collapse on the first step of the stairs.

"I could've killed him, I swear." My voice continues to flow out from me, vibrant and foreign. I stand up and turn to her. Now in her eyes shines the essence that I caught a glimpse of the first time I saw her, focused and bright in the meeting room, but which has appeared less and less often as the months have gone on. She takes a step toward me. She stops a few millimeters from my face, without breaking eye contact. Then suddenly she hugs me in a passionate embrace; I feel the tears running down her cheek and into our hair.

"Thank you," she whispers, her voice dry.

Her hug brings me back to myself.

"I have a joint in my room."

We move apart.

"Finders keepers!" Her expression is playful.

She plunges down the stairs; I run behind her, my heart in my mouth. We start laughing, trying to catch our breath, hiccupping. The moon, round and white above us, illuminates the expanse of grass and marble. We run through the night, jump the little square walls around the flower beds as if they are unassailable hurdles, chasing each other, coming back together. My legs move effortlessly and in my chest I feel a fire catching and reducing me to cosmic dust. I am new, virgin, untouched, I have never seen the light of day.

When we get back to the hotel we collapse against the columns at the entrance, getting our breath back and, facing one another, wait for the laughter to subside. In the elevator we keep smiling into the mirror, as if we have just robbed a bank.

"Gloria, do you or do you not have an underage girl in your room?" I ask her, suddenly remembering about Amanda.

"Oh shit, yes. I'd forgotten, she sent me a message. But maybe she's asleep now, because when she's awake she's always sending me messages. Shall we go to your room to smoke? Then I'll leave, I promise."

In my room we throw ourselves onto the bed. I take a thin joint out of my silver cigarette holder that has the initials L.G. on it.

"Who's L.G.?"

"My grandfather. Leone Gatti. Strange man. When he died, we found tons of little boxes containing snippets of newspapers. Not photos or articles, just the scraps of things he'd cut out and put God knows where. It's nice though, huh? It's silver. It means a lot to me."

Gloria watches me as I caress the little silver box. Then I put it on my chest and light the joint.

"You treat your things very differently from me."

"That's because I don't have much," I say.

"I can't remember what it's like to not be able to have something I want."

"It must be nice . . ." I reflect, "you can focus on less tangible things. People waste a ton of time thinking about physical things they can't have."

"Do you waste much time on that?"

"A bit . . . But maybe that didn't come out right. It's not that there's something I really want. I just wonder how I would live if I didn't have the problem of having to survive economically."

"Would you still work at the Galeone?"

"I think so."

"Would you still work for me?"

I inhale the smoke, it scratches my lungs, I make a circle with my lips and pass her the joint.

"I think so. Are you going to tell me about Amanda? Why is she sleeping in your room?"

Gloria sits up on the bed, then turns over and lays on her stomach. "Amanda is a fan. I met her like four years ago. She was one of the first. At the beginning I talked to my followers a lot because it's not like there were many of them. And I liked it, it felt like we were equals. As if we were all there, in my room, and I was no different from them. She was always writing to me, and I always wrote back. This work was nice in the early days, you know? Nobody really knew what I was supposed to do, hardly any brands were involved, and I didn't really care how I came across. I can't say exactly when things changed. I think it must have happened gradually because I didn't really notice. Anyway, this one time I did a show in a shopping center on the outskirts of Ancona. Amanda asked if we could meet. She was two or three years younger than me: I would've been sixteen, and she was thirteen or fourteen. My grandma and I took her to a restaurant after the show; she'd never eaten out before. Her mom had left, and her dad is kind of out of it.

We gave her a ride home, but when we got there her dad was out. We didn't know what to do, so we got her a room in our hotel. In the morning we had breakfast, and she was so happy because she had never seen a hotel breakfast before, see what I mean? And it wasn't even a super luxurious hotel. Anyway, when the time comes for us to leave, Amanda makes this huge scene. She says that I'm her best friend, that she thinks of me as a sister. She's crying so much, and I don't know what to do because of course it's not the same for me. In the end I gave her my hoodie, the one she was wearing today. She always wears it. Since that day she's been following me around Italy. She doesn't go to school, as in, she's stopped going and there's no one to really notice. So she gets on these regional trains that take days to get anywhere and crosses Italy to see me. She even turns up at my house sometimes and buzzes the intercom; I've had to ask the porter to tell her I'm not in whenever she comes. I don't want to be mean; it just gets a bit much."

"You don't need to explain yourself, I can imagine." I relight the embers of the joint, take a toke and pass it to her.

"But that's not all. At a certain point this thing happened. Last year, in spring, I went to do an event in Bari. My grandma is too old now to follow me to all these things, so Valentina came instead. We arrive at the venue and obviously she's there waiting for me. I tell her she can't come in—she actually wasn't allowed—and she makes one of her scenes. Valentina then has the idea to get her to wait in a restaurant nearby. She gives the server twenty euros and asks him to keep an eye on her. After three hours we come out and pick her up, and she's acting kind of strange. We take her back to our hotel again, and when we get there, she tells us that when all the other customers had left, one of the servers gave her a few beers and put his hand between her thighs. She tells me she doesn't know where to spend the night, and that she might have to sleep in the station. Which would be ridiculous, right? She wasn't even eighteen, who knows what could've happened to her. So I let her sleep in my room with me, while Valentina grumbled that I'm too available and that I should be more careful with the trust I throw around. I asked Valentina if we should call the police, but she said no, she was just attention seeking and we'd already done plenty, what with paying for her dinner and the room."

"And so . . .?"

"Next morning Amanda was back in full swing, as if nothing had happened. I asked her if she wanted to file a report, and she asked, 'for what?' 'For what happened to you yesterday,' I said, and she responded that it was nothing. Sometimes I wonder if she was telling the truth. Because if what she told us was true, that man could hurt someone else, and it would be partly my fault."

She chokes on the smoke and passes back the joint.

"What a tale," I say.

"Yep."

"Do you think it really happened?"

"I think that if that story wasn't true, there's a similar one that is. Life isn't easy for a girl like her."

"Do you feel responsible for her?"

"Yeah. But right now I really can't worry about other people because . . ." She pauses, her voice cracks a little, "because . . . I feel like I don't even know who I am. And everyone around me thinks I'm stupid, like at tonight's dinner. They say it to my face, or I overhear it when they think I'm out of earshot. They ask me to write books, but don't expect anything from me other than stratospheric sales. They ask me to be in a film, and even if I make a mess of it, they all just tell me how wonderful I am. Nobody tells me what they really think. Amanda reminds me of the careless me who had no clue what she was doing, and since I no longer recognize that version of me, it's like I can feel a ghost of myself every time I'm with her."

The smoke curls above us and hangs beneath the ceiling.

"Do you have any brothers or sisters?" she asks me suddenly.

"I had a sister, yes."

"Had?"

"Yes . . . She died."

Gloria holds her breath.

"I'm sorry, I didn't mean to."

"It's not like you killed her."

"How did she die? If I can ask . . ."

"Of course you can; we're talking about it. She committed suicide. Two years ago."

Gloria is frozen. I turn onto my stomach and lay my head on the pillow, my face turned toward her. I pick the tiny little bobbles off the duvet cover with my fingers.

"Do you feel responsible?" she asks me in a tiny voice.

"I don't know. Sometimes yes, sometimes no."

Her phone lights up. It's just past midnight. "It's Amanda," she says with a hint of disappointment.

"Tell her to come here."

Gloria obeys, relieved. After a few minutes the mahogany-haired girl arrives, though she must have dyed it with henna, because as she gets closer to the bed, I can smell fragrant earth.

"Do you want the last two drags?" I ask her.

Gloria glares at me.

"What? I'm sure it's not her first time. You've smoked before, haven't you?"

"Of course," she says defiantly. She feels intimidated in front of me and doesn't dare move closer to Gloria. She smokes silently.

"Do you have anything I can eat?"

"Haven't you eaten?" Gloria asks, a note of exasperation in her voice.

"No, if I spend money on food, I won't be able to get home tomorrow."

"Why do you do this?" Gloria mutters, frustrated.

"Don't worry, I've got loads of food," I announce. I take the packets of mini salamis from the train out of my suitcase and explore the packets in the minibar. I line everything up on the tray with plastic teacups, put a towel over my arm and serve Amanda as if she were a guest in a luxury restaurant.

"Here you are, young lady."

Amanda laughs and starts eating.

"I told you it would come in useful," I say to Gloria.

"Yep, you're all set for the apocalypse." She smiles.

When Amanda has finished eating, I take her to the bathroom to brush her teeth and hand her a T-shirt to sleep in.

"We've decided we'll all sleep here tonight, no fussing."

Amanda nods timidly. "Can I sleep next to Gloria though?"

I look at Gloria and she nods her head. Amanda lets out a squeal of gratitude and pounces, hugging her and lying down by her side. Gloria puts an arm around her shoulders and strokes her hair until she falls asleep. I put the light out and listen to the cars rumbling along the bypass. The breath of the two girls synchronizes and for a moment I feel that everything that is supposed to happen in the world is happening here in this room, right now.

In the morning, we wake up and go down to breakfast. Like the evening before, Gloria doesn't eat. Amanda, on the other hand, ravages the buffet. I go back up to my room and Amanda follows Gloria to hers. I light another joint which I've been hiding in my suitcase. Smoking weed in the morning punctures my brain, loosening it in my skull. When I meet Gloria and Amanda in the hallway, I'm on another planet. La(u)ra is also there. She doesn't mention last night's events; I suspect she's forgotten. The auditorium where the prizegiving is happening is just a short walk from the hotel. It's overrun with schoolchildren because the Super Winner, La(u)ra explains, will be chosen by the jury we met last night in conjunction with a group of middle-school students. Trying to enter through a side door so as not to be seen by the snotty-nosed kids, suddenly we are stopped by a bouncer. He grabs Amanda by the arm and holds her so firmly that he almost lifts her off the ground: she's not on the guest list so she can't come in with us. Amanda erupts into a hysterical wail and thrashes around reaching toward Gloria, who is, in turn, pulled by La(u)ra into the dark corridor that leads to the stalls. "Come on, let her in," Gloria begs. There's no way, she has to stay outside. Amanda's face contorts as if she has gills and can't breathe out of water. I remain in a daze until I hear Gloria calling me from the other end of the corridor.

"What's up with you? You seem out of it."

I don't have time to answer her because the ruckus has attracted the attention of the school students, who have now spotted Gloria and are approaching her like an army. I catch a flash of intolerance cross her face before she is swallowed whole by the greasy sludge of pre-adolescence. They touch her, pull her hair, take photos, ask for an autograph, two autographs, put copies of her book of poems in front of her to kiss, touch, dirty. When I catch sight of a slice of Gloria between the hot bodies and frizzy hair, her expression is desperate. She's standing on tiptoes looking around and when our eyes meet, she gestures for help, irritated. I shake myself awake and walk quickly toward a hostess—a woman in a bizarre salmon-pink pants suit—and ask her if she can please rescue Gloria and take us to our reserved seats. She barges through the crowd, shields Gloria with her body and takes us through a black door that opens onto the stalls of the theater. When we get to the front row, La(u)ra is already there, looking at her phone, seeming not to have realized she's lost sight of Gloria. As soon as we sit down, she nudges me with her elbow and points out the old woman sitting next to her. She's a well-known poet, lover in her youth of an even better known (and more talented) poet. La(u)ra takes Gloria by the wrist and in a sudden movement throws her onto the woman. "Photograph them," she hisses at me. I obey and take a picture of Gloria, wide eyed, next to the stranger with blue eyeshadow. They both look embalmed. "Now take one of me," and she too throws herself onto the poet, who would clearly prefer to continue reading the sheets of paper she's holding. In fact, that's exactly what she does as La(u)ra's face contorts into what she seems to think is a smile. I sit down, as does Gloria. I scroll through the photos I just took, giggling uncontrollably, until the salmon-pink lady returns and tells Gloria she'll have to say a couple of words on stage about her love of literature and poetry, writers and poets.

"No one told me," Gloria says.

"Oh, you don't have to say much, just tell us why you felt you needed to write this book of poetry, who your literary idols are, etcetera."

As soon as the lady disappears, Gloria turns to me: "You have to write it, I don't know what to say." She gives me her phone.

"Glo, I don't think I can right now. It's a ridiculously simple and personal thing, it has to come from you. Just write something down," I say, annoyed, and pass her back the phone.

"You are being paid to help me, so help me," she hisses.

I have never written anything for Gloria other than captions for her brand content. That's easy because at the end of the day the meaning is always the same: you are fine just how you are, you are beautiful, the aesthetic standards for women are unjust (buy this face cream). Now I'm being asked to do something completely different. I'm too stoned to ask her about her relationship with books. In a trance, I start typing the words that I imagine I would say if it were me doing it. I write about when I discovered Goliarda Sapienza, with her protagonist who was so amoral and obscene, after years of reading Jane Austen's boring, pretty, and good women; about science fiction blowing my mind when I read Fredric Brown's short story "Sentry," which made me reflect for the first time on the notion that we all think we are good deep down, even when we're not. A bit about the melancholic and mocking poetry of Nelo Risi; the solemnity of Giovanni Raboni's; Cavalli's poems that "won't change the world" but nevertheless changed mine; and finally about when I learned Pascoli's "X Agosto" by heart: not because I have any particular affection for Pascoli, whose poems we studied at school and are therefore classified as old and dusty, but because the poem goes like this:

> *A swallow was returning to her roof*
> *when they killed her. She fell among thorns.*
> *She had an insect in her beak:*
> *dinner for her brood.*

> *Now she is there, as on a cross, offering*
> *that worm to that distant sky;*
> *and her nest is in the shadows, they are waiting,*
> *peeping softer and softer.*[1]

These verses had made my sister cry to the point of exhaustion. Once I'd discovered this weakness, I committed the poem to memory so that I could make her despair on command. Great entertainment. Plus, after the swallow, Pascoli's father dies too, but Eva didn't give a shit about him.

After ten minutes or so I pass the phone back to Gloria, and a few moments later they call her onto the stage. For the whole duration of the ceremony, I stare at what's happening in front of me without my brain registering any of it. Dancers fling themselves around on fabric ribbons that hang from the ceiling; the jury asks the candidates questions. As well as Gloria, there is an excessively self-assured woman who has written a book of poetry for children, and a science writer who has put chemistry into verse. The questions are all about literary tastes: "who are your favorite poets?," "what are some of the classics you grew up with?" To the second question Gloria answers: "No one in particular, they all left a mark," and when the high school principal asks her what country her favorite writers tend to be from, she responds that it has never crossed her mind to

[1] Translated by Adriana Baranello

compare writers of different nationalities: "I don't see any differences," she says.

At a certain point in the ceremony a bunch of twelve-year-olds come onto the stage and read out their reviews of the three books in the contest. There are fifteen reviews per book for the three finalists. Torture. After the reviews, the ribbon dancers twirl around for a few more minutes, to then make way for the candidates and judges again. At that point I fall asleep, folded over myself. My conscience awakens only when an unsettling voice from another dimension floats into my eardrums. It's mine, but it doesn't belong to me. I see purplish squiggles on the backs of my eyelids. I want to open my eyes, but I can't. I tell the index finger of my right hand to move, just to test a small part of my body, but it doesn't. The voice continues to speak. It's Gloria's voice, lower and hoarser than mine. What is she saying? She's talking about when she learned Pascoli by heart to read it to her sister, how science-fiction moved her, how strongly she felt the absence of amoral female characters. I gasp for air, it's as if someone is sitting on my chest. It's me, that's my voice, those are my memories, she's wearing my identity and has left me naked. Only now that it's in someone else's mouth does my story restore to me some truth about who I am. Around me, frozen in my lucid dream, a roar of applause. I move my pupils to the right and left furiously. I manage to open my eyes. Gloria is on the stage, smiling timidly as the jury looks on in admiration. Even the poet who's less famous than her dead lover and who seemed dead herself until a moment ago is politely applauding. Gloria comes off the stage, runs over, and hugs me.

We come out of the theater into piercing sunlight. Gloria is besieged by school kids once again. They didn't make her their Super Winner in the end: their teachers, consciously or otherwise, had instilled in them a moralistic instinct to vote for the scientific poems. But this time she willingly embraces them, hugs them, kisses them. The Ultrapop! editor is waiting impatiently: he wants to formally propose a book, but not poetry this time.

I stand to one side, the unsettling sleep of a few minutes before has not yet dissipated. I look for Amanda but can't see her.

At every opening Gloria throws me a look of gratitude streaked with guilt. When we finally get to the car that's taking us to the station the only thing I ask Gloria, who is oozing joy, is what happened to Amanda.

"I have no idea," she responds, smiling, "but that's just how she is. She's crazy."

When Eva died, I had a few exams left and my thesis to write. I was already living at Filippo's, in Paris, in the apartment with the squeaky, worm-eaten parquet.

It was my father who called me to tell me. I was playing *Ni No Kuni II*, a video game in which I was a young prince with a tail and cat ears and a blond bob. Together with my team, I had to reconquer my realm, which had been stolen by a usurper mouse. The gang of heroes moved through enchanted worlds. I flew on colorful blimps over tropical seas whose beaches were populated by dragons and other monsters we had to defeat. I was carrying out missions assigned to me by the inhabitants of cities filled with temples built in crystalline waters. I met sorcerers who lived in magical forests where it was always night, and fought enemies armed with sabers and bows.

My father never called. Our relationship was suspended when, at twelve years old, I developed breasts. He decided it would be impossible to understand me from that day on. Our exchanges were reduced to a rare, half-swallowed greeting, and I was fine with it.

I read online that in the memories of many people who have gone through a sudden loss, the moments before hearing the news are cloaked in a prophetic aura. Everything conspiring to suggest the imminent tragedy. That's how it was for me too. But, unlike the people on the forums, I know for sure that the universe was not giving me, or anyone else, a warning. When humans are under stress, our cortisol levels rise. Cortisol has a non-linear effect on the memory. If the stress lasts for a limited period of time, its peak makes the memory more acute. If high levels of stress are maintained over time, then the constant presence of cortisol creates a cascade of problems, ranging from difficulty sleeping to memory loss to depression.

Of the minutes that precede my father's phone call I remember everything.

I am sitting on the couch with the controller in my hands. The shutters are down. The sun has just set, and a bluish light is seeping through the corners of the windows. I can hear the faint chirping of sparrows from outside. It's hot, and every so often I get up to submerge my wrists in cold water. The honking horns in the street are friendly sounds, whispering that, if I wanted, I could go downstairs and find proof that I have a body. I don't want to: I don't want to have a body. I'm smoking a cigarette that I rest in a round metal ashtray at regular intervals, a thread of smoke rises, and remains suspended in mid-air. When my phone vibrates and I read my father's name and surname, I feel like I already know what he's going to say. I pause the game. My hand moves toward the phone. My fingertips leave sweaty prints on the screen. I slide my thumb to accept the call. There's silence on the other end. I imagine my father in those moments, before saying what he has to say. When Eva started getting sick, a furrow appeared on his brow that gives him a look of constant confusion, as if he has just been presented with a dish he didn't order, but knows he has to eat anyway. It was his cheeks that fell first, onto the bones of his face. Joined soon after by his eyelids, his earlobes, and finally his hair. He has little white balls at the corners of his mouth. The blue of his eyes has faded, his hands swollen to the point where he struggles to use the phone. Little by little his whole body has given in to the struggles of recent years, surrendering to the force of gravity.

His initial silence on the phone is a mute prayer: you already know what I have to say, put the phone down, don't make me say the words out loud. I don't grant his wish. His unease stirs in me a quiver of pleasure. I want to hear the air slowly meander and make his vocal cords vibrate. I want his breath to form letters, the tip of his tongue to touch the roof of his mouth, his lips to join, his throat to close.

My father starts to cry. Wailing like a newborn baby, unstoppable. I wait. Finally, he falls silent. A deep breath, stony voice. "Come home, Eva is dead."

At the funeral there were almost only adults. Friends of my parents who we hadn't seen for years, with their now grown-up children. They came over to me to tell me they didn't know what to say. Livia, an old friend of my father's, gave me a ceramic necklace she had made herself: a horrible, varnished medallion with jagged edges. She put it around my neck, whispering that when her brother died, she started wearing eccentric clothes and jewelry to hide her pain. She was the saddest woman in the world.

Eva's body was in the coffin, which was closed. My mother didn't want to see her. I, however, had seen her when it was still open, before the black car arrived to take her to the church. I had never seen a dead body before. They are swollen, artificial seeming, how I imagine one day androids will look. Her skin seemed synthetic, pulled over her bones like a latex mask. Her blond hair surrounded her marbly face like a halo. It hadn't been easy to find a priest who would conduct the ceremony for a suicide, but eventually we found one who was more open-minded in another neighborhood. This too was alienating. We traveled along unknown roads until we found ourselves in front of a threatening-looking church built in the sixties. The shops in that area were almost identical to the ones that filled our own neighborhood: they sold curtains, flowers, footwear, but the signs had different letters on them. There were supermarkets with names we'd never seen before, trees that weren't the plane trees I was used to. Everything conspired to give me the impression that the family who had gone to mourn that death was not mine. They were strangers. We, because I was there too, were strangers.

Like my sister's, my mother's appearance had also changed: she no longer looked like the woman we used to live with in the house on the ground floor in the well-to-do neighborhood. In my memory she was beautiful, with soft cheeks and a gap between her teeth, the same as my sister's, which peeked maliciously through her lips every time she opened her mouth. She was always on the hunt for rare teas; she cultivated a little vegetable plot on some communal land that she'd been given permission to use. Like my sister, she saved birds, mice, and bats from the claws of the crows that had invaded the city, devouring all the other flying creatures that lived there before. In the new house on the edge of the highway, everything that had once been a sign of her grace became an obsession. Before Eva, she nurtured a sweet, almost silly, attention to domestic details: the apartment was a constant work in progress because she could wake up in the morning and decide that one wall of the hallway needed to be painted ocean blue. She constructed lamps from recycled junk. On their own they were kitsch but, placed by my mother in the living room, they made it feel like a holiday house, one of those with sand between the couch cushions that nobody bothered to brush away, because being carefree makes control futile. She could sew and she made extraordinary costumes for Carnival on an old Singer machine, while my sister and I looked on, terrified that the needle might prick her; no, more than prick her, pierce her and then lacerate her until all that remained was a pile of bloody sludge, leaving us alone with our father who we didn't really know. Eva's deterioration made looking after the house my mother's cross to bear. She would buy tiny objects to confront the smallest daily challenges. In the bathroom she hung a squeegee for wiping away the droplets that left limescale on the plastic shower door. For every cup, a little colored peg indicating its rightful owner, a result of her recent germaphobia. She spread a plastic sheet over our only couch, which took up the whole living room. She still used the Singer, muttering that she needed to sew the curtains but, like a modern Penelope, she never finished them. However, unlike when we were children and the needle never pricked her, as Eva's illness developed, our mother's hand and foot became less and less coordinated, leaving her fingers covered in wounds that turned dark as they aged. So she started wearing white latex gloves, but the latex made the skin on her hands peel, and she developed eczema. Sometimes, overcome by a dark restlessness, she would call me to say she was sewing me some clothes, and when I went to see her for Christmas, she would make me put on these pasty, misshapen dresses. I would stand in front of the mirror and look at her as she smiled blindly, as if her eyes saw something that was concealed from mine, and told me that I looked lovely, that I was beautiful, and I didn't dare question her.

My father would later walk out, leaving her alone in those few square meters. I wouldn't blame him. He would meet a woman a few years younger than him and without any great passion they would get together and move to the North of Italy, where he would open up another travel agency, using funds from a regional pot to promote tourism. I would look gratefully at the future he had made for himself, however pathetic it was, because it showed me that, somewhere, there was a way out. Toward my mother, however, I experienced a burning repulsion, because her whole body told me there was no escape. She was fading by the day, dragging me with her and abandoning me at the same time.

As an adult I would understand that my mother's behavior was the only possible option for her, because, ultimately, the only thing she had made in her life was us. And my father's behavior was the only option for him, too, because he had never truly been part of the family, had always had one foot out of the door, ready to run as soon as things got bad. The blood of my female branch was infected, sick, and like a virus it would keep me tied to Eva, to my mother and her dead plants, and to the unhappy shadow of fate that I can't shake off.

My sister's corpse, in my memory, has a giant head like a marionette. When I saw her lying in the coffin surrounded by flowers from people who hadn't seen her in years, she wasn't her. My family is mildly Catholic; I have never believed in God. Yet, looking at that hollow body, I found it completely plausible that the concept of a soul had been invented, and that it was often called the breath of life. Because indeed, when living beings die, they lose a magical element, without which they are nothing but objects, things. My sister was now just a thing, and you can never really love things.

After my father says the words, the mountain each of us, like the family of Sisyphus, has been pushing the rock of the illness up is conquered. The rock that rolled down to the foot of the mountain every night has toppled over the crest and is now rolling down the other side, free, into the valley.

When my father puts the phone down, the sky is almost black. The bank of smoke is still suspended above me. The honking has dispersed; the birds have stopped singing. The videogame is paused where I left it. I pick up the cigarette butt from the ashtray. The sound of the lighter echoes around the empty apartment. I inhale. The tar envelops my chest. I feel the phalanges of my index and middle fingers being warmed by the red embers. I stub the cigarette in the ashtray. I have a few minutes left before the news settles like snow on my conscience. The world is still the same as it was before the call. There's time. I breathe, press play, and return to fighting for the kingdom that was once mine.

After the prizegiving in Naples, I grow increasingly tired and as winter arrives my energy abandons me completely. All I feel is excruciating emptiness, like a cyclone into the eye of which all remaining fragments of things I thought my own have been sucked. I can't fast anymore: my hips grow, my body swells. I still go to the supermarket and buy the gummy crocodiles with the foamy white bellies, but I'm no longer capable of throwing them in the trash. Instead, I gobble them down as fast as possible, not questioning their flavors, attempting to run away from the threat of the past me, who I want back and, at the same time, am terrified of. Not even Olivia Benson gives me comfort: suddenly her botox injections, increasingly apparent with every new episode, sadden me. I feel betrayed, like a child whose beautiful mother comes home one day having altered her features.

I open Instagram and scroll through the faces of girls who look like adults—made-up, sparkling, skinny—until Gloria's talking image appears on the screen. When I turn up the volume, I hear that she's using my voice, my words, my inflection, my phrases, as her large hands move around in the air.

Since the speech at the ceremony in Naples, Gloria has begun to consume me, because I allowed her to, and now I am nothing. Taking possession of my body, she has lost more weight and now hers is slim and austere. She has seized my reference points without knowing their history. Her borders are growing stronger thanks to my bricks, which she extracts, one by one, from my boundary wall, leaving me crumbling. I often think back to Valentina's words and regret having ignored them: Gloria is using me to fill herself up, until a mask with my features appears in place of her face, and nothing of me will be left. My poems, my memories, and my pain will all look better on her, because she is lucky, luminous, rich.

And yet I feel good when I see her in the flesh. Gloria is good. Gloria is affectionate, she wants me by her side, she oozes respect and gratitude. Sometimes I catch her reading a book she saw me flicking through weeks earlier, or gazing dreamily at me while I'm drinking my coffee. When I'm with her it feels like I too am cloaked in the bright shadow that she has cast since birth. As soon as I get home, though, her figure turns gloomy and parasitic. Once again, I can't but talk ill of her to whoever happens to be around. Like my colleagues at the Galeone, even Angela, usually so reliable, has started to come up with excuses whenever I start gossiping about Gloria, running up to the cash register to pay and disappear. My resentment embarrasses them. I know it, but I can't stop. I can sense their unease growing at the intensification of my friendship with the flesh-and-blood Gloria, who I spend the majority of my time with.

The only thing that placates my anxiety is fantasizing about the death of all of Gloria's family. I imagine them in a car when a bolt of lightning hits the street, opening up a gash in the asphalt, their car sinking down into the abyss. Or—a more elegant scenario—it comes out that the family has been evading tax for decades. The fiscal police arrive, word spreads, they fall into ruin, and become pariahs. The economic and social breakdown crushes them, to the point that Gloria's little sister gets sick and dies. I come up with other variations on the theme, but the substance is more or less the same: death, humiliation, disgrace. The real Gloria, in the meantime, sends me little brown paper bags of medicine when I'm sick, bakes cakes and brings them to my house, and buys me an identical extra of everything she buys herself, which I never accept.

When Gloria and I land in Paris, the city is sealed in a glass bubble, like a snow globe full of water. The video of Gloria reading my speech at the prizegiving went viral and now it is not only brands who call her, but also cultural institutes. In Paris she is taking part in a conference at the Italian Cultural Institute with the director, a linguist, an editor, and a few other influencers. The theme: the language of young people on social media.

We stay in a studio apartment behind Place des Vosges owned by Gloria's mother's partner. Inside, it looks like the interior of a boat, each piece of furniture slotted next to its neighbor in a celebration of millimetric perfection. "He doesn't rent it out," she explains, "because he likes the idea of always having a refuge available. Have you ever been to Paris? If you want, we can go for a walk before we go to the Institute," she says, putting her suitcases under the folding table.

"I used to live here," I announce, enjoying her astounded expression. I like to keep some things to myself so that at least a few shreds of my life are shielded from her greed.

We go out, walking between the metal-ring-bordered flower beds of the gardens and into Rue des Francs Bourgeois, where luxury boutiques are nestled into cloyingly pretty buildings. Gloria doesn't speak, but every so often I see her breathe in the cold air deeply, as if to tame an annoying thought.

She seems distracted. I have a feeling that her unhappiness is my fault. Being near me has made her wither, like a piece of fruit infected by the mold of its neighbor.

"Did you know sighing is vital to your existence? It stops your alveoli from closing up, permitting the exchange of oxygen and carbon dioxide. There's a bunch of neurons in your encephalic trunk that program each sigh. Just think, the first patients who used an iron lung died because nobody understood the importance of sighing."

Gloria gives me a lazy smile before returning to her thoughts. The Pompidou Center rises ahead of us. In the square in front of it, Parisians lay on the cobblestones soaking up the shy winter sun. We head up the stairs inside the transparent shell. The people beneath us become smaller and smaller until they are just colorful dots. We buy a ticket and go into the half-empty rooms.

Gloria wanders around like a ghost, her gaze passing through the paintings without seeing them. Every so often, when I lose sight of her for a number of minutes that feels excessive, I discreetly go in search of her. When I find her, I pause and observe her from behind until the moment I sense she's about to turn around, then I vanish. Her wall of sadness is impenetrable, but within it I know she is magnificent; I want to reach out and touch her. We find ourselves in front of Klein's blue tree, which pulls us into a flow of thoughts that neither recognize as our own.

To get Gloria's attention I tell her about the time I contacted the son of the chemist who worked with Yves Klein and had a studio in Montmartre, to obtain a tin of the artist's blue paint. I'd tried to paint it onto a canvas, but that enchanted color is not like others: the exceptionality of it is dependent on the pure pigments remaining entrapped in a resinous glue that will destroy any paint brush. After many attempts I managed to produce a scruffy blue canvas to give to Filippo when we left Paris so that we would always have a piece of it with us. Filippo pretended to be pleased, but as we got to know each other better he explained that he was embarrassed to put it up because it reminded him of a Klimt print from Ikea that he had in his room when he was a pretentious and broke college student. The painting had ended up in the basement and got damaged by the humidity. At some point I threw it out, relieved to be liberated from the tangible evidence of my naivety.

"If you still had it, I would hang it in my house. It's the most romantic present I've ever heard of," Gloria says, and for a moment her features light up, before dimming once again.

When we get back to the apartment, the sky has darkened and the sidewalk is starting to shimmer in the rain.

"I have a surprise for you," Gloria says, pulling a tote bag out of her suitcase. I open it, and inside there is a black dress with forest green cut-outs. She pulls out another one that is identical but with yellow rather than green.

"Verle, a sustainable brand, asked me if I wanted to choose something from their new collection. I said yes, as long as I could have something for you too."

I try on the dress in the microscopic bathroom. It's clingy, hugs my thighs and shortens my neck.

I tug at the fabric to pull it away from my body, I can't breathe. I don't want to ruin Gloria's parenthetical good mood, so I come out of the bathroom with a fake smile that collapses as soon as I look at her. She looks amazing: her neck grows, candid, out of the fabric, so slim I want to squeeze it until my fingerprints are impressed on her skin; her legs are like stems on shining heels. I don't rebel, not even when she runs a treacly lipstick along her lips and tells me the car is waiting outside.

"You look great," she says radiantly, turning for a moment to look at me as we descend the stairs. In the car she hums a melody I can't follow. We get out on Rue Varenne, by the entrance to a neo-classical building. The cold air cuts my face, making my eyes water. We are escorted into a room with frescoed ceilings, which opens onto a dark garden. We sit at a table that takes up the whole room, waiting for the event to start. Next to us, in order, are: two YouTubers who started a production house as soon as they crossed the threshold that highlights the age difference between adolescent stars and their pre-adolescent audience; the Italian linguist, who is talking about how linguistic departments in France are made up almost entirely of Italians; and an independent publisher who specializes in French texts in translation. At the head of the table is the director of the institute: a plump woman with a silvered braid wrapped around her head.

"Come to the bathroom with me," Gloria whispers.

I hold her bag while she pees. When she comes out, she looks at herself in the brown speckled mirror.

"Pass me my phone."

I pass it to her, and she pulls me toward her, poses, and starts taking pictures. Her lips protrude in the shape of a kiss. I look bewildered, the faint light hitting me from above, throwing the shadow of my hair over my face. The caption reads, "Sisters."

I let Gloria go back to the table while I inspect my reflection.

My phone is vibrating like crazy with notifications from people who are now following me by virtue of my physical proximity to Gloria. I lift my eyes to the mirror. The girl who looks back at me through the opaque glass doesn't exist.

When I get back to the table, Gloria is confidently talking to the editor and the linguist in an unusually high-pitched voice. We can hear the buzz of the audience taking their seats through the wall that separates us from the room where the panel will take place. The director clears her throat: "Before we start, we're just waiting for our last guest. As I wrote in this morning's email, it will no longer be Anastasia Locci, since she had to cancel at the last minute, so we hope that won't be a problem for you."

The director has not yet finished giving her excuses when her braid-wrapped head turns toward the door to witness the entrance of an imposing figure. The majestic body of the new arrival leaves enraptured murmurs in its wake. It advances clumsily, as if there are springs attached to the soles of its feet.

It's Lavinia, but she looks nothing like the girl I saw at the party under the streetlight six months before; nor does she look like the child from her YouTube videos. The body that once concealed her spirit seems imbued with a new awareness, as if two warring factions have finally declared a truce after a millennia-long conflict. She's wearing a lilac blazer and soft pants with hems that swish over a pair of sneakers. She sits down at the table, apologizing for her lateness, aware of the effect she has produced: everybody there is hypnotized by her.

Gloria's bony hand squeezes my thigh with a surprising force.

"Why is she here? What email is she talking about? Why didn't you say anything?" she whispers in my ear.

An email flashes through my mind that I received this morning at the airport: I opened it quickly before going through security and didn't read it, then forgot about it. I don't respond. I turn to Lavinia: "So nice to see you again; you look amazing."

She smiles at me, revealing two dimples.

The director escorts us into the room full of young girls. On our arrival their excitement explodes like champagne into minuscule bubbles.

I go and sit at the back while the guests get seated on the stage. The director opens the conversation. The speakers' words unravel in the dense air that fogs up the windows. Gloria is wearing an Apple watch on which my suggestions for the discussion will appear. I'm sweating even though it isn't hot. My dress is sticking to my itchy thighs, which are glued to the wooden seat. There's a buzzing in my ears, my throat is closing up, and my fingertips are skating uselessly over the phone screen. Gloria keeps glancing nervously over at me. As I try to concentrate, the phone falls onto the floor. The sound of cracked glass. It's broken. I raise the phone in the air to signal the problem, but Gloria doesn't understand. She's furious, and I am furious too. I stand up and make my way through the crowd of girls. I look at Gloria one last time with a hint of malice. She lifts her chin to see where I'm going, and conceals her dismay with a rigid smile. I go outside and breathe in the cold air. I feel a tingling in my chest for my newfound freedom.

The sound of my footsteps follows me to the Panthéon and along the picture-perfect Rue Mouffetard. I get to Café Léa and turn down into the underpass where a homeless guy once showed me his soft, dark penis. I come back up to the surface on Boulevard de Port-Royal and stop at number 26. The red brick building is modern and elegant. I still remember the entrance code: 2317A. A warm light shines from the top floor, the same light I had seen years earlier and became my North Star: something to guide me in leaving everything behind and being reborn in the gleaming skin of a person with no past.

Six or seven years ago, if someone had asked me what the most depressing city in the world was, I'd have said Paris. I was living there.

I am twenty-one, Paris is cold and stinks of urine, and Eva has stopped being Eva. I change neighborhood after three months because, in the affordable suburban area I had initially chosen, two people had been attacked in the course of twenty days. I put my things back in my suitcase—which I hadn't finished unpacking yet anyway, because having it open next to the bed gave me the sense that my situation was temporary—and pay an exorbitant price to share the garret of a noble, elevatorless building in a more central area with a girl named Nadia from Calabria. Nadia has sequin-covered handbags and thick black hair. She got the bigger room in the garret because she'd been to see the place with her parents: her father a security guard and her mother a stationer. Her father is aggressive and drinks a lot; her mother has grayish skin, and when her father drinks he sometimes hurts her, I discover later, when our relationship has solidified.

At the beginning, I find Nadia repulsive: she speaks in dialect, writes sloppily, has no sense of style and isn't ashamed of any of these things, despite being in Paris. I spend the first two weeks studying the shabby chic style of my French counterparts and scouring thrift shops for a uniform that will make me look graceful like them and different from myself. To pay for these vintage store sprees I work in a Sicilian restaurant behind the Champs-Élysées. My parents gave me five thousand euros to start life in France: money that was languishing in a bank account my grandmother opened when I was born and added to for a few years, which was then forgotten when she died. I won a scholarship that covers a third of the rent, and my parents have no other money to give.

Nadia on the other hand, despite her family's modest background, is fully funded.

The psychobiology course I have enrolled on triggers such deep disinterest that I am cast into the throes of desperation. In theory, the subject is fascinating: the infallible logic of the mind's biological mechanisms fills the pages of books with brain teaser-like riddles and solutions. In practice, it is drowning in aseptic rooms where the brains of chicks and mice are cut into veil-thin strips, then inserted into machines that measure the changes elicited by markers injected before the animal's death. The professors lie about the numbers, lie about the statistics, and revisit their own data to try and make it adhere to their hypotheses, despite the fact that this theoretically invalidates any results obtained. My lab colleagues nervously roam the corridors. I haven't made friends with anyone on my course. Each time I've tried, I've ended up hunched over a flat beer with a sense of emptiness stinging my throat.

I have started running. I bought some brightly colored discounted Asics, and in the mornings I leave the house in the cold and bright or damp and gloomy air and crank up the steps until I get to the bank of the Seine, where I start to run against the flow of dog walkers. I don't run much at the beginning; run and walk, walk and stop. As time passes, I run for longer and longer, until the day I understand why people run: after six or seven kilometers, after my body has sent me all the signals available to tell me to stop, I no longer feel anything. Breathing becomes easy, my legs have no nerves or muscles, my head is empty, I no longer exist. I run farther and more often, until one day I strain my Achilles.

Forced to stay home, I get into bed promptly at ten o' clock each evening but don't sleep until four in the morning. Through the university health service, I see a psychiatrist who prescribes me a sleeping pill. I fall asleep immediately when I take it but wake up at five in the morning with an anvil on my chest and the taste of rust in my mouth. The only moments of relief are my fantasies of throwing myself into the Seine. I run along the bank in a straight line, then deviate decisively to the left, still running, until my right foot plunges through the air and into the water. I am embraced by the waves flooding my lungs. When I imagine it, I feel my chest cavity freeze, as if my organs were sponges, and an imaginary relief spreads from my toes to the tips of my hair.

Before Paris, I thought suicide was a violent, energetic, desperate act. In Paris, suicide is slow and sugary, like a stick of licorice to softly suck on. One day I recount these dreams to Nadia, who, unlike me, goes out drinking with her new girl friends and makes out with Turkish boys from her course. Even though I've only treated her with disdain, Nadia can't wait to help me, finally appointed to the role she has always dreamed of: mother hen.

"Let's call your parents."

"I can't call them."

"Why not?"

"Because I left precisely so that I wouldn't have to call them. It wouldn't help anyway; they have other stuff to worry about."

Nadia goes with me to a new psychiatrist who prescribes me another drug. It's a mood stabilizer that makes my fingers tingle and prevents my taste buds from perceiving carbon dioxide in drinks. It also takes away my appetite and desire to drink alcohol. After a couple of months, I start to feel better. I sleep easier at night; the waves of the Seine disappear from my fantasies. When Nadia drops a packet of cous-cous on the floor, I offer to clean it up while wondering whether moving out wouldn't be preferable to picking up all those grains. I find it funny if Nadia comes into pee when I'm in the shower. We share hairbrushes and sometimes I wear her T-shirts. Nadia takes me out, and I start to see her with different eyes: when she goes out with boys, she wears loads of make-up, sparkly heels, and a corset that squeezes her abundant curves. Every gesture is studied, every word carefully considered. When we get home, she removes her make-up, takes off her heels and puts on a fluffy giraffe onesie. Like an actor changing out of her costume, she can finally be herself again.

She receives packages from her mother that contain vacuum-sealed cutlets and delicious oils, and each time she opens one she unfolds the little table, gets two chairs, and makes me sit down opposite her. I am surprised to find myself envious: it occurs to me that Nadia never feels alone: her whole family is there with her when she cuts the edge of one of those pressurized packets and lets it sigh open. As she heats up what she has received, she tells me about the men she talked to last night or tonight and advises me on how to find one for myself.

"Men," she says, "are all the same. They don't look it on the surface, but deep down they're all the same. To get them to stay with you, you have to make them comfortable, but to get them to choose you, you have to make them uncomfortable. Once they've chosen you, you must never let them see you without make-up, not even in the morning, and you must never have sex on a first date."

Even though we're the same age, Nadia says these things with the air of someone who has been in the game for a long time: she talks about flirting like an eighty-year-old presenting her history of romantic liaisons. As the days pass, I understand that this is partly true, because her wisdom comes from the stories of her mother, her two grandmothers, and her older, married cousins.

Years later, on a trip with Filippo, we'd make a stopover at Jeddah. The airport is a single squalid room, and as the men file silently through the metal detector, the women go into a black tent. As soon as I stepped over the threshold I was greeted by a silvery bustle, like a hive of metal bees, women reproaching me, touching me, sneering at my too-small breasts. They laughed at me, and yet we were accomplices, equal in the ontological condition that united us all: being women and knowing things that men will never know. In Jeddah I would remember the complicity with which Nadia had shared her vision of the world with me, recognizing me as a sister in the name of that unwritten code that united us, a thousand-year-old testament that would keep me safe from the things I'd otherwise be vulnerable to.

What makes women feel like sisters today, now that the shared intimacy of dressing up as something we're not no longer exists, I would wonder in that dark tent, with those women whose faces only I was allowed to see.

The day I meet Filippo in Paris is the Friday of Carnival week in February. The department has organized a party at the home of a professor. My mood is more docile, and I feel ready for my debut with my course mates. Nadia helps me get dressed and does my make-up, she even lends me her straighteners.

"Stay here, I'll be right back," she says when her work is finished.

I wait, sitting on the edge of the bed, encased in tight jeans and a stripy crop top. Nadia has put foundation on my face, painted on my cheekbones with a little ochre sponge, and drawn midnight-blue eyeliner along my eyelids to make them look longer. When she comes back, she's holding a packet of cat's eye contact lenses.

"I got these for you. They're a gift; you'll look amazing in them."

"Come on, Nadia, I don't even know how to put them in, I'll look ridiculous."

"But it's Carnival! I bet everyone else is going to have at least one accessory. And contact lenses are so much cooler than cat tails or ears." She starts fiddling with the lenses, which slide all over the place.

When I look in the mirror, I see my reflection covered in make-up, my watering eyes. "I look like a clown."

"No, you don't, you look beautiful. Now go out and make friends with someone, I implore you."

I take a coffin-like elevator to get to the host's apartment and, looking in the mirror, notice that the contact lenses have moved from their original position. Now the vertical feline slit is horizontal, and I look like a goat. I put my finger in my eyes and try to reposition them, but after a few seconds they slip sideways again.

The door is open onto the hallway, and I hear dense chatter over the backdrop of insipid jazz music. The mixed languages of the guests are interwoven with the melancholic sound of a trumpet flowing out of speakers on either side of a fireplace. Nadia was right: everyone's wearing something carnival themed. I feel like I'm being looked at with some insistence and try to go unobserved by standing against the wall. I spot the table with the wine deep inside one of the two rooms and instruct myself to walk over to it as soon as the time spent standing next to the wall gets too long and reveals my unease. The table is covered in cheese and bread, but I have never eaten in public and won't start now. Some of the professors are sitting on couches, others come and go from the kitchen. Not all of their faces are familiar, so I conclude there must be some members of other departments here too. They are mostly young, and some of them are Italian, recognizable from their unmelodious French.

"We never seen you in class," Deema reproaches me as soon as I unstick myself from the wall. She is one of the people on my course who I had tried to go out with in the first weeks of term, an English girl with Palestinian heritage, curls hair-sprayed to her forehead and pointy, beak-like lips. She's sexy. "Where have you been?" she continues as I try to stay focused on pouring myself some wine.

"I work a lot and I haven't felt great lately. I hope to attend class more often from now on."

"More often sounds better than never," she says. I smile because I don't know what else to do. Deema disappears and I remain next to the table, making sure to look busy to a distracted eye.

Soon enough my only activity is pouring myself wine. On my fourth glass I feel my muscles melt and my head become soft. The voices and the music continue to merge, and every so often someone comes over and asks me questions that I answer without paying much attention: "Where have you been? Are you still attending class? Are you O.K.? We never see you at Friday drinks."

My judgment was wrong: the table is not the right place. I pour one last glass and practically run into the kitchen. When I get there I feel a coolness on my chest and realize I'm covered in red wine. Warily, I raise my eyes and find myself in front of a stripy red and white shirt. From the neckline appears a neck, and from the neck appears, naturally, a head.

The man's expression is as astonished as mine; green eyes, round gold-rimmed glasses. He has no chin; his shoulders are narrow and hips wide.

"*Desolé*," he says in an Italian accent, looking too insistently at the wine stain on my stripy top.

"Don't worry, it's my fault. I wasn't looking."

"I noticed. What is there that's so interesting in the kitchen?"

"What isn't there," I respond. "There are no people."

"There's me."

"You weren't expected."

We both look down, his eyes still drawn to the stain. I like it. I'm not used to such brazen desire. I look at him, perplexed, and he smiles.

"Come on, let me into the kitchen," I say.

"Can I join you?"

"But weren't you just leaving?"

"I was only leaving because you hadn't arrived yet."

I laugh.

He moves a few centimeters to one side, and I slip past. I am warmed by the radiation coming off my body.

I move around the table and sit on the sideboard. He stares at me from the other side of the room. I avoid his gaze; his desire is turning me on and it's making me uncomfortable. My experiences with men reside solely in adolescence, where everybody wants but no one desires. As I savor the tension, I can almost see myself through the eyes of the man in the stripy shirt: sensual like I've never been before, ankles crossed, a few centimeters off the floor, the fabric of my top transparent from the wine, and my lips encrusted in red. Every inch of my body is tense. He moves closer and finally I look at him. He has sweet, concealing eyes. They contain the ironic spark of someone who has already seen the script.

"What are you studying?"

"Psychobiology."

"A scientist," he lights up. "Do you like it?"

I don't respond right away. I feel myself wanting, for the first time in my life, to answer the question based on the asker's expectations. As if I have captured the idea this man has of me, and I can choose to embroider his projection or unpick it one stitch at a time until the real me is revealed.

"I love it," I say. "Right now, I'm working with genetic markers on mice."

I am learning to seduce in Nadia's way, even if I don't realize it yet: I am contorting myself into what a man wants.

I have never felt so powerful; I have never been less so.

The man lives in an apartment on the sixth and top floor of 26 Boulevard de Port-Royal. By Parisian standards the place is enormous: eighty square meters, windows everywhere, even a bidet in the bathroom. On the walls, however, there are no pictures, no bookcases, nothing that could be attributed to the personality of its inhabitant, except for a pile of books on the floor with an e-reader on the top.

He pours me yet another glass of wine. My head is spinning, I would like to lie down on the couch, but I don't want to seem like a child who can't handle her alcohol.

"There's nothing in this apartment."

"Things are useless. When you teach you are always moving from one university to another, and it doesn't make sense to accumulate stuff. People are obsessed with things; they think that if they have enough stuff their life will be more stable. But no life is stable, and admitting that is a sign of strength."

I am enchanted by those words. My garret is bare too, but my emptiness has always embarrassed me, like it was an admission of poverty. Those words give me new strength: a justification that legitimates who I am. The man is smiling at me, tenderly, I think.

"It looks like you've lost a contact lens."

I cover my eyes with my hands; I'm embarrassed.

"I'll go check." I head to look for a mirror, but he grabs my arm.

"Don't go, it doesn't matter: you look funny."

I don't want to look funny.

He moves forward on the chair, takes my chin between the thumb and index finger of his right hand, and kisses me. I feel his wine-coarsened tongue wander into my mouth, and I close my eyes. He bites me a few times and I don't like it, but I don't say anything. He leads me over to the leather couch, where he makes me sit on his lap. He grabs my thighs and continues kissing me. I can feel him swelling under his linen pants and I rub myself on it.

"How many professors have you fucked before?" he whispers in my ear. I have to stifle a laugh. I've hardly done it with anyone my own age, let alone professors. But he is eager for me to participate in his fantasy.

"I'm not telling you," I whisper back, his hair tickles my lips. He lifts me up and puts me down on the couch, pulls off my jeans and burrows his head between my legs. Then he grasps at my panties.

When they are down at my knees, I start. I'm on my period. I completely forgot. Now what happens? I don't want him to be grossed out; I felt so perfect in his eyes.

"Wait, I have to go to the bathroom."

"Are you crazy?"

"No, seriously, I forgot something."

"What have you forgotten?"

"I can't tell you."

"You never tell. If you don't tell me, you can't go to the bathroom."

I look up at the ceiling to hold in the burgeoning tears while he dives down between my legs again. As I stare at the ceiling, I feel a scratching movement and a familiar friction: he has pulled out my tampon, tossed it to the other side of the room, and is now licking me like it was nothing.

Is this what men are like, then? So different from boys my age, so experienced? Or does he love women so much he isn't disgusted by having blood all over his face, on his tongue, in his beard? I yield to his actions and let out a few groans that I hope are believable. Then he turns me over on the couch and penetrates me from behind.

"You're on the pill, right?" he grunts.

"Of course," I lie.

When he comes, one hand around my neck, I pretend to come at the same time.

He collapses, his eyes closed and legs spread wide on the warm, sweaty cushions while I make myself tiny at the empty end of the couch. Then, without a word, he drags himself into another room, looking drunker than before. When he doesn't come back, I go and peek into the bedroom and find him splayed out like a star fish, his breath puffing out of a gurgling stomach. I crouch next to his body, in the alcove left open under his arm. I observe him for a few minutes, and wait for my heartbeat to slow.

"What's your name?" I whisper in the dark.

"Filippo," he mumbles. And in that name, I am sure, my future resides.

Gloria is white as a sheet when she lets me into the apartment. Without speaking, she goes and lies on the futon on the mezzanine. On the journey from Port-Royal to Place des Vosges I prepared a speech to explain my disappearance: broken phone, Paris awakening certain memories. I am saddened by how little interest she shows in the reasons for my disappearance: she only cares about me when something unexpected happens, when I can be of service to her; as soon as circumstances change, she returns to being absorbed in her own world. She treats me like she treats Sara, like she treats her fans.

I grab a book and join her on the mezzanine and, instead of lying down next to her, I sit with my back to the wall ostentatiously turning the pages.

"What are you reading?" she asks, eventually.

"A story."

"What is it about?"

"A man who makes a plain-looking waitress fall in love with him when he just wants someone to fuck."

"Will you read it to me?"

I read out loud, raising the pitch of my voice when it's the waitress talking and lowering it when the narrator is the man. At the end of the story, Gloria squints her eyes at the ceiling.

"Do you think I could ever be a waitress?"

"I'd say it's probably best you stick with what you're doing."

"What is it that I'm doing?"

I venture: "Publicity? You've also written a book of poems. You've acted. You earn good money."

"Yeah, but I've only been asked to do all these things because I'm famous."

"Does it matter?"

"To me, yes, I think so." Neither of us speaks for a few minutes. "Sometimes, when I close my eyes before going to sleep, this strange angst creeps up on me. So, I turn on the light to try and shoo it away, but when I see my room with the posters from my fans, the gifts, the plushies—I mean, when I see the objects around me—they don't feel like mine. It's as if I didn't choose them; as if, at some point in my life, someone or something picked me up and put me in that room, and I have lived in it for all these years as if it were mine, forgetting what the one before was like."

After the conference, where she had managed to come up

with reasonable answers even without my help, she let girls take selfies with her and hid her impatience. The thing that really bothered her, though, was that Lavinia hadn't done the same thing. There was no trace of her. When the crowd started to flow out, Gloria went to the bathrooms to see if she was there, but the mirror reflected only her own image.

In the end, she went out into the garden and crouched down under the windows. The grass was wet and the hedges shone in the moonlight. After a while, she thought she saw a tiny spot of light moving around slowly in the dark. It was the ember of a cigarette. She crossed the distance between herself and the spot, hardly noticing her heels sinking into the wet earth, and found herself in front of Lavinia.

"I've been looking for you," Gloria said.

"And I've been waiting for you," Lavinia smirked.

They both looked down nervously. Lavinia crushed the cigarette filter under her shoe and lit another one.

"You didn't spend any time with the fans," Gloria pointed out.

"I don't need to."

Silence.

"It wasn't that bad," Gloria said, falteringly.

"I don't give a fuck. I just happened to be in Paris and they offered me some money to take part. I thought this shit seemed better than what we usually do, even if it pays less."

Gloria started. She hadn't been paid, she thought it was vulgar to ask for money from a cultural institution.

"What happened to you?" she asked, surprised by Lavinia's arrogance.

"What could have happened to you, but luckily happened to me."

Lavinia's face turned to wax. Then she started speaking as if reciting a part she'd been rehearsing for months. Her tone was measured but betrayed a certain pompousness when she emphasized certain words. She barely moved, as if her whole body was trying to separate itself from the words coming out of her mouth.

A year before, she had started chatting with Stefano, a friend of Giulio's who also had a Twitch channel. He wasn't good-looking—he had small eyes and a mousey face—but he was doing well at that time and emanated a mysterious, masculine aura. Lavinia had been chatting with Stefano for some time when he asked her out for a drink. She showed up at 10 P.M. on the dot, but as well as Stefano she found Giulio and a third guy, Davide. The three of them chatted as if Lavinia wasn't there. Feeling uneasy, she told herself she'd have one drink and then go. When she patted her pockets to make sure she wasn't leaving anything at the three guys' table, Stefano looked surprised and asked her to stay for another drink, disclosing that he had some pills he'd stolen from his mom. Lavinia accepted and he crushed two yellowish tablets into her gin and tonic, doing the same into his own glass. Giulio and Davide refused the offer, but they grew increasingly interested in Lavinia who, within a few minutes, started to relax and talk. She was having fun, she even suggested going to a club, and when they proposed going to smoke a joint at Davide's instead, she enthusiastically consented. That was when her memory started to cloud over. She remembered getting into Giulio's car because she had kicked a plastic water bottle that was rolling around on the floor. She remembered kissing Stefano, or at least she thought it was him. She had some images in her head of Davide's place—a shoe box—empty beer cans piled up one on top of the other and a screen on the wall where a DJ was playing in a desert, with no one around. The other vague recollections had come back to her over time in the form of dreams and flashbacks. They were sensorial footprints: the smell of beer and cigarette butts, a hand pressing on her neck, a pillow that smelled of stale smoke being pushed into her lips.

What was very clear, though, was that, in the morning, she woke up naked on the couch. She looked around, saw cushions on the floor, but felt nothing. She got up, gathered her clothes and went home. A few hours later she got a message from Stefano, who wrote that he'd had a lot of fun and that they should do it again soon. She replied with laughing emojis and clung to the clump of confusion that was nesting inside her. The subsequent days and weeks passed by in a thick fog, and she couldn't say what exactly she'd been doing. She certainly slept a lot, waking up many times over the course of a night. She argued furiously with her mother, a woman who lived her life in compliance and tiptoed around the house like a thief. She understood nothing of her daughter, and she'd never tried to. She only knew that she was able get hold of enough money for her to buy herself whatever she wanted.

Lavinia started taking Ativan and filming herself in her room so that, in her flashes of lucidity, she could watch back what she said when she was high. Each time one of the three guys appeared in her feed it made her jump and her lungs contracted, so she stopped following them and things got a bit better.

Then, a couple of months after that night, when the episode seemed so well insulated in the flow of her daily life that it had taken on the form of a silent embolus, the photos came out. They showed her nude on top of Giulio, and lying across Davide and Stefano. They had begun to circulate on some private Telegram groups, and eventually made their way to her from some fake Instagram accounts. She tried writing to all three of them on WhatsApp but got no reply. Then she tried on Instagram, but they had blocked her, and when she tried to call them, she learned they'd blocked her phone too. She would have kept trying if she hadn't been inundated by an avalanche of hateful messages just hours after the photos were posted. She was used to receiving comments that were far from flattering, but she had never experienced the effect that the virtual masses can produce on an individual. They were writing to her everywhere: on WhatsApp, Instagram, TikTok, Facebook; they searched for her on Telegram; they wrote to her mother, some boy who lived in her neighborhood even staked out beneath her apartment. The worst, however, were Gloria's fans. The fact that Lavinia had seemingly stolen the boyfriend of her goody two-shoes counterpart would never be forgiven. Men writing her filth was nothing new: she had never nurtured high expectations with regards to the male gender. It was the girls who she was hurt by. She felt betrayed and misunderstood, but that wasn't all: she perceived, even if she didn't fully understand it, that in this context, it was the girls, not the boys who truly held the power to expel her from her position in the social hierarchy.

She looked at the photos until she felt sick, and on some nights she fantasized about the possibility that the girl wasn't her, but a doppelgänger. She stared at the images on the screen and when she thought for a moment that she couldn't see her tattoos, she almost cheered, ready to proclaim to the world that the girl in the photos wasn't her. But, right on time, her tattoos jumped out, and a flame in her stomach burned all that was left of her.

The brands had stopped calling, spooked by the sex scandal she'd been struck by. Her mother continued to ask her for money to buy herself trash, and the servile, pathetic way in which she did it made Lavinia despise her more than ever before.

Swallowing her fears and a few Ativan, Lavinia went to the party in the post-industrial pavilion to confront Giulio, Davide, and Stefano, but they were nowhere to be seen. And yet, that was when everything changed. In the taxi Gloria paid for, after being degraded by the group of girls who had followed her out of the club, Lavinia received the photos of herself from the thousandth stranger, trying to make God knows what point, and Lavinia realized what she needed to do. She went home and set up an account on Onlyfans, a platform where you post content—photos, videos, articles—and people pay a monthly subscription to see what you post. She took some photos of herself in provocative poses, sometimes showing her nipples, sometimes her ass. She linked her Onlyfans account to her Instagram, with its two million two hundred thousand followers, and almost immediately got twenty thousand subscriptions, each of whom would pay ten euros a month to have access to her body. She had never made this much money in her life. And that wasn't all: her community on Onlyfans was kind. The men bought her things from her Amazon wish list, they wrote her declarations of love, and sometimes they told her they felt sorry for her and what had happened with the photos. There, men loved her, and she started to feel a closeness to them.

"I'm freer than I've ever been before. And in a few months, once I've earned the amount I need, I'll be even freer," she told Gloria as she pulled a leaf from the bush next to her and started deboning it. "You think you're free but you're not," she went on, "you think the money you earn makes you free, but it actually chains you down. You're forced to say things you don't believe, things written by other people; you've had to give up on producing your own thoughts. That's the only way you can function. I've never been as good at it as you are, but I know it's just as hard for you as everyone else."

Gloria muttered a few unrelated sentences about bending to the male gaze and selling your body, and Lavinia exploded in nasty, twisted laughter.

"My body and your body have always been for sale. There is no 'male gaze,' the men are not the problem. The problem is that we are locked in a box, all of us, all the people you know. We see only what they want us to see; we say only predictable things; we obsessively look at ourselves through the eyes of the audience we have in our heads. We no longer live inside ourselves, we observe from the outside, thinking about what our spectators would most like to see or hear."

She let the leaf confetti fall to the floor and started off toward the doors without saying goodbye. Halfway across the garden she turned back to Gloria.

"Thank you for what you did at that shithole party. When

you looked at me with that air of superiority, all spruced up in the hope of seeing Giulio, a lot of things suddenly made sense."

Then she wandered into the empty room and Gloria remained on the grass, still.

The light in the mezzanine is dim; every so often it seems to quiver like a candle, but maybe it's just me. Gloria looks close to tears.

"What have I done in all these years?" her voice shakes.

"Loads of stuff, you can afford a life that most people your age can only dream of," I respond with little conviction.

"But I don't feel like I chose it. I feel trapped. And what if one day I don't feel like doing this anymore? I'm not good at anything, I haven't experienced anything."

"You're still young, nothing you're doing now is set in stone." This I do believe.

"Maia, you don't understand," she says, shaking out her mane of red hair.

"What don't I understand?"

"There's nothing, in here," she murmurs bringing a hand to her sternum. Then she grabs my wrist and lays my palm over hers, closing it into a fist and knocking my knuckles on the bones. "Do you hear that? I'm empty, all empty," her voice is so low it could be a thought.

Eva is leaning into the mirror. With the index finger of her left hand, she pulls her eye toward her temple, and with her right, she draws a perfect streak of eyeliner along the edge of her eyelid. Then she dabs her lips with an orangey red lipstick and joins them together to produce a suction sound. Finally, she pushes herself forward slightly, moving her weight onto her bare toes to then rock back on her heels in an elegant, almost imperceptible oscillation. She winks at her own reflection and goes out of the bathroom, leaving the light on.

She's wearing jeans that belong to me and an aqua green

hoodie. At dinner she asks permission to go to a party outside the city and sleep there, swearing it's a friend's birthday at her house in the countryside.

"O.K. then," my mother responds, "as long as Maia comes with you."

I protest, I don't want to spend the night with a bunch of fifteen-year-olds, but a flash in my mother's gray eyes confirms that I have no choice. After dinner, Eva takes me into her room, makes me sit on the bed, and explains the situation.

"So, it is a party in the countryside, but it isn't Valeria's birthday. It's organized by some friends of friends. You can come if you want." A hopeful expression appears on her face.

"Don't worry, I have zero intention of coming."

Eva's face darkens, and whatever appeared a moment ago quickly disappears again.

"Lend me your jeans and your red top and I won't tell mom you're not coming."

"No. You can borrow the jeans, but you don't touch the top, and I won't tell mom that it's not Valeria's birthday."

She looks at me for a couple of seconds, as if gauging whether there's room to negotiate. There isn't. She swiftly turns around, the whip of her blonde hair generating a gust of air that brushes my cheek.

I reluctantly call Caterina, the only friend I know well enough to ask to sleep over.

Before we go out, my mother takes me to one side and gives me twenty euros: "In case of emergency. Be careful, please, and text me before you go to sleep."

I get in the car followed by Eva, who opens the passenger mirror and with her eyes reduced to slits examines her face as if trying to catch sight of a defect. I drive to where she's meeting Valeria, who is just as dressed up and waves her hands at me joyfully.

"Don't make me regret covering for you," I tell them, bloating with magnanimity.

Then I say goodbye, warmly to Valeria and coolly to Eva, a classic tactic to hurt my sister. She hardly notices anymore. Before heading to Caterina's, I hand my sister the twenty euros. "Maybe you'll need it."

"Maia . . ." Eva comes over to the car. "Thank you." She looks at me and, in her blue eyes, I see a momentary glimmer of the submissive, worshipful abandonment I'm so familiar with. I don't know it yet, but this moment, in the car that smells of plastic and our father's pipe tobacco, will be the last time I see that look in her eyes. The last time Eva is still Eva, foolish as cotton candy.

The next morning, I wake up and call Eva to meet up and go home. She doesn't answer the first time, or the second, or the third. I text my mother to say she's still sleeping. I try again around eleven. No answer. I call Valeria. On the second attempt she answers in a sleepy voice, and it takes her a minute to realize who it is.

"It's Maia, wake up and find Eva, I'm begging you. I have to take her home before my mother kills me."

"O.K., give me a minute."

Valeria calls me a while later: there's no trace of Eva. My head starts to feel heavy on my neck, my breath shortens. "O.K., tell me where you are." On the other end of the line, I hear Valeria's slurring voice asking a stranger to give her the address of where they are. They're thirty-odd kilometers away, in an abandoned farmhouse in the countryside. I don't wake Caterina, I just text her telling her I had to leave. I drive to the address Valeria gave me. It takes me a while to get there because it's not on the map, I keep calling until, an hour and a half later, I see a dilapidated building surrounded by colorful blotches that I assume are sleeping people. As I get closer, I recognize Valeria.

"What the fuck is this place?" I ask her. Her eyes have dark circles around them, and she looks absent.

"There was a rave, it was cool. I swear we'll find Eva."

We start calling out for her, between the irritable grunts of the other bodies lying like stray dogs on the wet earth. Nobody responds. We scour every corner of the house, comb the land around it, but there's no sign of Eva.

The only place we have not yet looked is a little bamboo grove a way from the crumbling building. We trek over to it; Valeria stumbles and has to stop frequently to get her breath back. The only thing running through my head is the task we need to carry out. I think nothing, I imagine nothing. By the time we reach the trees the sun is beating down mercilessly, the gnats gathering in a frenzy around our eyes and mouths.

Then, through the thin canes, our eyes snag on an aqua green smear. We move toward Eva's body slowly, as if not wanting to wake her, even if we both know that this sleep is not natural. There is a puddle of brown vomit next to her. The hoodie is hunched up around her chest, a bra strap has been pulled so hard it has snapped. Valeria and I watch her in silence. Eva's back, curved into a strange shape, rises and falls quickly, like that of a small animal. I'm scared to touch her. It's Valeria who moves first. She crouches down next to her, strokes the bluish skin of her cheek. My sister's body jerks. When she opens her eyes, her face contorts into an indescribable expression, one which bears the stamp of a fear so deep it is nameless. I crouch down next to Eva. I take her face in my hands, bring it close to mine and remain still. I start to shake her, first gently then harder. Her body is like a puppet, wobbling like jelly, her head following a few moments later. I shout at her, saying she's an idiot, stupid, that I've always known I couldn't trust her. I start ranting about the twenty euros that my mother gave us and that she's lost, and as I'm shouting these things, I put my hands into the pockets of her jeans and root around in a senseless search. Eva does not react. She stares with glassy eyes at what's around her without seeing anything. Valeria is trembling but doesn't dare speak. After two minutes I pick Eva up off the floor and drag her toward the car. She is stumbling everywhere but I don't care.

As we march across the sun burned field, leaving the abandoned farmhouse behind us, a sensation surfaces for the first time that would resurface increasingly often after that day. I would feel it when I first met Filippo; at Eva's funeral; every time I saw my mother after her death; at the party when Lavinia was harassed by that group of girls: I suddenly stop living life as it is, and sense that until this point I have been living in a moving body of water, but now I can get out, sit on the bank, and watch the water run by without ever really touching it. And little by little, this certainty, solidified by adrenaline, would infiltrate my memories too: I would no longer be truly alive in them, they would turn into anecdotes about something that once happened to me or to someone else, with no real difference between the two.

After that morning in the bamboo grove, Eva would no longer be Eva. I would tell my mother that my sister had implored me to let her go to the rave, swearing she'd be extremely careful. My mother would get angry, then overwhelmed by the void that had taken her daughter's place, then forget—or maybe she made herself forget—all about my responsibility.

The psychiatrists would say it was a mixture of substances and perhaps a traumatic experience that triggered the distress that would, for the next few years, squat in Eva's guts, in her blood vessels, her veins, her bones, in the chemical reactions of her synapses, the receptor distribution of her neuro-hormonal circuits, in her ears, her cerebral ventricles, her prefrontal cortex, her amygdala, the memories in her hippocampus, her long eyelashes, the gap between her teeth, her genetic code. A distress that was always there, waiting to explode, and we can't know if it would have exploded regardless, or if it would have continued to run silently through her healthy body if she hadn't gone to that party.

But I remember the color of pure fear in her eyes, not of dying but of being annihilated, disintegrated, until she disappeared.

I know better than all of them that my sister has never suffered from any disease but that of being broken into tiny pieces in a place so deep and sacred that no treatment could ever work, because there is no process that can reconstruct what makes us human and free once we have been turned to dust.

# PART THREE

After the trip to Paris, time passes more quickly. I'm sometimes caught out by how much I've changed, even since the previous week. I can't say precisely what these changes are, but when I think back to something I did or said in the recent past, it's as if I'm watching someone else in my place.

I confide in Gloria about this feeling: her eyes open wide and she says it's the same for her. In fact, her appearance betrays much more of this change than mine does. She has regained a bit of weight and her jawbones no longer protrude so sharply, even if I sometimes catch her massaging them, as if checking she can still feel them through the skin. Unlike Gloria's influencer friends, who display a suspicious concern about her eating habits, I say nothing when she eats and nothing when she doesn't; I just take mental notes in a silent surveillance—sometimes in a spirit of care, sometimes of envy. For the most part, I am amazed when I see her eat and witness her body becoming less skeletal: it means I haven't infected her. She is still untainted. Feeling this protective of someone else is new to me, and although it is entangled with other less noble sentiments, it makes me wonder whether, deep down, I'm a better person than I thought I was.

We work all the time. We go to publicity events where we smile like a pair of fools; we go to photo shoots where Gloria is told to get into awkward poses that make her uncomfortable. What we're really doing is prostrating ourselves to the bizarre requests of the brands and the Instagram algorithm. The latter is continuously changing: sometimes it wants Gloria to post ten-second videos, sometimes it wants her to put up photos on her grid without sharing them to her stories. But they both demand the same thing: that Gloria be herself, without ever really being herself.

We haven't talked about Lavinia since Paris. Or rather, I have tried several times to find out how that night affected Gloria, but whenever I ask, she shakes her head or gives me an evanescent smile. Then I try to intuit her mood in other ways. I find her crying in the toilets on photo shoots, or, when she invites me to her house, I find her lying on the bed in a onesie, eyes empty, staring at her phone, surrounded by a tide of half-opened packages on the floor. Each time she is called up to perform as her public avatar, another tiny piece is chipped off of whatever remains of her core after so many years of inhibition.

In April, Anna Ricordi had the first in a long series of little accidents. On a windy day her car, a small silver CityCar, crashed into a pole. It didn't cause any damage, but the way the accident happened was cause for concern for herself and Valentina, and then also for Gloria. Apparently, Anna's left leg had started to hurt, to the point of freezing completely. After that first accident, she started to behave in ever-stranger ways: one day she summoned her granddaughter, saying she wanted to buy a house near the sea within three weeks maximum; the next day she went out shopping dressed as if she was going to a gala dinner, tripped and twisted her ankle, and since then has to walk with crutches.

Gloria adopts a clumsy avoidance strategy when it comes to these episodes and responds to my questions about her grandmother's health evasively, until one evening, at an event hosted by a sportswear brand, she bursts into tears right before the photo shoot. Between sobs, Gloria tells me how when she was little, her grandmother got it into her head that her granddaughter was getting too fussy. To counter this, she organized trips where she'd have her wade across streams and ponds full of leeches. Or, when Gloria refused to eat a cherry that had fallen on the floor, she dragged her to a stable yard and made her touch the horse manure, all in the name of toughening up this little girl who had grown up wrapped in cottonwool.

"She's a complicated person, she's tough, but she's also the only one who . . . before you, no one ever took so much interest in me, just her. What will I do if she dies? I'm not an independent person." I say nothing. I mechanically stroke her calf, which is sticking out of a pair of running leggings.

The truth is that Gloria, when she's not Gloria Linares but just Gloria, is becoming more and more independent. She haggles at the market with the Arabs who sell the first soft apricots, and who get her the best ones from a basket they keep hidden behind their big iron scales. As she negotiates the price, she has her grandmother's imperiousness, but unlike the reverence her grandmother evokes in the person in front of her, Gloria incites in her interlocutor a sweet shedding of responsibility, a sense that it is really she who knows what's best for them.

One afternoon in the car, we are stopped by the police. We pull over, forgetting that we have a little tin of weed sitting on the dashboard. I feel my heart slide down to my knees when we are asked to explain, but Gloria gets out of the electric car and tells them with the necessary calm that the tin must belong to whoever rented this car before us. She touches them on the shoulders, speaking with passion, her nostrils trembling as if she might burst into tears at any moment, and as she brings her hands to her chest, she explains that she doesn't smoke weed, just like she doesn't smoke cigarettes, due to an unspecified heart problem. The policemen find themselves nodding. "Yes, young lady, you're right, the real problem here is that the checks on these car-sharing vehicles are so poor."

Gloria can talk to anyone without arousing anger or annoyance. But there's another form of power making its way to the surface: how she sees things. When she is not exhausted and feels like chatting, she reflects an image of the world around her that does not correspond to what I see, even if we are immersed in the same reality. When her empathy settles on a person, however wretched they look to me, Gloria is able to overturn, at least momentarily, my impression. For example, when Valentina goes off on one of her venomous rants, sparking a murderous rage in me, Gloria justifies it like this: "Valentina lost her parents very young and she moved to Milan from Basilicata when she had just turned twenty," she explains. "Before working for my grandma, she did leafleting in the metro for a dodgy plastic surgery clinic. One day, my grandma saw this young girl clinging to the handrail of the stairs down to the Porta Venezia metro. She told me she was really pale and her legs were shaking. My grandma went and asked her if she was O.K., but Valentina couldn't speak. She was having a panic attack. My grandma took her to a nearby pharmacy where they gave her a few drops of an anxiolytic. When she had calmed down, Valentina explained that she lived outside Milan, was struggling to pay her rent, and had no one. My grandma gave her a job as her assistant. Valentina is an unpleasant person but she's doing her best, like we all are."

At the Galeone, Gloria has made friends with all the Fays. Unlike me and the other girls, the Fays respect her. They go to her one by one to ask for advice on their love lives, and listen as if she were Pythia, despite her being twenty-five years younger than them and never having been in a relationship longer than three months. When she receives them, her eyes light up with a kind authority, and she listens attentively as my colleagues offer her drinks.

When I told her about my photographic pact with the short Fay, Gloria looked me straight in the eyes and asked: "Do you want to send him these photos?"

Yes, I would have liked to respond. It would have been the truth. Instead, I told her no because that was the answer she seemed to want to hear, and I didn't want to disappoint her. So, Gloria went to my Fay and simply asked him for the name of the contact he got weed from. The next day, when I arrived at her house, she took me to her room and showed me a tin bursting with weed.

"Where did you get it?" I was stunned.

"From the guy who sells it wholesale to your friend. Yesterday I went to his house and made him give me everything he had left."

"You're telling me you went there on your own?"

"Yeah. He's a nice guy. He told me he sells other stuff too, if we ever need anything. Now you don't need to send those pictures anymore."

I felt sad and told her that she should never go to a drug dealer's house alone again.

Really, I knew that nothing would have happened to her. Her regality places her above all risk. What really annoys me is her newfound capacity to handle the world without feeling in danger, without needing me.

I continue to send photos to my Fay anyway, because the process of taking and sending them feels like something that defines me. Even just scrolling through the folder of images that portray me in violently sensual poses makes me feel like I have existed, exist still. One of the last times I meet him, he has a surprise for me. As well as a sealed plastic bag of weed, he puts three little squares of colored paper in my hand. When I ask him what they are, he says it's acid.

"LSD," he whispers in my ear.

"How do you take it?"

"You put one in your mouth and let it melt on your tongue. Maybe you can split it with Gloria."

I nod, pretending to weigh up that possibility. I will take it alone and tell her nothing, because this little square of paper marks a boundary between me and her.

It is because of Gloria's new assertiveness that the day I meet Edoardo I tell her nothing. I don't feel like seeing her eyebrows rise and arch in accusation: I already know she doesn't like Edoardo, just like she doesn't like Filippo, even if she never says it openly. If I talk about one of them, she sighs and her chin stiffens. When I proudly showed her the message thread where Edoardo wrote that although I'm not his type physically, he can't wait to "get to know me better," she said: "You are so smart, but when it comes to understanding what people are really saying, you're an idiot."

I can't fathom where she finds the nerve to cast these judgments at me from her mere twenty years of age. "Perhaps it's that you're too prudish, since you never fuck."

She squints her eyes: "Could be," then continues folding her clothes and putting them away. Gloria has the power to make me feel ashamed of my choices. I don't want her and Filippo to meet because I know that, if they did, I would never be able to see him through eyes other than hers again, and that would make him ugly and I would be mortified, and then I'd be furious with myself for having given more authority to a little girl than to my boyfriend, a grown-up, cultured, important man. Whenever I distance myself from Gloria, Filippo regains the value I saw in him from the start, and when I get closer to her again, I see all the pitiful aspects of him that make me recoil.

Edoardo started messaging me after the summer. He contacted me from a private Instagram account with zero followers. I was flattered; I couldn't believe he was interested in me. In Greece, between Francesca's incursions and my problems with Filippo, we hardly talked. At first it was just the odd short message. He had seen me reading an essay about leaf-cutting ants on the beach and wanted to hear my opinion. I had found the essay boring and spurious, and stopped reading halfway through. I didn't mention that to Edoardo though.

Only after months and months did he start to show a more obviously erotic interest. He would write to say goodnight and that he hoped I'd dream of him, something I found ridiculous for two reasons: firstly, the banality of the phrase; and secondly, the fact that I spent my nights sleepless, unsettled, or blank from benzodiazepine. Nevertheless, just like I'd done years earlier with Filippo, I responded that I was sure I would dream of him and that I hoped he would dream of me too.

After another few weeks, more explicit requests started to arrive. He asked me to send him photos of my lips, my neck, my hips. At that point, exhausted by indulging such dishonest requests, I decided to send him a photo of my butt hole, just to hurry things along. He didn't respond for a few hours, and when he did it was cold, as if I had insulted him. He told me that he wasn't used to such disinhibition and that he preferred to maintain the mystery: girls didn't behave like that in his day. Nonetheless, every so often he would say that he wished to see me and when I sent a picture of my face, part-hidden by hair, I sensed a hint of dissatisfaction in his words. So then I'd send him one of my clitoris and he would tell me I was brazen. He disappeared for a while and when he showed up again, he was even colder than before. At some point he wrote that even though my body was too thin, he found me intriguing, and this revelation filled me with pride, because it made me feel superior to Francesca, with her voluptuous curves, her order, her wisdom. Perhaps, I tell myself, it is Edoardo who makes her what she is, and not the other way around. It is he who waters her with his intelligence, his austerity, his gentle sarcasm, and his good manners. Perhaps I too, in proximity to Edoardo, would be fertilized with the same substance, and it would make me feel new, fresh, give my skin the same oily scent that wafted from her wrists.

Edoardo is waiting for me at a table outside the bar where we have arranged to meet. He's thinner than I remember, and he looks like he's melting into the seat, with no spinal column holding him up. He's wearing a pair of aviators that I never saw him wear in the summer, and two thin, white arms poke out of his rolled-up shirt sleeves. His unshaven beard gives him a sensual coarseness.

The day before, exasperated, I had written that I liked to

be submissive: the same thing I said to Filippo after our first encounter to convince him to see me again. For many men, these words are sufficient to plant a seed of love that germinates from the knowledge of having absolute power over another human being. I hadn't lied to Filippo: I wanted to be with him; I wanted him to save me, and for my destiny to belong to him, and so everything necessary to obtain his closeness became desirable. His desire for my body, when my body stopped belonging to me, was the closest thing to love I had ever experienced.

I walk over, smiling.

"There you are." Edoardo drawls. He pulls one of the chairs out from the table and gestures for me to sit down. Then, as if he has known her his whole life, he looks complicitly at the waitress, and she giggles before going into the bar and coming back out with two beers.

Edoardo's fingernails are short and round. There are a few white hairs in his beard. His hair, though, is black and wavy, identical to how I remember it from when Francesca pushed it back off his forehead in the summer. We talk without listening to each other about books, his lessons at the university, and Francesca's jealousy, a topic that has also come up in the chat, and which in his opinion is the disease that has infected their relationship, forcing him to do just what she expects and fears.

"If everyone thinks you're something, you become that thing," he sighs.

As he talks about the competition entries he's been sorting through for weeks, complaining about all the students who write down their pronouns when signing their name, who he eliminates immediately, his hand slides onto my knee.

"It's already a lot to ask us to use 'they' in official communications, to be inclusive,"—his hand moves up to my thigh, —"I mean, fine, I am happy to use 'they' as default, sure, everything is neutral, gender is a construct, whatever, but remembering everyone's pronouns is unbearable." His hand moves up to my underwear.

Edoardo is different from how I saw him with Francesca. He's more sure of himself; he holds his hand between my legs as he talks to me and flirts with the barista.

"Do you want another drink, or can we go up to the room?" he asks without looking at me.

I choke on my beer. I hadn't thought about what would happen afterward. The fact that we are both in relationships and that the courtship has gone on so long made me think we wouldn't be consummating our passion any time soon. Before meeting with Edoardo, I imagined coming across as light-hearted and easy-going. We would joke, I would be charming, he would fall at my feet and abandon his sanctimonious reservations, bending to my liberty. At that point I would tell him I had to go because I had made other plans, and I'd enjoy having recouped my power, corroded over months of virtual small talk.

"That's where we're going," he points in the direction of a yellow building fifty meters away.

"I have plans," I respond, but the words wilt in my mouth.

Edoardo doesn't seem to hear me. He calls the waitress over again, asks her name, and whispers something in her ear. She laughs and adjusts a strand of hair that doesn't need adjusting. He finishes his beer, gets up, and gestures for me to follow. I get up too, as if under a spell. I feel my sweaty thighs peeling off the seat, leaving a shadow of sweat. With his hands on my shoulders, he steers me like a farm animal toward the hotel.

The walls of the room are covered in a tired wallpaper. The furniture is from the seventies, and the windows, set at an angle, illuminate the room with a harsh light. The bed is unmade.

"Take off your clothes," he orders. I obey. Nothing of what's happening bears any resemblance to what I had expected. He takes my panties off under my skirt and, as I pull the skirt down, I notice fabric marks impressed on my stomach. I find myself wondering if he will still find me attractive. Then I take off my T-shirt. I am naked. Edoardo looks at me with an indecipherable expression, then comes close and whispers that he didn't think I would be so shy, but if I had been as brazen as the girl in the photos, he would have liked me less. I try to reconstruct the hypnotic effect of Xanax, in the hope it might make the whole situation more bearable. Edoardo unbuckles his belt with a whistle and suddenly I hear a dry sound, like a snapping branch, and a piercing pain across my back. I bury my face in the bed, open my mouth, and the sheets return my warm, wet breath.

In the darkness where my eyes are pressed into the cotton, I see Gloria sitting on the windowsill with a cigarette in one hand, her phone in the other, and her legs folded up into the small space. Her eyes are tired and her red, greasy hair falls on her shoulders in defined locks. As she lazily scrolls through her phone, biting her lip, she asks me: "Do you like having sex?"

"Why do you ask?"

Gloria speaks quietly, looking down.

"I follow some sex positive accounts on Instagram . . . they talk about sex and how to do it well, that you shouldn't be ashamed, and how important consent is. It's just that when I find myself actually doing it, it's not easy to put all those things into practice. Then there are these girls who say they're always doing it and trying out all these things, and they say it as if it's a given that all women want the same thing. Also Sara, my friend, told me about all the men she's been with, but I . . ." She pauses, her eyes open wide. "Do you think it's possible . . ."—her voice reduced to a breath— "is it possible that there's something wrong with me because I don't like it that much?"

I can't remember my answer. I can only picture her, legs all tangled up like a spider, with an air of expectancy. Then her image is replaced by one of Nadia with her drawn-on eyebrows and fake eyelashes. Perhaps she would have answered that pleasure is not that important.

I inhale again as the hiss of the belt behind me merges with Edoardo's gravelly voice. I hold my breath. I grip the fabric of the sheets, damp from my sweaty palms. Slowly, I get up. Without turning around, I stretch across the bed and grab my skirt and T-shirt.

"What are you doing? Are you tired already?"

I don't respond. I pick up my panties and denim jacket. The pain numbs everything else.

When I start walking toward the door Edoardo takes my arm: "Where are you going?"

I turn to face him: "If you don't let me go, first I'll scream, and then I'll call your wife."

He loosens his grip with a comically worried expression that reminds me of the man Eva and I caught masturbating at the pool. I leave the room. I walk past the concierge, who looks at me sideways. I was in there for less than half an hour, he must think I'm a prostitute. I look back with a flash of amusement in my eyes, as if confirming his suspicion. I step out into the fresh air and walk toward a bus stop, my chest swollen and an unnatural warmth emanating from my crotch. When I get home, I climb into bed, take a Xanax pill, and touch myself, rubbing my fingers over the wet cotton of my underwear. I fall asleep before I come.

The days following my encounter with Edoardo are viscous. Filippo is in Germany for the whole week for a conference. Milan is cloaked in a milky sky and the temperature is unusually high: the papers are blaming it on climate change. Fires are breaking out in Southern Italy; Instagram is full of people raising money for the civil protection services, and generic tips against waste and in favor of products that don't contain microplastics. Gloria does not take part in this collective virtual mobilization, and I don't ask her why: the cloak of mugginess deadens any desire to provoke her.

In "Law & Order: Special Victims Unit," Olivia Benson has

adopted a child: her transformation into a maternal figure, ever more empathic and embracing, is complete. The gummy crocodiles stick to one another, and I no longer even try to resurrect the me who would eat just a few of them. The sense of unreality merges with, or is generated by, the sticky air. In the morning I wake with the feeling that my past and present are not arranged along a timeline, but that they have collapsed one on top of the other, giving life to a kaleidoscope of emotional scraps that melt together, losing all sense. Perhaps this is why, on the third day of Filippo's absence, I start to think of him like I used to at the beginning of our relationship, and for a few minutes at a time, sometimes whole hours, I am full of grandiose feelings, I love his memory like one loves a sacred effigy. I call him, which astounds both of us since our communications when he's traveling are usually kept to the bare minimum. I feel like we are the same people we were when we lived in Paris and would drive up to see his eccentric friends who lived in a commune outside the city. Their utopic project would crumble within a few years, when it was discovered that one of its founders, Max Babionishev—the son of emigrants from the Soviet Union and a reasonably successful artist whose work had been shown in Manhattan—had been coercing his apprentices to engage in a certain amount of promiscuity. At the time of our visits, though, all this was still unknown, and I remember the adoration with which many of the women who would later accuse Max looked at him. I was euphoric during those trips, but I tried to contain it so as not to embarrass Filippo, putting on an impassivity that was so tiring that often, before falling asleep, I would get a stomachache from tensing my abdominal muscles so much.

His voice on the phone is sweetened by my flattery and he tells me he'll be back soon.

Exhilarated, I decide I'm going to take half a tab of LSD on the morning of his return. A Google search tells me that the effects last a while. I have to attend a Glow event in the afternoon where Gloria will be the guest of honor, but I calculate that if I take it at nine in the morning I'll have plenty of time to get over the most intense effects, and by the evening, on Filippo's return, I'll be almost completely lucid but still tingling with little bursts of magic.

As soon as the square of paper melts on my tongue I sense a knot of anxiety near my sternum, which doesn't loosen until lunch time when I ascertain, with a mix of annoyance and relief, that the substance has had no effect. Maybe I didn't store it correctly, or maybe my Fay gave me a tab with too little acid in it. I roll a joint, relax for a few minutes of an episode in which Olivia Benson is dealing with an Epsteinesque politician who has been running a racket of underage girls, then take my bike to meet Gloria at the event where her task is to entertain an audience of young fans.

That's when the acid starts to stir. I realize because it takes me forty minutes to get to the former train and tram carriage factory rather than the fifteen it was supposed to.

My lateness is caused by the fact that I mistake every double-parked car for a car waiting at a signal, and while waiting for a non-existent green, I get lost in phantasmagoric light games created by a courtship between the rays of the sun and the emerald green of the plane trees. I park my bike and with extreme slowness try to chain it to a pole, but my hands seem to have lost their muscle memory. I give up.

My brain is melting, I don't want anyone to talk to me. I plan to explain to Gloria that I feel very ill so, unfortunately, I can't stay. I just need to find her. I weave my way through bodies dressed in garish colors and leave the room where the event will soon take place. I stand on tiptoes to look for her and see her in the middle of a large group of strangers sitting around a wooden table. Her head is shining like it shone on our first meeting, I remain still for a few moments, enchanted by her peach and apricot hues, by her white hands. While I'm still lost in this contemplation, she lifts her head and her face beams gratitude. She says something to the people around her and walks over to me in long strides, quick and light. I am ready to tell her what I need to when, to my dismay, her features liquefy in front of my face. She bursts into tears. Her tears are stained black from her mascara. She hugs me, desperate, and my only desire is to lie down in a dark room.

"Maia, you have to help me," she hiccups. "The Glow people have done nothing. They haven't written a script, haven't thought about how this shitshow of an event should happen, and I am contractually obliged to go and entertain seventy little girls. What do I tell them, Maia? Help me."

I feel trapped in the body of a newborn baby. The idea of being a giant newborn baby makes me laugh. I wonder whether I should hug her, but I suspect that if I did, I wouldn't be able to detach myself from her soft skin and then I'd be forced to get up on the stage clinging onto her. The image of me on Gloria's back as she talks to the audience makes me laugh even more.

"What are you laughing at? Are you a moron? Can you not see the state I'm in?"

"Glo, I have to tell you something," I stutter.

"Oh God, you're pregnant," she says, squinting her eyes.

I let out a howl, I can't hold back the tears, even if mine are from convulsive laughter. "It's you who wants to be a mother, not me! No, no, I'm not pregnant. I've taken acid."

Gloria doesn't seem to understand. "What do you mean?"

"LSD."

Gloria takes a deep breath, clenches her fists, and closes her eyes. When she opens them again, she looks resigned.

"O.K., get lost. Actually no. You don't deserve it, stay. Make yourself a tiny bit useful and go and buy me some cigarettes. There's a tobacconist just outside, on the piazza."

I wander away, happy to be of help to this beautiful, patient, girl. Unfortunately, in the time it takes me to dodder out of the complex, I've already forgotten my job. I decide that a few minutes' sit-down will help me remember, so I choose a flower bed out of which rises a tree trunk adorned with grooves that depict funny faces in the bark. I think I sit in the flowerbed for at least an hour, unburdened by thoughts of my task. I sit there under the curious gaze of passers-by, tearing strands of grass into tiny strips, playing with my shoelaces, watching the hairs on my arms—they have thinned out and turned ash blond since I've gained weight—slither around on my skin like little worms. I put my earphones in and listen to a song. Then another. At a certain point I decide it's time to go back inside: I stand up, walk back to the building, and enter the room where I find Gloria on the stage addressing her ridiculously young followers on a random subject. How long has it been?

Gloria is talking about how often people on social media ask her for advice on their love lives.

"Girls often ask me if they can make the first move. Of course you can, of course! In fact, you should. When I get this question, I always say: 'Go on, declare your love, do it!' We shouldn't be afraid to open ourselves up."

I emit a convulsive groan that transforms into unrestrained laughter. Gloria has turned the same color as her hair and shoots me a furious look that makes me roar even louder. The shiny little heads of the girls start to wobble until a cloud of laughter is released from the audience, filling up the whole space and eventually reaching Gloria, who, laughing along, loosens up and says: "In both senses!"

I am standing there, enjoying the jovial atmosphere, my chest swelling with pride at being its cause, when my wrist is grabbed by a boney hand that drags me out of the room and into the courtyard where the sky is now white and heavy. It's Valentina. The pink of her gums clashes with her violet lipstick. She is uttering insults, something about shame (mine) and professionalism (not mine). I want to listen, because she seems very tense and I feel bad for her, but my attention is swinging frenetically between her lips and her T-shirt, which reads: I DON'T HAVE TIME TO REPLY TO YOUR TEXT. The sentence makes me feel deeply sad. Why would you brag about working so much you don't have time to reply to a text?

"Wouldn't you like to have time to reply to texts?" I ask, interrupting her rambling. She stays silent for a few seconds, confused by the question. She is wheezing lightly, her breath causing the writing to inflate and deflate.

"What?"

"Your T-shirt, the one you're wearing. It says you don't have time to reply to texts."

She starts shouting again about how irresponsible I am, how she would have time to reply if only I did my job properly, and so on. What a drag. I imagine that I'm a shiny pearl in an oyster shell at the bottom of the ocean. If I concentrate hard enough, I can feel the weight of the water on my shell, the currents running through the moss and algae that live on me. It's dark and I am surrounded by a round silence. I am safe, I'm in my shell. Sadly, I am brought back to reality by Valentina's face, now folded into a painful grimace. It's incredible: every expression she makes looks fake to me, as if she learned it from a handbook of facial expressions. She's crying. Today seems to be the day of crying. I try to tune into what she's saying.

"You're behaving like this, but it's only because you don't know what I know." Did she already say what she knows while I was distracted? I can only hope not. I wait while she noisily blows her nose into a tissue with a unicorn printed on it. I would like one too, but I'm too scared to ask.

"Anna is dying. Do you understand how selfish you are? And when she dies, what will happen? Who will take care of Gloria? We'll lose our jobs, both of us."

This information about Anna punctures my ears but I don't absorb it. Instead, I ask her if she remembers when, months earlier, she told me she was looking for a new job. Wrong question: Valentina emits a sort of growl and takes up insulting me again.

When she finally calms down, I try to climb back into my

oyster shell, but she, set on ruining my evening, gives me a taxi voucher and tells me to wait for Gloria to finish and take her home, because she can't be seen by the Glow team with her makeup running. Before disappearing, she hisses: "Don't say anything to Gloria, Anna hasn't told her yet and she wants to do it herself." I nod. I hear a thunder of applause from inside, which, in my head, is not a sign that the event has finished, but rather a generic sentiment of joy and gratitude directed at me from adorable strangers.

It is Gloria who interrupts my contemplations, shaking my shoulders and demanding me to call a taxi immediately. In a daze, I get up and follow her toward the open space where I had been sitting a few hours earlier instead of buying cigarettes. A group of excited girls follows us, asking Gloria for an autograph, which she gives them.

"I have to thank you," Gloria says once we're in the taxi.

I look at her suspiciously. "Are you sure about that?"

"Yes, I am truly lucky to have met you, you make all this seem," —and she nods her head in the general direction of the complex we're leaving behind us— "unimportant, how it should be. You remind me of what matters."

"Thank you," I say, proud.

"Let me finish. I am lucky to have met you, but if you don't let me try acid, I'll tell my grandmother. It's up to you."

I snort. She's really something. "O.K.," I say.

"Promise?"

"Promise," I sigh, leaning my forehead against the dark window of the taxi. I suddenly realize that I am holding a piece of information that has the power to change Gloria's mood. I would like to keep her happy and naïve for the rest of her life, I would like her to never be touched by pain. She must sense my turmoil, because she weaves her fingers through mine, resting her head in the cavity of my neck. Her hair brushes my arm, and I shiver.

When I get home, Filippo is back. I turn the keys in the lock and open the door to a waft of his sour smell, which, like all smells, you forget exists until you are exposed to it again. I hear the hum of the TV from the living room and Filippo's voice, a sequence of words I can't distinguish. I put my keys and wallet down on the varnished shelf over the radiator by the entrance and go into the bathroom. After a few seconds my features in the mirror start to melt and I see myself older, my cheeks fallen, bags under my eyes, burst blood vessels. I quickly look away and am about to leave when I realize that, in the few minutes I've spent in the bathroom, my conscience has created the expectation that, on the other side of the door, I will find the old chancellor from years earlier in Paris. Time no longer exists, my internal and external realities are lined up along the same plane: my parents await me on the veranda on the ground floor, in the apple green light of our old apartment; Filippo, Paris, and the chancellor are all gathered in the study; Eva and her stuffed toys are still alive. The only person absent is Gloria, perhaps because I saw her so recently, or perhaps because Gloria is such a dazzling novelty that she refuses to belong to the symbolic universe that is unfolding in front of my eyes.

I tiptoe to the living room door and look in. Filippo is on the phone with his back to me and moving around the room along a trail that I feel I can almost see, as if he is leaving luminescent footprints behind him. I am still Maia, and he is still Filippo, the man who once unlocked blazing feelings in me and without whom I couldn't exist. The narrow curve of his shoulders, his oval head, his small body, his reddish, silvering hair, the arms of his gold-rimmed glasses resting languidly on his tiny ears, like the ears of a child. Yes, Filippo is still Filippo. My heartbeat accelerates as I watch him gesticulate and move around the room. Then he turns and sees me, and his face relaxes for a moment. A dizziness tickles my head. He puts the phone down, comes over and takes me in his arms. I feel the heat of his body wrap around me. I go to kiss him, but his rotten breath penetrates my nostrils and, like a wave washing a sandcastle away, Filippo becomes a stranger. His gray eyes are inexpressive, his sloping shoulders make me feel like I'm about to fall, his silvering hair is the sign of his defeat. I hold my breath to kiss him and he guides me to the couch that still holds my shape. He undresses me with what feels like a pretend voraciousness, as if we are actors in a passionate movie scene. Jeans down, panties down, jumper off, all the while pushing me into the coarse cushions. He spits into his hand in an attempt to make the penetration smoother but when he enters me, I feel only discomfort. I lay my chin on the armrest as he holds my hips, panting and moaning in a display of virility. As he pushes me forward and back, forward and back, my gaze catches on a fly on the wall a few centimeters from my face. As I consider brushing it away, everything stops. Filippo has frozen behind me. I turn to look at him and see his eyes fixed still on a point on my now bare back. I am about to ask if everything's O.K., and then I remember. My skin is littered with the marks of Edoardo's teeth, and his belt lashes run down my spine. We remain immobile in that position. It is Filippo who takes control of the situation: he grabs my hair, pulling it toward him until my neck is bent into an unnatural angle, then he grabs my head and pushes it against the cushion, so forcefully that for a few seconds I wonder if he is going to kill me, an event that feels both legitimate and coherent with my life: Maia, 27 years old, asphyxiated on the couch on which she spent her twenties. Detective leading the investigation: Olivia Benson.

Filippo doesn't kill me. Instead, he grunts as his hip bones thrust into me with increasing violence. Every so often he lets out a high, feminine whimper, and, unable to finish, he reaches for the metal box where he keeps his poppers. I feel sorry for him; I would like to help him finish, to save him those clumsy gestures. He gets back into position, erect behind me, inhales the pungent alcoholic aroma from the vial and returns to his brutal thrusts. I want to laugh, but I manage to conceal it with sounds that could be taken as sexual. When he finally flops on top of me, spasming, he is like a wounded animal. I curl up at my end of the couch, cover myself with a cushion and watch him as he sits, legs spread wide, panting.

My head is still shaken by the electric shocks of the acid, which lays a filter of comic solemnity over everything around me. Filippo's sweaty stomach overflows onto his thighs, his back is curved, and his forehead is beaded with sweat. He stares off into space, his lower lip trembling quietly.

I have the impression that his face is losing its specificity. It's as if I can recognize in him the matrix that generated all men. He is the same as Edoardo, the same as my Fay, the same as Nadia's men, the same as the Galeone owners. He is a man who is nothing if not the reflection he sees in the eyes of others. And I am just as pathetic—as are my colleagues at the bar, as was Eva, as is Gloria, as are the efforts of Nadia and those of Valentina—because I, like so many others, sought in him nothing but a fragment of that reflection.

I try not to make a noise as I get dressed and leave the house, as if the sound of me leaving might shatter the gypsum statue of Filippo with his legs spread wide on the couch, turning him to dust.

I turn up at Gloria's house. Anna Ricordi opens the door with a strange brightness in her eyes. She doesn't ask any questions—perhaps noting my sloppy appearance—and with a nod of her head directs me to her granddaughter's room. I open the door and Gloria is on the bed, calm, her face bathed in the synthetic light of her phone. She lightly pats the mattress next to her and I obey. I stretch out on the bed facing her, as she remains lost in TikTok, in photos of her peers smiling at her as they promote a product. I reach over and slip my hand into the inlet between her back and the mattress, enjoying the light pressure on my palm which, if I close my eyes, could be holding her whole body.

* * *

The house is silent. The honey-colored parquet creaks under Gloria's feet as she goes into Anna's studio. Her grandma is reading a Wodehouse book on the old turquoise velvet couch that they chose together so many years earlier for the shape of the seats, soft and round like soap bubbles.

Anna, lying on the couch, her eyes made comically large by her reading glasses and her gaze running swiftly over the pages of the book, doesn't immediately register her granddaughter's presence.

"Nonna, it's me."

Anna starts and looks up at her granddaughter leaning against the door frame. Sometimes, in the haze of that age she insists on ignoring, Gloria reminds her of her son when she looks at her big brown eyes and long eyelashes, or her mother, when she rests her gaze on her chin, round like a little apple. In both cases she experiences a faint unease, as if her heart stops beating for a few seconds until her feelings make their way back to the present, letting go of old times that have peeled away.

She loves Gloria more than she ever loved her own mother and her frustrated stiffness, and perhaps more than she loved her son, who grew up with an education the opposite of the one she was given, and who life unceremoniously took from her. With Gloria she finally felt free to love somebody without the onus of duty, without the specter of fear that she would fail to give the little girl everything she needed.

"Come here, child."

"Why are the blinds closed?" asks Gloria, sitting on the edge of the couch. She has the curious sensation, even before anything happens, that this moment will remain impressed on her memory.

"I called you because I need to talk to you about something," Anna says, sitting up on the couch and stroking the smooth velvet. Gloria moves closer to her.

"You're sick, aren't you? Is it the leg that hurts when you drive? Are they going to operate on it?"

Anna continues moving her fingers over the cushion cover, as if scrutinizing the craftmanship. She realizes that telling her granddaughter about the illness marks the moment it becomes real. The doctors' words aren't important, nor are the futile treatments she has already started to undergo, or the curt phrases uttered to her colleagues, or the pragmatic ones pronounced to the notary and lawyers. Nothing she knows has been true until this moment.

She takes a deep breath, feels the air filling her diaphragm.

"It is my leg, yes . . ."

"So, are they going to operate? Will you walk with a stick? We'll get you a wizard one, or one with an animal's head on it. Or one with a bottle opener: at least then you'll know where it is!

"We don't lose it, you steal it."

They laugh through their noses. Gloria knows that what her grandmother is about to tell her won't require them to buy a stick, but feigning naivety seems like the right thing to do, even if she couldn't say why.

"I went to have the pain in my leg checked out. Gloria," she coughs, "they found a metastasis in my femur. I have lung cancer; it seems I've had it for many years."

Gloria strokes her grandmother's hand, her fingers swollen as if they've been blown up.

"How long do you have?" she asks.

"Around six months. I've already started the radiotherapy, but soon I won't be able to walk on my own and I'll have to use a wheelchair."

"I'll push you around like when I was little and you put me in the shopping cart; I'll finally be able to return the favor," Gloria whispers, looking down.

She lays her head on her grandmother's lap, and Anna strokes her temples. Gloria closes her eyes and inhales the mothball scent of the fabric of her grandmother's jeans, which hold a record of all the changes of season they have seen. Gloria doesn't know it yet, but that scent of fresh and silent darkness will remind her of her grandmother many times throughout her life.

Anna rests her head on the back of the seat, her eyes turned toward the center of the ceiling, where a white stucco medallion, long abandoned by the chandelier, winks down at her. She feels her granddaughter's wet lips creating a circle of warmth where they brush against the fabric of her jeans, and for a moment, before feeling ridiculous, she imagines that this warmth could heal her.

* * *

We put up our tent in a part of the pine woods full of tired trees, branches lying face down on the bed of stones below. The buzz of the cicadas is so loud I fear I won't get used to it.

Gloria isn't speaking. Every centimeter of her face is tense, taking in all the things she can see: fifty meters away a group of men with leathery skin and bare feet are setting up the stage for tonight; there are bare-chested boys and girls putting up a tent near ours; children chasing one another, squealing; dogs barking playfully, creating a party atmosphere. The air smells of resin, salt, earth. And weed, lots of weed, floating up in creamy clouds from the tents, its sweetness merging with the scent of the pines.

Gloria is wearing a light pink bodysuit, denim shorts ripped at the hems, khaki and black rubber sandals. She has straightened her hair, which is the same golden red as the tree trunks at sunset, and her eyes shimmer with silver glitter. Despite being beautiful, she keeps moving her hand across her belly, as if trying to conceal the effort inherent in choosing what to wear and how to make herself up, surrounded by all these people who have made no effort whatsoever.

"Let's bring a tent like theirs next time," Gloria says, pointing at a regal structure with numerous rooms a few meters from us.

"Yeah, if you help put it up. Otherwise, you'll have to sleep in someone else's tent."

"Sorry, you're right," she laughs, and starts pretending to help me.

The national park is in Cilento; it's private land where construction is banned. On the train we realize it's the first non-work trip we've done together. It was Gloria who organized everything: a month earlier she turned up at the Galeone with a thick paper envelope decorated with PVA glue and glitter. Inside the envelope was a handwritten letter in her curly handwriting that explained the surprise she had planned. We were going to a rave by the sea in Campania. She had already bought the tent and the train tickets.

"You promised me acid," was how she concluded the letter.

I accepted, glad of the opportunity to leave my new living situation behind for a few days. It was Anna Ricordi who found me a place to stay after the break-up. Now I am living in a house owned by one of her old friends, Lucrezia, an alcoholic with a bunch of cats. I do her shopping and clean the house in exchange for a bed. It's a temporary arrangement; it better be, because for some weeks I have been sharing a minuscule room in the basement with a plague of roly-poly bugs, tiny black creatures with an armor of coils that, if touched, contract into little balls like stones or seeds. To get rid of them I have sprinkled insecticide around the perimeter of the room, which is now littered with dried-out crustaceans. The way they curl up into a little ball when they die—just like when they are alive and afraid—makes me sad.

From the station in Agropoli we have to hitch a ride, but it's easy because so many people are going to the same place. A white gate with a security booth marks the entrance to the park. It's unsupervised because the guards have been paid by the organizers to turn a blind eye. A long white road stretches from the gate through the pine woods, bordered by the sea on the left, and stretching for a few kilometers on the right until giving way to watermelon fields and vineyards that climb the slopes of a small mountain. On the top of the mountain sits a ruin that everyone calls "the observatory." We take two beers from the cooler and head toward the edge of the woods, where they open onto a sloping clearing. Our steps disturb clouds of gray crickets with red and blue wings. When we look down, we see highways of ants carrying little blonde spikes. We walk past a few small bays that are already occupied until we find a free one. We tumble down over the sea-polished stones and perch on the only flat rock, the water caressing our feet. We drink our beer in small sips as the sky turns pink, then indigo. At a certain point, Gloria ventures into the water in her rubber sandals and squats down in the shallows with her hands cupped.

"What are you doing?" I ask her.

"I'm catching tiny prawns."

"And then what?"

"Nothing, I catch them and let them go. They're tickling my palms."

I get up and go to join her.

"No, wait."

"Why?"

"I've just peed."

I squat down next to her.

"I'm peeing too."

"No way!" she shouts, moving away disgusted, but can't help laughing as I follow her clumsily, my flow pausing every time I stand up.

We return to our rock with our lips still crinkled from laughing. I take off my bikini top. Gloria looks down, embarrassed.

"You seem better since you broke up with Filippo," Gloria observes, lighting a cigarette.

"I don't know, nothing much has changed. Before I was miserable in luxury, now I'm miserable in a basement invaded by crustaceans."

"But at least you're not lying to yourself anymore. Before you were always covering up your sadness with things that didn't belong to you. Now you're a broke twenty-seven-year-old who serves drinks, works for me, and lives in a dump. Things can only get better."

"If they get even marginally worse, I will become a crustacean."

We both laugh. Gloria looks attentively at her blue-painted toenails, puts her cigarette out on a smooth stone and drops it into an empty box in her fanny pack.

"You know," she says slowly, "my grandma says that, for women, men are like the Wizard of Oz."

"Meaning?"

"Women are like Dorothy: they make a huge effort to reach the Wizard of Oz, expecting to get from him whatever they think they don't have. But then they find him and discover that behind the curtain there's just a little man projecting shadow puppets onto the wall. My grandma says that we already have everything we need to get home, we just don't realize it."

The song of the cicadas has disappeared, taken away by the incipient night.

Gloria stretches out, squints her eyes, and holds her breath for a moment: "My grandma is dying," she says flatly.

"I know."

She turns around, shocked.

"Vale told me, at the Glow event."

Gloria nods and starts singing a little song. Then she stops.

"What did you feel after Eva died?" she asks in one breath.

"What do you mean?"

"Recently I've been wondering what pain feels like, because I've never really felt it."

"It doesn't feel like you expect it to. It's a process, and it feels different for each person."

"What does it feel like for you?"

"Pass me a cigarette."

Gloria obeys. I light it and inhale the bitter smoke until my lungs feel saturated.

"It's hard to explain," I reflect. "Do you remember in Paris when you told me you didn't recognize your room anymore, that it seemed like someone had filled it with things that didn't represent you, things that weren't truly yours?"

"Yeah."

"Well, it's as if . . . it's as if, when you're born, you come into the world in an empty room. The walls are white, the temperature is mild, you watch the cycle of seasons through the glass of the windows, and the sounds that come from outside seem interesting but nothing more, because you know they can't reach you. There's someone looking after you and as you grow, little by little, the room is filled—by you and those who love you—with signs and objects. Notches appear on the wall that record your height, and there are drawings and photos . . . traces of the time that has passed since you first opened your eyes in the room. But there's also damage, which might be big or small, deep or superficial: a hole in the wall that has never been filled, a leak that stains the white of the ceiling. And then there are the alterations that work under the surface, the ones you don't notice. They gnaw away at the walls and run along the floors, but they do it slowly, too slowly for the progressive deterioration to be noticed and stopped in time. Until one day you wake up and there is no longer any trace of the room you once knew. And, for the first time, you see that you're alone; you realize that the walls will no longer protect you and that you'll have to look after yourself. But since you don't know how, the only solution you can think of is to try and enter someone else's room in the hope you'll find your own again, which will never happen. Then, even the hope of finding that place disappears, and all you can do is accept that something fundamental has been lost forever: the faith—implicit, stupid, and beautiful—that you are safe."

Gloria fiddles with a round, flat pebble: "Do you think that Eva's death changed you?"

"Of course. But I don't think enough time has passed to know exactly how. Whatever I told you would be false."

"How did you feel in the days afterward?"

"After her death?"

I take the pebble from her and start to pass it between my palms.

"Light. As if everything I'd thought was important up until that moment suddenly wasn't anymore. All the angst, the studying, the exams, the future, the expectations . . . everything gone, puff. I felt like I was levitating when I walked, I had no fear."

"And did they come back? The angst and the fear, I mean."

"No. Nothing came back."

The final rays of sun paint the surface of the water with red, almost purple, streaks. Crests of brown rock emerge from the sea.

"So that's what you mean when you say you changed?"

"Yeah, that's part of it. It was like I had lost all interest. At the beginning it was kind of pleasant, then it was just . . . empty. And it stayed empty until . . ."

"Until?"

"Until I met you."

I blush. Gloria rubs my knee.

"Right, that's enough. Why would you ask me these things now?" I say, pushing her affectionately.

Gloria smiles. "You're right, sorry." She picks up her fanny pack and the empty bottles, which clink. "Let's go back to the tent," she says after a while.

Before we start walking Gloria takes the pebble from my hands, bends her knees, and skims it into the water making it bounce twice across the surface. We watch the stone sink.

When we get back to the pine woods, the preparations for the party are almost complete. In front of the stage, fairy lights look like they're carrying messages from one tree trunk to another. The DJs are gathered around the decks. They open small suitcases that contain petroleum-colored vinyls, touch their beards, and gesticulate. People wander around under the lights; their bodies are electric, and the air crackles with excitement.

We sit down under a thin pine. Gloria's eyes are red from the weed and the beer. She looks funny so I take a photo.

"Let me see."

I pass her the phone and watch her eyes light up with amusement.

"I love it, send it to me."

"You want to post it? You look like a rodent."

"No, I don't want to post it. I want to keep it for myself. It's strange, but before I met you, I didn't have any photos where I looked silly. Promise you'll take only silly photos of me from now on."

"At your service."

"Now I'm going to take one of you."

The girl on Gloria's phone smiles back at me. I don't recognize her, but she looks happy. Is this how Gloria sees me?

The music is starting, and Gloria grabs my wrist. The lights dim and people start moving toward the stage.

"Let's go!" she exclaims, exhilarated. A thread of sounds slithers out of the speaker, marking the start of a mysterious future. Then the bass starts. First stealthy, then velvety, then it explodes. The sea of people around us moves like a flock of birds swirling across the sky, and we are a part of it.

Gloria looks around and whispers in my ear: "We're all the same here." Then she closes her eyes, and her lips stretch into a hint of a smile. We dance on the spot.

"The time has come," Gloria says, struggling to conceal her excitement. I nod and take two dark squares out of my pocket.

"Keep it in your mouth until the paper melts," I whisper in her ear. Gloria nods that she understands. Her tongue shoots toward the tip of my finger where the paper is balanced. I take a photo of her with flash, then put the other little square on my own tongue and taste only paper, nothing else. I keep dancing with my eyes closed, moving the paper around in my mouth until it's turned to paste. I open my eyes again when a girl taps me on the shoulder. Her pupils are enormous in the intermittent blue from lights flashing on the stage. Her jaw is rigid and her face tense.

"Sorry, could you tell me what it says on my phone? I've lost my friends, but my eyes keep crossing and I can't read their texts."

I take the phone from her hands. "It says they are on the right of the speakers, where the biggest pine tree is. They're waiting for you there," Gloria explains from behind me.

"You're angels. Wait a minute," she says, pulling a little colored box out of her fanny pack. She opens it to reveal some white crystals.

"It's MDMA, do you want some?"

I hesitate, but Gloria's index finger flies into the little chest and she gets hold of a couple of grains.

"Thank you," she says to the girl. "You too Maia."

I imitate her. But when the crystals come into contact with my tongue, they taste bitter and disgusting and I retch. The girl moves away from us smiling idiotically while Gloria explains the benefits of the LSD+MDMA mix.

"Sorry, but how do you know these things?"

"These Dutch guys have a YouTube channel where they try all different drugs and explain them. This combo works miracles, trust me."

"And I should trust a group of druggy YouTubers?"

But she's already turned back to the stage, her hands reaching out toward the sky. I feel another retch coming. Only for a moment, then suddenly my head turns soft. I immediately open my eyes and the lights are melting together, making golden and silver arabesques. I look at my hands, then at Gloria's: it seems like hers are mine and mine are hers. She has also opened her eyes, in ecstasy. The music moves through us like a luminous chemtrail, and when I look at the sky, I can see a streak of the milky way. Maybe that's where the music is coming from. Gloria's face looks glazed as it sways from side to side in a pearly light. Then I feel something else. A wave rises from my belly button up to my throat and shatters my tongue, at which point I open my eyes wide and let myself fall into an ecstatic wonder that runs fast from my big toes to my hair and locks my jaw. The music is more defined now and surrounds me like amniotic fluid. I look at Gloria again and see a shiny white net sliding all over her skin. I want to ask her if she feels what I feel, so I reach my hand out to touch her, but my fingers don't reach, as if I am moving too slow. I try twice more before I manage to get her attention. I brush her arm, she turns, and I'm left speechless. For a fraction of a second that lasts a lifetime, it is Eva looking back at me. The little gap between her two front teeth; her big, sad eyes, animated by a hint of malice; her blonde hair dancing over her white skin. Her face appears and disappears in the flashing lights, and every so often its expression changes. One moment she's angelic, then sad, then sly. Now she's scared, wearing the aqua green hoodie, and even though I can't see them I am certain she's wearing my jeans. Am I mistaken?

Suddenly I hear the hoarse voice of a gangly boy calling out to her, and when she turns around her image remains suspended for a few moments before crumbling into a million pieces. Now in her place, turned toward the boy, is Gloria.

"Gloria?" says the boy. "Gloria Linares? I can't believe you're here; my sister is crazy about you. Let's take a photo, you know you've got druggy eyes. Do you come to these parties undercover?"

He thrusts his phone in front of Gloria's joyful face—she's enthused by the idea that someone wants to immortalize her inhabiting, at long last, her own skin—but I am faster than him. I push him back. "Don't touch her!" I shout. He stumbles into a group of guys dancing behind us who start on him, grabbing him by the sweaty cotton of his T-shirt. Gloria takes my hand. "Let's get away from here," she whispers. In a few seconds we are out of the crowd.

Gloria leads me through the pine woods as my ears welcome the growing silence as the music withdraws.

"Be careful here," she whispers. We go down the same slope that took us to the little cove in the afternoon, but the beach now looks like the surface of a foreign planet that we're exploring for the first time. We reach the flat rock we were sitting on hours earlier; I can hear only the quiet lapping of the sea. There is not a single thought in my head. Without realizing, I start to cry.

Gloria gets undressed, her body is mother-of-pearl. She caresses the sea, then comes back to me and wets my neck and temples. She says nothing, just goes back and forth between the sea and the rock. When I stop crying, her voice is asking me to undress. I do it and leave my clothes next to hers. She stands in front of me, wipes away my tears with her fingers, then slips behind me and puts her hands on my shoulders to drive me toward the sea. The water skims my feet. "Let's go in," she whispers, and as she says it she walks past me and glides into the dark water until she disappears. I reach her where she has stopped: on a rock covered in slimy moss, which we explore with our toes with no fear or disgust, both of us sure that everything on that beach will welcome us as if we too are seaweed, stones, crystals of salt.

Gloria is in front of me again. She takes my face in her hands and brushes her thumbs across my eyelids to close them. I feel her lips on my eyelashes, then on my cheek, and finally on my mouth. Her tongue is soft and smooth, her skin smells of child's sweat. We have just one mouth. Eventually she pulls away, bursts into laughter, and plunges under the water. She disappears for a few seconds, but before I can worry, I see her resurface at the shore.

I follow her out of the water, go and get my phone from my jeans pocket, and take a photo of her, then another, then a close-up. I sit down next to her. We try to look at how they've come out and I realize I took other photos of her when we were dancing. Our eyes, though, are like those of the girl who gave us the MDMA, and we can't make out what's on the screen.

Now the moon is high in the sky and the few visible stars have blurred into one another. Gloria points at a section of the night sky: "Someone is definitely watching us; we are guinea pigs in a beautiful experiment."

"Or it's the acid."

"Yeah, but even if it is, who invented acid? Why are we here, right now, in this moment? For thousands of years, we thought the Earth was flat and now we think it's round: how do you know that in a few more years we won't discover that we're all inside a simulation?"

Feeling lazy, I tell her she's right.

Then the blue of the ocean becomes speckled with pink, orange, and lilac and, bewitched, we watch the clouds as they fray, leaving colorful trails in their wake.

"Shall we go back to the woods and sleep?" Gloria asks in an empty voice.

I slowly start getting dressed. I don't want to go to sleep. I don't want this day to end. I want to preserve it in a glass jar so I can take it out again every so often.

When we get back, we can see people still swaying to the music in the distance, but we stop at our tent and climb into our sleeping bags. Gloria's hand rubs my shoulder. I don't know how long it takes me to fall asleep, but in my half-sleep, I think of something I once read about the Battle of Arezzo in Dante's time: the knights opened up their own horses' stomachs and hid inside. Gloria and I are the horse and the knight. But I don't know who is which.

The summer days slide into one another, and I am steeped

in their static stuffiness. My housemate Lucrezia's mood is also worse in summer: in the evenings she drinks and takes her pills, which make her muddled and melancholic. Then, her cheeks empurpled by the heat, she sets to recollecting her bastard ex-husbands and ungrateful children. Sometimes she raises her voice and curses them as if they were sitting next to me on the couch.

I try not to think of Gloria. The morning after the party, we woke up, empty, and hardly uttered a word to one another as I tried to take down the tent. In the end, I gave it to some guy, on the agreement that he got it back into its original form and took it away. We passed the train journey in a catatonic silence, and when we got to the station, we just nodded goodbye. In the days after, I didn't dare to call her: a strange tension had fallen between us that I can't explain.

A week after we got back, Valentina called to tell me Anna's health had taken a turn for the worst. When I asked her how Gloria was, she said: "How do you think she is?" Reluctantly, I sent her a message saying that she knew where I was if she needed me. Gloria responded with an intentional-sounding coldness: "Thank you very much for your kind thoughts."

Now and then, the image from the party of Eva looking scared and about to crumble to pieces flashes across my mind. The more her face appears, the less sense it makes, like when you say a word too many times and it becomes a string of meaningless letters. That's how it is with Eva's face in summer: a symbol so crumpled by my obsessive looking that I never quite manage to grasp it.

At the beginning of August, the Galeone closes, and with it my only contact with the outside world, my Fay included. I look at photos of him on holiday with his wife, a woman with dark hair and a round, sweet face. He has stopped requesting intimate photos, and I start to miss our exchange, especially since there are no mirrors in Lucrezia's house, and I don't know what my body looks like anymore. If nothing else, my Fay confirmed its existence and even its desirability.

Every so often I think about calling Filippo, pleading for forgiveness, and going back to the big apartment with the flat screen TV showing "Law & Order: Special Victims Unit." One night I dream of him and Edoardo exchanging stories of my wrongdoings while I intently clean a toilet that refills with excrement as I scrub. For the whole of the following day my heart beats too fast, until the evening when I take a Klonopin pill from one of Lucrezia's packs, not before crushing three into her cocktail to ensure she will sleep without needing me.

Anna Ricordi passes away at midday on Wednesday, August 11. The air is dense, and the sky is white. I am surprised she has decided to go on a day like today, when everyone is on holiday and only the poor and the mad remain in the city. You can accumulate all the money and power you want in life, but maybe if you are born poor, you are destined to die in the summer, surrounded by the same nothingness as when you came into the world.

I hear the news in a brief message that Valentina has sent to all her contacts. She expresses condolences that sound rehearsed, even in writing, and invites me to the funeral, which will take place in a small temple at the only cemetery that offers secular services.

It dawns on me, painfully, that without Gloria my life is lousy. I try calling her, but the phone is always disconnected. So I write to her on social media saying that I want to talk to her in person. She replies that it's a tricky time: she is swamped by everything that's going on, and she'll get in touch when she can. "Anyway, I'll see you Friday," she writes.

Anna's funeral is nothing like my sister's. The service is at eleven in the morning, but I get there early in the hope of finding Gloria and talking to her alone. Or rather, in the hope of seeing her arrive and being able to observe her from behind a cedar tree, because I want to see what her face looks like before my presence transforms it.

I wander through the shrines of wealthy families to while away the time. My eyes are drawn to one that a rich businessman had built for his son, who died aged four from diphtheria on a trip to Argentina with his father. On the door there is a ship that looks like one of Christopher Columbus's caravels from an elementary school textbook, alluding to the return journey of the body. On the right-hand side of the cube, the trio of Fates keep vigil over a cradle, and on the left, there are engravings of some toys. On the back wall, a man and a woman, the parents, embrace. I wonder how guilty the father must have felt for taking his son with him, and whether the mother had held a grudge. Here I am, in front of the tomb of this child who is no different from all children who are dead, and yet I know who he is because his parents had enough money to ensure that the memory of their son—or at least an echo of it—is impressed onto every pair of eyes that falls on this block of marble.

I touch the marble, expecting cold on my fingertips, but the surface is smooth and warm. As my fingers travel along the grooves of the sad engravings, I feel absurdly close to this family and this boy who died more than a hundred years ago. If Eva had died a century ago, her death would not have disrupted my life the way it has. Tragedies were a common matter: everyone died, that was life. Now, however, I feel like the custodian of an experience that distances me from others, a participant in a secret that nobody wants uncovered.

Suddenly, the thought of seeing Gloria makes me feel sick.

I walk along the gravel pathway, flanked by rows of lime trees. I want to leave; I walk faster, anticipating freedom just a few steps ahead, but in that moment the funeral car appears at the entrance to the cemetery, gleaming under the alabaster face of the sky. I quickly hide behind a tree.

Just behind the car, I see Gloria, Rebecca, and their mother, Viviana. The latter is wearing a headscarf, darker than her linen tunic, which covers her hair except for an escaped red curl at her temple. She looks like she learned how to wear grief from the television sets she used to work on, and that she has passed this knowledge down to her daughters. A few steps away from them, the stepfather looks at the ground and fiddles with the metal strap of his watch. Behind him flow all the stars in Gloria's galaxy: the alcoholic uncle staggering along and holding his daughter's hand; Viviana's colleagues, now famous actors, walking next to their husbands; Gloria's influencer friends, among whom are the twins with matching little cylindrical hats, one forest green, the other sea blue. And then, all wearing an air of contrition: directors of museums and trade shows, newspapers and magazines, a film producer, a couple of editors. Some furtively look at the person walking next to them, trying to work out who it is. At the back of this cluster of people who have returned from vacation just for the ceremony is Valentina. She mechanically passes a crumpled tissue under her nose and over her eyes. She's the only person dressed in black.

As I consider what to do next, I spot, about fifty meters from Valentina, a group of four or five people dressed informally. I can't figure out who they are until I see their cameras. Journalists.

I wait for them to pass my hiding place and then join the line. The procession stops in front of a small, square temple made of white stone. The coffin is placed inside the building, at the center of a semicircle fringed by three rows of chairs. A strip of light streaming in from above makes the ebony, surrounded by regal arrangements of flowers, shine. I wait for everyone to sit down before I enter and stand next to a heavy curtain. I have never attended a secular funeral. The first person to speak is Gloria's mother, who talks about how the mother of her late husband was at her side throughout her grief and how she took care of her first-born over the years. I know from Gloria that there was bad blood between Viviana and Anna: the former felt she had been deprived of her eldest daughter; the latter accused the former of being an inattentive mother.

An old man gets up on the stage: a colleague from the newspaper Anna worked at as a young woman. He tells the story of when she ended up in the Horn of Africa as a photographer. Food supplies didn't always arrive on time and so she was taught by the locals to set up sophisticated ostrich traps. I wonder if it's true. Every detail, every suit, every word that leaves the lips of those who get up to commemorate the deceased, seems false, as if the most important people to express their pain to are not the family members, but an invisible audience.

Surprisingly, the only one who comes across as earnest is Valentina. She jumps up, enveloped in dark robes, gripping the shreds of tissue in her left fist. Then, shaking, she starts talking about what a wonderful boss Anna Ricordi was: "She picked me up off the street when I was having a panic attack, she saved me, I owe her . . . I owe her everything. I was just . . ." Her voice breaks; she can't go on. The audience starts to fidget nervously, as if everyone there is part of an entity assigned the task of judging everything that is said as appropriate or not. And then Viviana, with a compassionate smile, lays a firm hand on Valentina's shoulder and tries to lead her back to her seat. Valentina is moved by a ripple of rebellion: she doesn't want to leave the stage like that; she doesn't want this to be the memory left with those listening. Maybe I was wrong. Valentina is not naturally sincere, but her unfamiliarity with the rules of this world is heart-rending.

Finally, it's Gloria's turn. When she stands up, I hear the quiet rummaging of the journalists taking their phones from their pockets to record her speech.

She clears her voice and looks around. She doesn't look for me, nor does she see me. The light from above makes her look sinister. Her long eyelashes project a shadow over her cheeks, and her hair is tied up in an elegant but calculatedly messy bun.

"With my grandma it was like I lived in this beautiful room with a four-poster bed, silk sheets, and a warm light. She protected me from pain, and I, having experienced it rarely, and never like now, always imagined it would be linear. Something sad or ugly happens and then you cry and you're miserable. Today, for the first time in my life, I understand that it doesn't work like that. What I feel having lost my grandma is different. Little drops of freezing water are seeping through the ceiling of this room where I have always lived, and I know that, little by little, a dark patch is developing that will change the room forever. But the thing that hurts the most, the thing that is also the most paradoxical, is that the only thing I want is for my grandma to be here, to hold my hand during the process—because that's what pain is, a process—that will make my memory of her gradually fade."

Gloria's eyes are teary. She is still, statuesque, in the middle of the room. The guests seem like they want to applaud, before realizing it would be inappropriate. The band of journalists hurries to stop their recordings and scribble down notes.

I struggle to swallow. Suddenly I feel like the curtains are exhaling dust into my lungs.

Gloria has taken everything.

I press my hand to my chest as if trying to tear my skin from my ribs; I close my eyes, then reopen them, wet with rage, and leave the temple. The daylight is blinding and sick. I drag myself to the cemetery gates in a daze, go down into the metro, climb over the turnstiles, and take the train going in the wrong direction and only realize after a few stops. When I finally get home, I collapse onto the bed, barely registering the piles of roly-poly bug carcasses around the edge of the room. I breathe. I accept the oxygen that fills my lungs, mixing with blind resentment. My heart slows. My head empties.

Who am I? You can't define yourself alone; you don't exist if nobody sees you. Who sees me? My parents, but they no longer exist. My sister, but she no longer exists either. Filippo saw me, but I showed him something that didn't exist, the product of his fantasies. My Fay saw me, but only in pieces. Edoardo saw me, but he was just a faded copy of Filippo. None of these people really saw me, I never let them. Only Gloria managed to worm her way inside. I let a thief into my house, one who has always had everything but a voice. Now she has one, and it's mine.

The morning after the funeral, I wake up disoriented from the sleeping pills I stole from my landlady. The first thing I do is open Instagram. I search for Gloria's profile, click on her stories, and find a bunch of accounts reposting a shaky video that one of the attendees must have taken while pretending to be just recording the audio. The video is everywhere, even Gloria has reposted it. The comments are enthusiastic. Hearts, applause, people brazenly sharing their own traumas. "That's exactly what it's like!," "I love you Gloria," "You have to write a poem about this," "I miss you Gloria," "Gloria," "I talk about grief on my page, follow me!," "Gloria I'm in love with you!," "Write my life story, Gloria," "My mom died a year ago and I expected things to be better after a year but instead it's just how you say it is," "Gloria I'm begging you, please follow me," "Gloria you're our queen," "Who wrote that for you?" (I smile), "Like one of my posts, Gloria," "So true," "Queen," "I'm crying," "There's something in my eye," "You're beautiful," "So deep Gloria," "Can we be friends?" "I loooove you," "Only hearts for you," "Babe," "It will be hard, but all experiences, even bad ones, help us become who we are," "Anna is definitely watching you from up there," "Goodbye Anna."

I know what I have to do. My fingertips tingle as I scroll through the album of photos on my phone, all the way back to the rave by the sea. I open the photos of Gloria. In one, she's topless and has a joint in her hand. In another, her pupils are swollen and she's showing her index finger to the camera, her nail covered in crystals of MDMA. In another, she's sticking her tongue out with a square of paper on it. In another she's laying on the rock, her face contorted into a synthetic smirk. Her abdomen is swollen and her thighs, pressed against the rock, are a strange shape. I get a new email address: maia8765@gmail.com. I open an account on Instagram and Twitter. I upload the photos to both social networks, using hashtags I know the algorithm will like. Then I write to a few accounts that post gossip about online personalities and to the editors of the gossip magazines you find in hair salons and under beach umbrellas. Then I take two of Lucrezia's Klonopins and wait.

When I open my eyes again it's early morning. I find my phone buried in the sheets. On the lock screen I see the date: August 15. The Galeone reopens tomorrow. It's a thought I welcome with gratitude. When I unlock my phone, the Instagram icon is accompanied by a red blob with a three-digit number on it. There are also twenty-six missed calls, all from Valentina, apart from one which is from Gloria. WhatsApp is overflowing with messages from Valentina, too. I delete the conversation without reading any of it. Instagram, however, interests me.

Firstly, my fake account has been reported and the photos I posted removed. Never mind, they're already everywhere. Now, under the video of Gloria's funeral speech, there are more than six thousand comments. The most frequent are along the lines of: "druggy," "slut," "so this is the example you're setting for our children?," "shame on you," "disgusting," "you don't deserve anything you have," "maybe now you'll have to find yourself a real job," "is this what your grandma taught you? Maybe that's why she died, so she no longer had to live with the shame of having a grandchild like you," "can I get high with you?" "I thought you were thin," "tiny tits," "god I love seeing you humiliated, you're a cancer," "people like you should kill themselves," "good girls are always the biggest whores," "go back to school." Among the comments there are various mentions of the brands Gloria works for, making sure they won't work with her again: "@glow, shame on you for the brand ambassadors you choose," "@nike, so do amphetamines keep you fit?" "@amazon, a match made in heaven."

I follow the flow of insults from one account to the next. Some brands, the smaller ones who are most afraid of the damage to their image, have uploaded apology posts and stories. They disassociate themselves from Gloria and say they had no idea, that they'll do better in future. The comments underneath do not let them off.

Pervaded by a sense of peace, I let myself be transported by the torrent of mentions. One minute I am in the bubble of Gloria's colleagues, where her lifestyle is condemned with a mellifluous sweetness: "I understand that pain can play brutal tricks on you, but we have a responsibility. I hope this call-out helps her figure some things out." The next I am in a bubble of micro-influencers who are trying to make the big time by producing six-minute videos revealing their own opinions on Gloria. I even go and comb the macho lair of Twitch. There, Gloria's face is photoshopped onto Lavinia's half-naked body. There are also videos going around of a government campaign against the use of substances in which the actor's face has been substituted with Gloria's.

After a few hours of scrolling, more sophisticated morsels start to come in. There's one about a presumed abortion Gloria had when she was sixteen. Another claiming that, as well as being an influencer, she works as an escort. On the male-only Telegram groups, meanwhile, users share Gloria's contact information and send her rape threats.

After a couple of hours, I put my phone down on the mattress, swallow the final pills, make a mental note to steal some more, put on "Law & Order: Special Victims Unit" at a random episode, and fall asleep, light as a kite.

Olivia Benson is wearing a blue suit when she arrives at the crime scene. Detective Tutuola is with her. It's late afternoon, the air is warm, and they are both dizzy from the final stretch of unpaved road. They joke that if they'd known where the crime scene was, they wouldn't have had lunch first. The car stops in a field full of weeds. In the distance are the remains of an abandoned stone building around which colorful tents are scattered. People who, to Olivia, look like toothpicks, drag themselves around under the spring sunshine. The forensic police call her over and Olivia realizes that Tutuola is touching her arm, prompting her to follow him. She turns toward the little bamboo grove covered in white signs and numbered tags, follows her colleague into a tiny clearing, and feels the familiar sensation of being about to witness something she would rather not. In the clearing lies the body of the victim. The young girl is wearing an aqua green hoodie, her jeans are around her thighs, and she is just about still breathing. Next to her, on the dusty ground, are darker stains of dry vomit. Olivia reads the scant victim information she got from the precinct, then bends down and starts to talk in a very low voice. You wouldn't be able to hear what she was saying even if you were next to her, only the sound of a reassuring song. Suddenly the victim opens her eyes, stamped with a mute, horrible fear. Olivia strokes her temples.

"You're safe now."

As I open the door to the Galeone, a rancid smell wafts out. In just a handful of days, the heat and residual sugars of the alcohol have rotted. Some of the owners are still on vacation, and the only one who has gathered up the strength to drag himself to the bar is Michele, the one who pretends to read. I don't even notice him at first. Giulia the Sardinian is behind the bar, lazily rinsing out glasses that don't need rinsing out. I can hear the swishing of the water in the sink, the mechanical clinking to Giulia's rhythm, and the coughing hum of the ancient AC unit, which hangs above a bookcase containing travel guides at least ten years old.

Giulia beckons me over to the bar and asks me how my

vacation was, with the clear intention of telling me about hers. With a vaguely maniacal look in her eyes, she tells me about her island and how it's going up in flames. But the real scoop is that she has fallen in love. I catch only the odd fragment of what she's telling me:

"Tall . . . skinny-dipping . . . bonfire . . . my parents . . . I'm thinking of going back . . . are you listening?"

"Yes, yes," I respond absent-mindedly.

"Why aren't you saying anything? I'm moving back to Sardinia, it's a really big deal for me."

I smile weakly, still in a fog from the pills.

"You look like the heat has gone to your head—do you want some water?"

Without awaiting my response, she fills one of the just-rinsed glasses to the brim. Passing it to me, she asks in a higher pitch: "Where's Gloria? I heard that her grandma died, so I imagine she didn't go away."

"I want to see her too. I need to talk to her about some business of the heart." Michele's voice behind me makes me jump.

"You're so insensitive, she's just lost her grandma," says Giulia.

"And you want to see her so you can offer your condolences, do you? Not to tell her that you're leaving us up shit creek and going back to Sardinia?"

Although the exchange is fast, it feels like they're speaking in slow motion. Before Giulia can respond, the swing door that opens onto the back room squeaks open and another waitress, Stefania, appears, hastily drying her hands on her black apron.

"I don't think Gloria will show her face any time soon. Didn't you see what happened to her? Actually, I wanted to ask if you knew anything about that," she says, turning to me.

"I know nothing, I just got back last night!" Giulia exclaims, her eyes excited by the gossip. "What did I miss?"

"Some really awful photos of Gloria came out. Her on drugs, half-naked. Wait, I saved them," Stefania responds.

"Let me see," the owner butts in.

Stefania takes her phone out and the other two gather around, mumbling things like: crazy, who would've thought, poor girl, yeah but she should've thought about that before she did it. They seem to have forgotten about me and I take the opportunity to move stealthily away toward the row of hooks where the aprons hang. As I stand on tiptoes to get mine, I feel a hint of nostalgia: the last time I touched that fabric, Gloria and I were about to set off for the rave. A vibration runs along my skull. I push the feeling away and tie the apron around my waist, then go out to the back to get some tea towels. When I turn around, Giulia is blocking my way with her phone in her hand. On the screen there's the photo of Gloria with her tongue out and the paper square in her mouth.

"What do you know about this?" she presses me, scrolling onto the next photo. Now Gloria is half naked. Seeing those images so many times has made them feel alien to me. Who took them? Who is the girl in them? Giulia plunges back into the phone and shows me the umpteenth picture. I freeze for a moment; I don't remember sharing it. It's the one I took of her sitting under a pine tree, before we started dancing. Gloria has a sweet smirk; I remember thinking she looked funny. It's true. A shiver runs down my neck.

"What's up with you today, you're in a world of your own," Stefania teases. "Come on, tell us something," she repeats. She flicks to the next photo. I don't remember this one either. It's Gloria on our rock. Or at least it looks like Gloria. If I stare at her for long enough, her features change. I take the phone out of Giulia's hands.

"Hey, hey, give it back!" she is getting worked up. I take a few steps back and zoom in on the girl's mouth. She has a gap between her teeth. Is it possible? And in the light of the flash, her hair looks blond. Another shiver. I drop the phone and it clatters on the floor.

At that point my legs suddenly become alive. I head toward

the exit, then turn and start running. As I run, my breathing becomes rhythmic, and my body starts to sweat. In my haze, I feel for a moment like I'm running along the Mostra d'Oltremare in Naples. Gloria is just a few steps away from me, I just need to reach out a hand and I'll touch her fingertips. But no, the sun is still out, the sweat is running into my eyes, and they start to stream. The effort of my legs runs parallel to the awareness of my conscience. I'm not saying it's not there, but it's dissociated, I can ignore it. I run to Anna Ricordi's building.

I make eye contact with the porter, who recognizes me and says something, but I am not listening. Out of the corner of my eye, I see him coming out of the little booth he sits in doing his crosswords. I run up two stairs at a time and knock on the recently varnished dark wood door. No answer. I ring the bell. Nothing. Then I look around and spot one of the small landscape paintings in the hallway. I pull it off the wall and grab the emergency key.

I enter the apartment as the porter's breathless steps follow me up the stairs. I close the door behind me; I hear the click of the lock and the indistinct voice of the man shut outside. I breathe in.

The house is submerged in darkness. The languid light of the summer dusk seeps through the old shutters. The wooden floor creaks as I step. I try to make as little noise as possible, even if I don't know why. I find myself in the doorway of the marble kitchen, where more than a year ago I heard Anna scolding Gloria for being friends with me. Now it's empty. The refrigerator hums in a corner. In the sink, there's a plate and two pieces of cutlery. I step back and walk past Anna's study. Her documents are no longer there, nor her computer. The desk is clear. I walk along the corridor to Anna's bedroom with its pink marble en-suite. As well as the huge double bed there's a worm-eaten wooden dresser. On top lie some silver hairbrushes with blond strands caught in them. The bristles are soft. The pieces of old furniture in the room squeak as if talking in a language only they know. I leave and pass the blue bathroom, then the black one. Finally, I'm in front of the door to Gloria's bedroom. I know there's no one in there but I knock anyway, softly. The sound of my knuckles on the wood makes me jump. I have interrupted the house's rest.

I open the door with its golden handle. Gloria's bed is made up. Posters drawn in felt pen by her fans droop sadly from the walls. Various plushies gifted over the course of her teenage years sit tidily on a dresser in the corner. There are no half-open packages strewn across the floor. The mirror covered in lipstick declarations is now clean, reflecting just my image. The colorful book—the one full of exercises she once forced me to do—sits on the bedside table.

Bewildered, I remember being a child and coming home from vacation with my family and finding the house quiet, fresh, and dark, the familiar smell of our history taking us by surprise every time. After the parallel life of the vacation—a space where it was impossible not to wonder if you were happy enough in normal life—each one of us breathed a sigh of relief when we were welcomed back by that friendly darkness. This was our home; there was nowhere else in the world we would rather return to.

I sit down on Gloria's bed. I don't know how many minutes I stay there: maybe an hour, maybe less. I only know that at a certain point the resigned shouts of the porter reverberate somewhere in my perception. I get up from the bed and silently, as if not wanting to wake Gloria, walk back along the corridor. I must look terrible when I open the door because all his intentions—visible in his knitted brow, glowering eyes, and chest swollen with air ready to be transformed into admonishment—dissipate.

I look at him and shrug. I'm about to descend the stairs and leave when the man stops me.

"Miss Linares asked me to give you this, if you came." He passes me an envelope identical to the one Gloria gave me the details of our journey to the rave in. Only this one isn't decorated. I hold it tightly and, as soon as I'm out on the street, I open it, careful in my haste not to tear the letter I anticipate it contains. But all that slips out of the envelope is a note the size of a small hand, that says:

By humiliating me you have freed me, and for this I will be forever grateful.

Don't look for me, I already know what you'll say, and I'm not interested. I don't want to think about you, let alone see you.

Bye,

G.

I turn the card over, but that's it.

## About the Author

Born in Rome in 1991, Irene Graziosi started writing after getting a degree in developmental psychopathology. She writes for several magazines and newspapers, has co-founded a YouTube cultural channel for young people (with almost a million subscribers), and a new cultural magazine.

EUROPA EDITIONS UK

READ THE WORLD

Literary fiction, popular fiction, narrative non-fiction,
travel, memoir, world noir

Building bridges between cultures with the finest writing from around the world.

Ahmet Altan, Peter Cameron, Andrea Camilleri, Catherine Chidgey,
Sandrine Collette, Christelle Dabos, Donatella Di Pietrantonio, Négar Djavadi,
Deborah Eisenberg, Elena Ferrante, Lillian Fishman, Anna Gavalda,
Saleem Haddad, James Hannaham, Jean-Claude Izzo, Maki Kashimada,
Nicola Lagioia, Alexandra Lapierre, Grant Morrison, Ondjaki, Valérie Perrin,
Christopher Prendergast, Eric-Emmanuel Schmitt, Domenico Starnone,
Esther Yi, Charles Yu

*Acts of Service*, *Didn't Nobody Give a Shit What Happened to Carlotta*,
*Ferocity*, *Fifteen Wild Decembers*, *Fresh Water for Flowers*, *Lambda*,
*Love in the Days of Rebellion*, *My Brilliant Friend*, *Remote Sympathy*,
*Sleeping Among Sheep Under a Starry Sky*, *Total Chaos*, *Transparent City*,
*What Happens at Night*, *A Winter's Promise*

Europa Editions was founded by Sandro Ferri and Sandra Ozzola,
the owners of the Rome-based publishing house Edizioni E/O.

Europa Editions UK is an independent trade publisher
based in London.

www.europaeditions.co.uk

Follow us at . . .
Twitter: @EuropaEdUK
Instagram: @EuropaEditionsUK
TikTok: @EuropaEditionsUK